FIELD OF STONES

Also by Marilyn Dungan

SNAKEBIRD

THE TAPE

FIELD OF STONES

Marilyn Dungan

Arcane Books
Paris, Kentucky

Published by Arcane Books
P.O. Box 5102
Paris, Kentucky 40362

ISBN 0-9666478-7-4

Library of Congress Control Number: 00-090997

First Edition 2001

Printed in the United States of America

For Doris & Linda

Acknowledgments

I wish to express my appreciation to the following people whose knowledge and cooperation helped greatly in the gathering of research material for this book.

Emily A. Craig, Ph.D., Forensic Anthropologist; R. Berle Clay, Ph.D.; Hardy Dungan, D.V.M.; Dr. Marcia Eisenberg of Labcorp, North Carolina; Nancy O'Malley, Assistant Senior Staff Archaeologist, University of Kentucky; Bruce Stephenson, Ph.D., Adler Planetarium & Astronomy Museum; Katie Bales and Doris Hamilton.

Again, I thank Patty Adams, John King, and Linda Hertz for their creative and time-consuming efforts preparing *Field of Stones* for publishing.

Prologue

The night sky opened like a dam gate. He gasped at the power of the waterfall cascading over the brim of his hat. In seconds, his jacket was sodden. The roar of the frigid March wind and the rain that was fast turning to sleet muffled his steps. Stiff fingers clutched the knotted neck of the bag ever tighter, and below, the almost weightless bundle slapped against his leg. In his other fist, he gripped a shovel like a walking stick, thrusting the spade into the sod with every stride.

In a sudden fury, the ice storm drove into him, taking his breath, forcing back his curses. As he pushed ahead, looming skeletal maples rattled icy branches. He slid across the blacktop and struggled up a slight grade until his shovel clanked against the fence. Still grasping the burlap, he leaned the handle against a plank and climbed. His broad face caught the sting of sleet as he swung the sack, topped the slippery board and dropped to the ground. Pulling the spade through the rails, he plunged it into the crunchy turf at his feet and dropped his burden. From his jacket pocket, he removed the flashlight and cast the beam across the small paddock. In front of him, glazed blue-gray tips of stones rose from the earth like a miniature Stonehenge.

He propped the light against a rock, seized the shovel and drove the blade beneath one of the smaller stones. It heaved and flipped on its side to expose a flagstone below. He found an edge and chiseled the spade under the stone. It barely moved.

"Damn it," he said, his words puffs of white ripped from his mouth by raw gusts.

Pitting his strength against more limestone forms, he levered while wave after wave of freezing rain slammed against him and set his teeth to clattering. But one by one the stones toppled until the large slab beneath was clear. He dropped to his knees and inch by inch, his numb fingers dragged the giant stone aside revealing several tiny rocks and a small pocket of earth in the shelf below. Clawing at the dirt, he unearthed a cavity before again feeling rock.

He reached for the sack. Sleet shattered and crumbled off the burlap as he crammed it into the crevice and covered it with the dense wet dirt that he had removed. With hands numb with cold, he shoved and pulled at the slab, fitting the rock back into the opening like a giant, jigsaw puzzle piece.

"Perfect!" he said smugly as he replanted the upright rocks. "No fear of a plow or disk turning it up some spring. Gone forever under the field of stones."

1

"Come on, you two, there's no need to look at me like that," Malcolm said from the hospital bed that was set up in the den of his newly acquired home. "I was just trying to spiffy up the place for Shar's visit."

"You sure as hell accomplished that," Gray Prescott said, lifting a newspaper from one of the two straight chairs that he had pulled up near the invalid and sitting down. "Now myself . . . I never would have thought of gilding the shrubs the same bright yellow as the house." Gray's turquoise eyes squeezed into smiling crescents before his left one tweaked a wink at Laney McVey who sat down next to him.

"And this elegant decor," Laney continued with a dramatic flourish of her hand over Malcolm's full leg cast. "An art nouveau, ornamental plaster molding, perhaps? How clever, Malcolm. I'm sure Shar will agree."

Malcolm groaned. "All right . . . I concur. I never should have ascended the ladder to paint the house." In frustration, he pounded the rumpled Lamont tartan throw tossed over his form. His other hand flew quickly to his tortoise shell glasses, knocked awry by his motion.

The woman who had been hovering in the shadows near the fireplace immediately rushed to his side. "What can I get you, sir?" she asked, plumping his pillow and making haste to the foot of the bed where she gently duplicated the gesture under his cast. She smoothed the summer weight throw.

Good Lord, Laney thought. The man can't even draw a breath without "Florence Nightingale" swooping to assist him.

Earlier, when the woman had greeted Laney and Gray at the front door, introducing herself only as Ivy, Laney was reminded of a photo she had once seen of the "lady with the lamp." Like the famous nurse, Ivy was quite striking in a serene, simple way. Her thick chocolate colored hair was severely parted in the center and pulled back in a knot behind a cap that, to Laney, looked like a lacy kerchief. The matching collar of her navy dress was secured at the throat with a gold oval pin. She wore no makeup because her steady blue eyes were naturally penciled with luxuriant lashes and shaded with dark eyebrows. But it was her skin that was her best feature—a creamy white silk flowing over her high cheekbones, straight nose and wrinkle free brow. So unlike her own, Laney thought ruefully, her carefully applied makeup fast melting away in the humidity, and her freckles undoubtedly forcing their way back to the surface like popping corn.

Malcolm struggled to his elbows and quickly waved the handsome woman away as he pleaded, "Ivy, please don't fuss . . . and please don't call me sir."

"Mr. Lamont . . ." Ivy began, tucking an errant wisp of hair behind her ear.

"Please . . . Malcolm," he corrected, dropping his head to the pillow, his own thick brown hair in moist curls from the heat, but curiously, his goatee and mustache neat and unfrizzed. He sighed, then suddenly brightened. "Ivy, perhaps some iced tea? It's so stifling."

"Certainly, sir . . . Malcolm. Right away."

Laney watched as the full breasted woman glided to the doorway, pausing only to glance Malcolm's way for an instant, as though she must assure herself that he would be all right until she returned.

"Where ever did you find her, Malcolm?" Laney asked, after the paneled door closed quietly behind the housekeeper.

"She was recommended by Manor Caretakers in Hickory. I was fortunate to find that she was between jobs and willing to take on temporary work. I understand she has worked for several families in the area and comes with outstanding references."

"I'm changing the subject a bit, Malcolm," Laney began. "But have you informed Shar of your "recent redecorating?" Laney giggled, tickling a pale toe peering from the end of his plaster.

"I haven't, Laney. How can I explain to her that instead of gallivanting about the Bluegrass with me, she will have to put up with a shut-in?" Malcolm's usually lively brown eyes dimmed behind his lenses. "I was so looking forward to her visit and now I've gone and spoilt it."

Laney recalled Shar Hamilton's first visit to Kentucky three months before. Her Pittsburgh friend had fallen hard for the Scotsman, and Shar's own Scottish heritage had drawn the two of them together like kilt and bagpipes. But other than their interest in any and everything Scottish, the affinity between the two ended there. Shar was conspicuously unconventional, fiery as a hot coal, and torturously inelegant, whereas Malcolm seemed to have been spawned from the European school of propriety. Only occasionally was his correct and exemplary demeanor pierced by Shar's outrageous behavior. But somehow the relationship flourished. That Shar was over six feet tall and the little Scotsman no more than five feet, seven in his argyle socks only emphasized their differences.

"You should have your walking cast before long so you'll be able to get around on crutches," Gray said, scooting his chair back and walking to the open window. The veterinarian unsnapped his blood speckled beige jumpsuit to his midsection. Not finding a breeze, he fanned his chest with the limp newspaper.

"Damn, it's hot. Never seen such weather." He glanced at Malcolm. "I thought this house had air conditioning."

"I'm afraid I removed the window units when I moved here in May, never thinking that Kentucky had Florida-like summer weather. At least we had an afternoon shower most days."

"This long dry spell is most unusual, Malcolm," Gray said.

"Smitty tells me my cattle are really stressed," Malcolm said with a scowl.

Only a few months before, Malcolm had moved his entire purebred Angus herd from Ocala, Florida, along with his farm manager and his wife, Eva, and their two children to the newly acquired Taylor Ridge Farm near Hickory.

"But back to human comforts," Malcolm went on. "A heat pump is being installed as we speak. I hope it will be in operation by the time Shar arrives in a couple of weeks—if, indeed, she will still come after she hears of my doltish mishap."

Laney glanced at her watch as Ivy returned to the den, toting a large tray. She offered the sparkling amber tea to each of them, set the tray on Malcolm's adjustable bed table and rolled it over his bed. She tucked another pillow under his head, slipped a straw into his frosty glass and lifted it to his lips.

"I can handle it, Ivy," Malcolm said, but smiled gratefully at her. Laney detected a flutter of Ivy's lashes as she stepped back. Suddenly, Malcolm raised a brow. "What are these?" he asked, lifting a corner of a linen cloth that covered a bulging plate on his tray. "Oh my," he exclaimed. "Surely not." He raised a golden square to his mouth and bit down softly. "Scotch shortbread," he sighed with pure pleasure, light crumbs catching in his beard.

Ivy smiled demurely. "My mother taught me how to make them when I was a child."

Laney chuckled quietly. If Shar were here, she would probably open her mouth and cram a finger down her throat. But when Malcolm passed the plate around, she had to admit they were delicious—obviously made with real butter and as light as air.

"If you don't have any other tasks for me, Malcolm, I believe I shall retire to my room for a small rest before dinner," Ivy announced. Malcolm thanked her profusely for preparing the shortbread, and, after plumping his pillow again, she took his napkin and brushed the crumbs gently from his beard before leaving the room.

Shar definitely would puke, Laney thought and checked her watch again. "I really must be going, Malcolm. I want to get back to the farm to see how they are coming along on the dig. I've been so busy with the bed and breakfast the past few days, I haven't had a chance to take a good look at it myself."

"Do you still have qualms about it?" asked Malcolm.

Laney, who had risen from her chair to leave, looked down at Malcolm and hesitated before answering. "Perhaps a little. I admit that when Bucky . . . Dr. Gage, approached me last fall and informed me that my sister had given him legal permission for the dig before she died, I was hesitant to convey the same authorization."

"Because it appears to be an Indian burial ground?" Malcolm inquired.

Laney nodded. "The thought of disturbing a cemetery was abhorrent to me but Bucky explained that this is not a burial mound that by a gradual addition of bodies grew into a huge cemetery over the years. Instead, most likely this is a single episode Late Woodland Indian stone grave—a one-time event. Anyway, burial mounds—at least on public land—are protected by law. After long conversations with Bucky about what they hoped to unearth in my field of stones, I was intrigued." Laney checked her watch for a third time and decided she still had a few minutes so she settled back down in her chair.

"Apparently, several years ago, a site similar to this one was excavated in Bourbon County, only that site had been disturbed somewhat by recent farming. Archaeologists uncovered a male laid out in a fully extended position—like we bury our dead—but several other burials were either greatly displaced or buried in what archaeologists call "bone bundles," Laney explained.

"What's a bone bundle?" Malcolm asked, finishing his tea and pushing the bed stand aside.

"Bones gathered up and buried in a grave after some other facility was first used to flesh the dead," Gray said, with his ready Bucky knowledge.

"Sorry to appear so ignorant but how do they flesh the dead?" asked Malcolm.

"It's believed that Indians laid their dead in another facility to allow the flesh to decompose by natural means," Gray continued. "When there was nothing but bones remaining, they collected them and buried them all at one time—in bone bundles."

"Then why was one individual buried in an extended position in the Bourbon County excavation?" Malcolm asked.

"I asked Bucky that," Laney said. "He said that the extended burial could have been of someone who had died close to the time the bone bundles were being buried, so they just included the individual at the same time."

"What's so special about this site?" Malcolm asked.

"Bucky believes that this site is intact—that no farmer has ever disturbed this field with a plow or disk harrow," Laney said.

"In other words, the dig could give a more accurate accounting of Late Woodland Indian burial customs?" Malcolm said.

"Right. And since the Department of Anthropology of Parker Webb University had already surveyed and mapped the site, I gave my permission for the excavation," Laney concluded. She jumped to her feet. "With that, I really must run, Malcolm. Gray, I know I said I would accompany you on your last call, but could I take a rain check? We've stayed longer than planned and I want to see the excavation and Cilla before she goes home for the weekend."

Gray didn't answer.

"How's that arrangement working out?" Malcolm asked, trying to get his visitors to remain a bit longer.

"That's a situation I'm not too comfortable with, but Malcolm . . . truly . . . I really can't linger any longer. I'll fill you in on my next visit . . . I promise." She tickled Malcolm's toe again, then leaned over and kissed him on the cheek.

As Laney and Gray pulled away from the house, Laney saw the curtain in an upstairs window move aside and lovely Ivy standing in the opening. Laney was certain that Ivy was watching her from the bedroom that Malcolm had shown her just before his accident—the one he had expressly redecorated for his fiancée, Shar Hamilton.

2

"When do you start removing the stones?" Laney called to Bucky Gage, who was studying something he had lifted from a three-tiered screen set up at the south side of the excavation.

The archaeologist raised his head and brushed his damp blond curls off his forehead and smiled so spaciously that his dark eyes almost vanished behind his bushy brows.

Laney watched as Toby Hart, a well-built member of the junior crew, struggled with a heavy bucket of dirt. He lifted it to shoulder height and dumped the load onto the top half-inch mesh screen. Dust filled the air, settling on Toby's arms already streaked with brown rivulets of sweat.

"First thing tomorrow morning, we start on the good stuff—," Bucky said, "removing these stones." His massive arm swept out over the scene.

Laney, sitting on the top rail of the black plank fence, gaped at the thirty square foot area in front of her. Most of the surface sod and dirt had been being removed, exposing layers of stones. Her lips parted in amazement. Some of the rocks stood upright with weathered blue tips saluting the hot sun. But the dusty gray majority rested flat on their sides forming a parched platform of rocks protecting something, Laney surmised, sacred or precious below.

Superimposed over the site were sets of parallel lines of twine, each intersecting the other at right angles. Bucky had explained to her that the grid divided the area into squares for precise labeling of specimens and features. Each square would be excavated in ten-centimeter levels.

"Bucky, I've never seen anything like this. There must be thousands of stones here," Laney exclaimed, her fingers trying to comb through her red hair but instead getting hung in the damp frizz.

Toby began spreading the new dirt over the surface of the box, pressing it into the screen and sorting out larger stones, throwing them into a pile next to him. The dirt sifted down onto the middle quarter-inch screen then to the bottom eighth-inch mesh before dusting a cone of fine soil beneath the structure.

Bucky dropped the specimen inside a paper bag and lifted it from the screening. As he thrust his burly frame toward Laney, he pulled a marking pen from behind his ear and wrote information on the bag. Halting just inches away, he fastened his eyes on hers as though daring her to be the first to turn away. A hint of a smile twitched his lips. She averted her gaze to the field of stones once more.

"Amazing, isn't it?" he said in his lusty voice. He rested a dusty, oil-tanned leather boot on the lowest rail of the fence near her foot. He labeled the bag and added his initials. His knee was almost touching hers and she wondered if the heat she felt was from his thick bronzed calf or whether it was from her own leg. She shifted her body ever so slightly. Below his short khaki sleeves, sweaty silvery hairs glistened on his forearms. "I expect to find multiple burials beneath that rock pile," she thought she heard him say.

From behind her, Laney felt soft arms grasp around her waist. "I'm going, Aunt Laney," a voice whispered. Turning her head, Laney looked down into the face of Cilla Sands, a teenager who was not really her niece, but the daughter of a close friend, Tina Sands. Laney had invited her to spend the summer at the bed and breakfast as a favor to Tina who was desperate to help her daughter snap out of a deep depression. Blackberry, Laney's Border collie who had followed Cilla from the house, fell listlessly into the patch of shade created by Laney's body.

"Luke's waiting for me," the pretty sixteen year old said, motioning to the beat-up gray Ford pick-up waiting in the lane about thirty feet away. Her eyes, the color of chicory flowers, were rimmed with pale lashes as fine as cobwebs. They watered in the late day sun. Her cheeks were shiny clean from her shower but already flushed from the heat. Tiny beads of perspiration sprouted at her blond hairline.

"I didn't hear him come in," Laney said, giving Luke a wave. Luke hauled his torso out the driver's window and sat on its sill. He waved a skinny arm, then played drums impatiently on the roof of the cab with his hands.

Toby Hart sauntered over to the fence. "Think I'll call it a day," he told Bucky and winked at Cilla and grinned, his teeth white against his tawny skin. Laney caught her blush.

Toby and Cilla were the only teens that had been selected by the Senior Staff Archaeologist, Bucky Gage, to participate in his field school. Both youngsters were in a challenge program in the public schools that gave outstanding teenagers the opportunity to participate in hands-on careers during the summer before their senior year. Both Toby, a local student from St. Clair County, and Cilla, from Mason County in northern Kentucky, were avid history buffs and had signed up individually for the Parker Webb University dig.

Toby dallied at the fence, pulling at a splinter of wood in the top rail. He stood about six feet tall with overly developed thighs that were putting a strain on the seams of his blue denim cutoffs. YMCA weight lifting gym, Laney speculated. He had a severe, square-jawed face with serious, almost navy-blue eyes that made him look older than his seventeen years. He stepped on the lowest rail, smoothly vaulted the fence and headed toward the camp in the yard. He grabbed a striped towel off a clothes line strung between two branches of a wild cherry tree and ducked into the shower that Bucky had constructed from a wooden flat, two fifty-five gallon drums, a plastic curtain and a shower head.

Laney had loaned Bucky the farm's gasoline powered water pump that drew from the cistern in the yard. The cistern was also the source of their drinking water. Close by, five tents of various colors and sizes and two portable potties made up the remainder of the summer camp.

Assistant Staff Archaeologist, Cam Dalton, his wife Bonnie, and four graduate students lulled in the shade of an ancient maple in the yard, trying to capture an elusive breeze before dinner. Two other students were preparing the grill by the carriage house. Each day, two members of the crew shared culinary responsibilities and there was much competition to prepare the most outstanding meal on their limited budget. Those not cooking had clean-up duty. The crew's meals were cooked on the giant barrel grill that Laney had provided, and in case of rain, on an electric skillet and a battered range with only two working burners inside the carriage house She had donated the spacious building for the duration of the dig that was scheduled to last for another four weeks. Not only did the structure serve as a dining-kitchen, but also as headquarters where the crew could study and store artifacts found at the excavation.

Cilla squeezed Laney's arm, moved quickly to Luke's piece of junk and scrambled inside.

"So far, Cilla and Toby have been positive additions to the team," Bucky said, drawing a cup of water from the five gallon water jug on the sorting table and tossing it down with a couple of loud swallows. "This is hot, backbreaking work for teens but I never hear them bitching—and I admit I throw a lot of the dirty chores on the junior crew. I'm glad you recommended Cilla to me."

"She's still having a tough time over her father's suicide last winter."

"She shows no evidence of depression here at the dig," Bucky said. "Or, maybe I just keep her so damn slogged, she doesn't have time to think about what's depressing her."

"Going to work her fingers to the bone, are you?" Laney asked. She giggled, "No pun intended."

Bucky guffawed. "You can bet your sweet ossicle on it," he boomed, reaching under her damp ringlets and pulling on an ear lobe.

She felt the tingle all the way to the house.

As soon as they were out of Laney's and Bucky's sight, Luke braked. He grabbed Cilla's arm.

"Luke, you're hurting me," she winced, pulling her arm from his grip. He backhanded her, his hand glancing off her chin as she raised her elbow to protect herself. He punched her upper arm hard for spite. She cried out.

"If I ever see you do that again, I'll do more than that," Luke snarled. He reached across her and unlatched the glove compartment, exposing the Bowie knife in its leather sheath that he often wore.

"What did I do?" Cilla whimpered, staring at the knife and sliding across the seat to cower against the door. But she suspected that Luke had seen Toby wink at her.

"You think I didn't see that jerk come on to you?" he said, once more accelerating down the lane. "Liked it, didn't ya?" he said, his hands pounding the steering wheel, his words punctuated by angry spittle that hung on his scanty buff colored mustache. His thin, greasy ponytail slithered below a dirty white baseball cap.

"I didn't, Luke . . . honest." She inched her way back toward him and hugged his thin arm. He tensed but didn't push her away. His wet skin was warm against her cheek. She hated for him to be mad at her.

"You know how I love you," she murmured, tears beginning again as her arm throbbed.

Luke stopped the truck on the lane and pulled her to him, sliding a hand beneath her T-shirt and fondling her breast.

"Someone's coming," Cilla said, pulling his hand away. She moved back toward the window and Luke started up the engine. He slammed the glove box shut and kicked an empty beer can under the seat.

Luke slowed as the vehicle approached, and he waved to Gray in his Jeep Grand Cherokee as they passed each other.

"Let's find somewhere to park," Luke said hoarsely, placing his hand on Cilla's thigh. She felt it creeping under her shorts.

"I have to get right home today," she said, her fingers grazing her bruised arm. She could feel the heat and the pulse of pain. "Mom went to an antique show for the weekend and I have to keep an eye on Aggie. She's with Grandma at the shop until I get home."

Her Grandma Lucille lived next door to the Sands' house and antique shop in the village of Washington, Kentucky. She worked in the shop and kept an eye on Cilla's younger sister, Aggie, whenever she could. Eugene Finley, Tina's boyfriend, stayed with the girls when Tina had to take a buying trip—usually on a weekend. This evening, Lucille was going out for dinner with Cilla's Aunt Margaret, so Cilla was in charge of Aggie until Eugene arrived.

Luke stopped at the end of the lane and pushed in the truck's lighter. "Shit, Cil . . . what about tonight . . . after little sister goes beddy-by?" he sulked.

"Mom's boyfriend is staying at the house while she's gone. He'll be there by dinnertime."

"What about tomorrow night?" he said, pulling a cigarette from the pack on the dash and lighting up.

"Eugene's taking us to a movie in Maysville."

"Ah, skip it," he said, then sucked deep on the cigarette.

"Luke . . ."

"Goin to have to get me another girl. I have needs ya know." With his mouth alternately pursing and widening like a fish, he blew out three rings of smoke. As they floated above him, he stabbed through the circles with the cigarette.

"Please, Luke. I'll . . . think of something."

"You'd better, Cil," he snapped, as he shoved the gearshift into first and turned onto Hickory Pike.

3

Gray's Jeep swung into the circle drive just as Laney and her Border collie reached the front porch. Blackberry, who sensed she would have to share Laney's attention with Gray's tabby cat, Puccini, ran off the porch and down her well-worn path behind the house for a quick dip in Stoney Creek.

When Laney opened the heavy oak door, Puccini squeezed by both of them and disappeared into the cool dark hallway. Gray made a sharp left into the parlor while Laney followed the cat into the kitchen to get the ice for toddies. She sifted through her mail that her farm manager had left on the front porch for her while Puccini stalked into the pantry to check out the dog's dish for any treats that might have accumulated during the day.

Laney tossed several bills on the built-in desk on the way to the refrigerator, filled the ice bucket and moved slowly back down the hallway.

When Gray took the bucket from her, he kissed her neck behind her ear—the ear that still tingled, pleasantly.

"Fix me a vodka tonic instead of a Bloody," Laney said, settling into the green Morris chair. She stared mindlessly at the rich, Victorian floral painted on the fireplace screen that covered the opening for the summer.

Gray handed the drink to her and instead of fixing one for himself, sank to the floor facing her, his legs stretched out in front of him with ankles crossed. Laney noticed his fresh haircut for the first time. He looked cutely geeky.

"Wanna talk about it?" Gray asked, his brows arching inquisitively.

Laney's eyes dropped to her drink and she jabbed at the ice with her finger. She didn't feel like answering, so she didn't.

"The book?" he asked.

"Book . . . ?"

"You're thinking, 'I'm a lousy writer.' "

She glanced up for a moment, then resumed bobbing the cubes. "I've received six rejections," she said.

"And a request for sample chapters," Gray added.

"It's been a month."

"Laney, you've been on the other side. Remember when you were an assistant editor at *Three Rivers Magazine*? How many submissions passed over your desk before one caught your eye?"

She shrugged, then mumbled, "Lots."

"How long did the process take?"

"So many submissions . . . a long time."

"You used to tell me that writers were so impatient. They'd write. They'd phone, wanting to know the status of their article. Drove you nuts."

Laney felt a smile tugging at her mouth. "You're right, you know. I should know better. But this isn't an article. It's my novel based on what happened to my sister."

"Laney, editors don't care about that. It has to be what they are looking for or they reject it no matter how good it is. All I'm really saying is, hang in there. You'll get published. Meanwhile, start another novel."

"Another one?"

"Another one." Gray crawled over to Laney and circled her waist with his strong arms. His mouth explored her neck and sucked its way to her jaw-line. A hot wave of pleasure swept down her body but just as his lips found hers, the doorbell rang. She startled.

"Oh my, I bet it's my guests," she said raggedly and cleared her throat. She jumped to her feet, knocking Gray back on his rear. "Sorry, would you get that casserole that Mother put in the fridge for us this morning and pop it in a three fifty oven. Shouldn't take long for me to get them registered and settled in."

She left him there and dashed to the door. Puccini slipped out and a damp Blackberry slipped in followed by a middle aged couple. The Griffins were in the Bluegrass for the Keeneland summer yearling sales that would begin on Monday. Laney learned that they were planning to attend a pre-sale party that evening at one of the large thorough-bred farms along with another couple staying at her bed and breakfast. A single room had also been reserved for Brice McIlvaine, a bloodstock agent from Ireland.

"I couldn't help but notice the camp in your yard," Kenneth Griffin remarked as the three of them mounted the cherry staircase to the Griffin's room.

"Parker Webb University from Louisiana is conducting a dig on the farm," Laney explained. "You're welcome to observe at any time as long as you stay on this side of the plank fencing," Laney said. "And please, no smoking," she added, recalling the bulge in Mr. Griffin's shirt pocket. "Ashes can effect radiocarbon dating at the excavation. Here at the B & B, smoking is allowed on the porches."

They were passing the family pictures above the mahogany wain-scoting. Her father smiled down at Laney's sister, Cara, who had died over a year ago. Writing the novel had become a catharsis for her grief and she could once again look at the oval portrait without crying.

"Tell me, what are they excavating?" Mrs. Griffin asked as Laney unlocked the first bedroom on their right."

"An Indian stone grave," Laney answered over her shoulder.

Laney heard a sharp intake of breath. She turned in time to see Mrs. Griffin shoot her husband a pained look.

"Ms. McVey," Mrs. Griffin said. "I'm afraid we cannot stay in your bed and breakfast. We are canceling our reservations."

4

"I should have known," Laney said. "Her name . . . Orenda . . . it's Native American," Laney said, palming her forehead. "The blackness of her hair . . . and so straight." She slapped a huge scoop of chicken rice casserole on her plate and tore a chunk of crunchy French bread off the loaf, slathering a thick layer of butter over it.

"Cool down, Laney. At least the Harneys decided to stay and the Irishman, too. In fact, they seemed truly excited about the dig," Gray said, taking a bite of salad.

"A stroke of luck," Laney said. The Harneys are acquaintances of the Griffins and I think, out of loyalty, they probably would have followed them to Hickory House if they'd had a second vacancy. By the way, thanks for phoning the hotel and making the reservations for the Griffins. I think they thought under the circumstances, it was a gracious thing to do. I didn't think of it, myself."

"You were upset."

"I still am," Laney said, scarfing up the rest of her casserole in three bites and swilling her chardonnay.

"Laney, not everyone feels the same about archaeological excavations. Some believe it's exciting to learn about our history and to try to understand how people lived and died. Others feel that the past should be left undisturbed."

"Well, I learned something tonight—inform my guests ahead of time about any special events that are going on at the farm," Laney said, mopping up the cream sauce on her plate with her bread.

With Puccini stretched out on his dashboard, Gray disappeared down the lane accompanied by the voice of Leontyne Price begging the gods for pity in *Aida's* "Ritorna vincitor!" Laney remained standing in the circle drive until the aria faded and the lights of his Jeep disappeared. The crickets picked up the sudden lull with their melancholy call. She felt suddenly weary.

The phone had rung eight times before she lifted the receiver in the library. "Shar, I was going to call you."

"Woman, what the hell is going on down there? I've tried to call Malcolm for three days and no one answers the phone. Then, when I call this evening, some woman answers and says he can't answer the phone . . . that he's asleep. Asleep! Who is this bitch and what's she doing in his house? So help me, if Mal is screwing around on me, I'll kill the little bastard."

"Put the brakes on, Shar. It's nothing like that."

"Then what?"

"Malcolm's had an accident. He fell off the ladder while painting the house."

"Acci . . . oh my God . . . when?"

"Three days ago. He fractured his tibia."

"Tibia? Where's that? Is it below the belt?"

Laney had to chuckle. "Well, it's below but not where you're thinking, Shar. It's the big bone in the lower leg . . . you know . . . the shin bone. He spent Wednesday night in the hospital and they did surgery Thursday . . . put a pin in. He didn't get home until today."

"There's something you're not telling me. I can hear it in your voice."

"He has this housekeeper . . . Ivy something."

"Ivy? Like in poison?"

Laney began to giggle.

"Fess up, woman."

"Malcolm's laid up for awhile." Another giggle.

"Laid? . . . that bitch!"

"May . . . maybe 'laid up' is the wrong choice of words," Laney said, laughing so hard she snorted. "I didn't mean—"

"What in hell *do* you mean?"

Laney took a long spasmodic breath to gain control. "Ivy plumps his pillows . . . makes him Scotch shortbread."

A lengthy pause followed.

In a small controlled voice, Shar asked, "How often will she be there?"

"Shar, from what I can determine—"

"Cut to the chase, woman."

"She's moved in . . . the whole kit and caboodle."

"The hussy!"

Shar called Laney back an hour later with the flight number and her arrival time on Monday morning at Blue Grass Airport in Lexington.

"It's no big deal, Laney. I just moved my vacation up two weeks. I told John Barnard if he said no, I would just take family leave."

"Shar, Malcolm isn't family."

"We're engaged. That's almost family. And if I have my way, we'll set the date before I fly back to Pittsburgh."

Laney, continually amazed by her friend's audacity, was secretly glad that Shar was coming back to Hickory. Those query rejections compounded by the abrupt departure of two of her guests had left her feeling discombobulated. If anyone could put her back on track, it would be Shar Hamilton.

5

The morning broke hot and hazy. Laney cracked the French doors to the screened porch and the brief sultry exposure convinced her that shorts were again in order. By seven o'clock, the thermometer read seventy-four degrees and the weather report predicted a high of ninety-eight. Below, Stoney Creek—the color of pea soup—lay shallower than normal. She stepped to the door. Bucky and two of the crew sat on the front step of the carriage house eating what looked like scrambled eggs and bacon off paper plates. Instead of hot coffee, Bucky held a soft drink can. His khaki shirt, already damp with perspiration, clung to his chest.

Laney's guests had left word they wanted their breakfasts in their rooms, an option that Laney actually preferred these days. Lately, she hadn't felt much like chitchatting with her guests early in the morning.

She had filled each basket with carafes of freshly squeezed orange juice, coffee, and an assortment of homemade muffins and orange marmalade sweet rolls that her mother had baked earlier in the week and placed in the freezer. Covered china plates held thick slices of peppered hickory bacon and generous portions of mushroom quiche. At eight, when the breakfasts were fragrant and piping hot, she left the meals on large serving tables that were stationed at the bedroom doors. She tucked blue and white checked napkins into sunny yellow mugs, knocked lightly at her guests' doors and tiptoed downstairs.

After her own coffee and muffin, Laney dressed in pink and white striped seersucker shorts and a pink T-shirt. She wove her damp hair in a plump braid and was about out the front door when Ginny Harney and the Irishman, Brice McIlvaine, caught up with her.

"We'd like to view the dig if we may," Brice said with a fading Irish accent. "If I can make it that far after that delicious breakfast." Ginny, dressed in a bright apple green sundress and leather sandals explained that her husband, David, was just finishing his shower and would join them directly.

They crossed crunchy brown grass to the fence surrounding the excavation. Laney noted that three canvas canopies had been erected to protect the crew from the relentless rays of the sun—one over the southwest corner square of the grid and a second over the northeast corner. A third canopy shielded a sorting table near the three-tiered screen.

The crew, all but Cilla, who by pre-arrangement returned each weekend to her home in Washington, Kentucky, had finished eating and were meticulously removing one stone at a time from the two sections and placing them in a wheelbarrow. When the barrow became so full that Laney thought no one could possibly push it, Bucky lifted the handles, wheeled and unloaded it in an area behind a pile of back dirt. Sweat poured from his body and dripped from the red kerchief tied around his brow.

Laney had just decided to return to the house, when from the southwest square she heard a cry.

"Dr. Gage," Toby called, his shiny face beaming. "We've found something."

Bucky returned the empty barrow to the far corner and rushed toward Toby and Dr. Cam Dalton, the assistant crew chief who was supervising Toby on his first dig. With a soft brush, Cam gently brushed dirt away from an item that had been exposed when the two of them had lifted a flat stone.

"It's metal," Toby said, clicking the point of his trowel against the circular object.

"Damn," Bucky exclaimed. "I'd hoped we wouldn't find any recent farming evidence here."

"It doesn't look like any modern farming implement I've ever seen," Toby said, "and I've worked on a farm every summer for as long as I can remember. Anyway, it was found under a flat stone the size of a dinner plate. And that stone was under several vertically laid rocks."

Laney saw the glance of respect that Bucky shot at Toby. "Cam, this calls for a measurement. Bonnie," Bucky called to Cam's wife who had wandered over to look, "photograph this before removing it." Bucky rushed to get his field notebook and waited for the measurements and for Bonnie to complete her shots before mapping the exact location of the artifact on a large sheet of graph paper clamped to a rectangular board, his artistic skills evident on the precise, measured drawing of the site. When the ring was fully exposed, Bucky lifted it carefully and carried it over to Laney, Brice, and Ginny, who had been joined by her husband. The rest of the crew who hadn't seen the ring crowded around also.

"The dark patina . . . appears to be brass," Bucky said, wiping an edge with his broad thumb. "About six inches in diameter, I'd say. Too large for a watch." He turned the ring over. "There's a groove that might have been meant for a piece of glass."

"Dr. Gage, there's something else next to where we found the ring," Toby called.

Laney and the visitors waited impatiently while the whole photographing and measuring procedure was completed. This time, Bucky carried over a couple of shards of cloudy glass and another brass piece, this one about seven inches long with an inch long slit that ran through the quarter inch thick metal.

"Must be an instrument of some kind . . . from the Historic Period," Bucky said.

"When did that begin?" asked Laney.

"Around 1650 is the earliest time Europeans reported seeing Indians in this area and that European trade goods were found."

"How old do you think that is?" asked David Harney, nodding at the objects in the archaeologist's hands.

"I think we'll have to identify what it is before we can answer that," Bucky said. "Back to work, you guys. I still have hopes of finding something older than this. Keep working toward the center. That's what interests me."

6

Two of Laney's yearlings were in the summer sales and Aaron Sloan, the farm manager, had called Gray to check them over before he hauled them to Keeneland that afternoon. When Gray drove up from the barn, the crew was just breaking for lunch. Laney prepared a simple lunch for the two of them and when she saw the crew drifting out of the carriage house to find a cooler place to eat their lunch, she suggested to Gray that they join them. After the discovery at the site, Laney's guests had driven into Hickory for lunch and to explore the many antique shops.

Under the maple in the yard, the crew ate grilled hot dogs with chips and fresh apples, all the while vying for the tree's shrinking circle of shade as the blinding sun rose higher in the sky. Several of the guys went back to the carriage house for seconds. Bucky had just returned with more hotdogs. An insulated aluminum five-gallon drinker dispensed endless iced tea. Everyone was still chattering about the morning's find and when Toby offered to do some research on the object, Bucky assigned the project to him.

"I have Internet access if you think that would help," Laney offered. "The computer's in the library."

"Maybe tomorrow when I'm off work," Toby said. "If I can't find anything, I'll have to hit the library some evening."

"Blackberry, get over here," Laney yelled suddenly, spotting her dog on the other side of the fence that separated the yard from the dig. Blackberry scurried back under the plank.

"Bucky, I understand you're from Lexington. How did you end up at Parker Webb University in Louisiana," Laney asked.

Bucky leaned back against the tree and crossed his legs. "I did my undergraduate studies at UK and got my masters at Tulane. By then I was married. My wife was from New Orleans, so naturally when I had a chance to work on my Ph.D. instate, I jumped at it. Parker Webb University later offered an assistant professorship."

"Must be hard on your family when you're away on digs," Gray murmured, glancing at Laney.

Bucky's eyes dropped to his lap. "We're divorced. No kids."

Blackberry trotted over to Laney and deposited a present in her lap. Bucky, next to her, gaped at the object. Laney, nibbling on a bologna sandwich, was so interested in the conversation, that it was a moment before she felt his gaze and glanced down.

"Jeez, thanks a lot, pooch," Laney said, picking up the treasure with her thumb and forefinger. "Ugh!" she said with a shiver, tossing it from her lap in disgust.

Like a lion, Bucky sprang to his feet and pounced on it as it hit the ground.

"A phalange!" he roared, his leonine mane of blond ringlets tumbling over his forehead as he landed on his haunches. Triumphantly, he held up the human finger bone.

After her discovery, Blackberry had been immediately banished to the house to keep her from digging up and running off with other bones in the site.

"God, Bucky," Laney began, as Bucky assisted her over the fence. "I promised to keep her away."

"No harm done this time," Bucky said good-humoredly, holding her hand a bit longer than necessary. He viewed the area where the dog had removed the bone—the same general area where the artifacts had been found. "You can see where it had been." Bucky placed the bone back in the indentation adjacent to the next group of stones to be removed. "It must have been barely covered with dirt, or we would have seen it." His eyes were glowing. "I bet if there's a skeleton, it's under these stones."

The crew was in a buzz. Toby, Cam, Cliff and Polly were quickly assigned to continue clearing the area of stones. The work was tedious and hot. The canopy, though it provided shade, seemed to trap the heat. Perspiration streamed down the faces of the four workers. In the background, resounding cracks and gray dust filled the air as Bucky crashed the stones onto the others in the growing pile. He removed his khaki shirt and Laney couldn't miss his powerful shoulders, shiny with sweat, tapering to his tight belly.

"Laney," Gray began.

When she turned her head, Gray's expression revealed that he had followed her gaze to Bucky.

"I . . . I have several calls this afternoon. Want to go?" he asked, his demeanor suddenly somber.

Distracted for a moment, she stammered, "Well . . ."

"Another rain check?" he asked derisively and walked away.

7

Cilla arrived at Laney's earlier than usual on Sunday afternoon. She was the first to alight from Tina's Voyager, but at the front door she darted by Laney into the hall. Laney heard her sandals slap the stairs as she rushed up to her room.

"What's all that about?" Laney asked as she and Tina hugged and kissed air before Laney led her to the kitchen for a cool drink.

"I'm afraid we've had words," Tina said.

"Eugene again?" Laney sighed, but immediately thinking of Gray who had left without saying goodbye.

"Uh-huh. She complained about him all the way from Washington. She hates it when he stays at the house when I go to antique shows." Tina sat across from Laney at the round kitchen table and cooled her hands on the frosty glass of limeade.

"Same old problem?"

"Yes. Don't get me wrong. Eugene loves the girls. It's just that he makes all kinds of plans for the three of them while I'm gone."

"And she just wants to spend all her time with Luke."

"Right."

"That's normal for her age, you know."

"I let her see Luke a lot when I'm home. And he calls her all the time. I don't think it's too much to ask for her to spend a little time with her sister and Eugene . . . especially since we'll be married this fall."

"Maybe she thinks Eugene is trying to replace her father."

"Could be. She says he puts too many limits on her," Tina said, her brows furrowing.

"And how teens hate limits."

"How has Priscilla been around here?" Tina asked, her blue eyes hoping for a positive response.

"According to Bucky, she's topnotch."

"That's not what I mean. The depression. . . ."

"Well . . . she's a little down when she returns Sunday night, but by Monday morning, her old enthusiasm is back."

"Eugene again. But I just can't help being away most summer weekends. These shows are a large part of my business."

"Want me to talk to her?"

"Would you?"

"First chance I get." Laney stood. "Do you want to see the site?"

"Sure."

Just as Bucky predicted when Blackberry unearthed the finger bone the day before, a complete skeleton had been found. The bones lay on a dirt pedestal in an extended position, the rest of the site still covered with black plastic to protect it from animals and the weather. As though it's ever going to rain again, Laney thought wryly.

The crew had taken Sunday off, going to church and then on to brunch at the Finish Line in Hickory. Toby and Bucky, however, had remained behind to brush dirt away from around the bones. Studying the bones just before Tina had arrived, Laney was astonished. If indeed it was a Late Woodland burial, the thousand-year-old skeleton was in remarkable condition.

Laney and Tina approached the fence. As Toby sifted a bucket of dirt in the three-tiered screen, he suddenly reached into the box and removed an object. Instead of dropping it into the paper bag on the box screen, he handed it to Bucky.

When Laney introduced Tina to Bucky, he seemed preoccupied with the find.

"What do you think of our main man here?" he asked her, thumbing at the bones over his shoulder.

"How can you tell it's a male?" Laney asked excitedly

"There's a small V-shaped indentation on the edge of the hip bone. It's called the sciatic notch. On males it's narrow, as is the pelvic opening."

"Can you tell anything else about him?" Tina asked, suddenly very interested.

"By the build-up of bony growths on his vertebrae, I believe he was between forty and fifty years old when he died—closer to fifty by my estimation. And he's over six foot tall. Toby here measured him."

"That's tall for an Indian, isn't it?"

"I don't think he is Native American. Remember that brass ring buried next to him? Historic period. But his teeth tell the story the best. This gentleman doesn't have shovel shaped incisors like most Native Americans. And the narrow nasal opening and wide roof of his mouth points to a Caucasian. Something else. The rocks covering the skeleton appeared to be at a higher level than the rest of the site." He dropped the flint object he had been fingering into Laney's hand. "This compounds my confusion."

"It's a tiny arrowhead," Laney said, showing Tina, then handing it back to Bucky.

"A serrated triangular point in perfect condition found in the dirt near the ribs of the skeleton," Bucky said.

"Could it be what killed him?" Laney asked.

"Possible. I see no trauma to the bones but I guess it could have hit a vital."

He appeared perplexed as he continued. "The remains are oriented east to west with the skull at the west end. In many ways, it seems like an Indian burial." He shrugged. "Finding a projectile point with a Caucasian is odd unless it was what killed him or . . . "

"Or what?" Tina asked.

"It could have been placed with him as part of a mortuary ritual." He walked over to the screen and dropped the artifact into the paper bag and labeled it. "I'll have to think about this."

He and Toby carefully covered the skeleton with the plastic and called it a day. As the two of them climbed over the fence, Toby called, "Ms. McVey, can I search around on the computer after I shower up?"

"Sure, come on in when you're ready. I'll get you started."

"Would you happen to have any beer?" Bucky asked her. "I'm fresh out and the Kentucky Sunday blue laws have instantly put me on the wagon."

For a moment, Laney had second thoughts about inviting him to the house for a drink. But whom would it hurt? Gray was miffed at her anyway, Laney thought, remembering how he had walked off the day before.

The three of them started toward the house but when they reached the circle drive, Tina restrained Laney with her hand. "I believe I'll head on back. Aggie and Eugene are cooking Italian." She glanced at the house. "No sense stirring Priscilla up again. She'll get over our fuss by next week." Laney gave her a hug and watched her friend drive down the lane.

Bucky insisted on drinking his beer on the front porch, collapsing on the porch swing and chug-a-lugging two thirds of the can before Laney had a single sip of her wine.

Her three bed and breakfast guests pulled into the drive and parked in the space that Tina had vacated—the last available spot in the black-top circle. Laney's 1989 Nissan sat in the ivy edged drive that cut across the yard from the front circle to the carriage house behind Toby's pickup and Bucky's red Chevy Blazer. Laney ran back inside and fixed drinks for them and brought out a couple more beers for Bucky. The four of them listened transfixed as Bucky spurted archaeology for the next forty-five minutes. When the grandfather clock inside the front hall chimed six-thirty, the Harneys and Brice excused themselves so they could change for another pre-sale party in Lexington.

Bucky stood up abruptly. The wicker swing creaked. "I'd invite you for dinner with the crew but you'd distract me and I'd end up not catching up on my field entries." His eyes twinkled like brown garnets. His lips pursed and he blew her a kiss. "Thanks for the beers." He grabbed the last can from the tray and with a half-smile, swaggered off the wooden porch and around the side of the house.

"What? . . . " Laney murmured as she entered the house. The library door was open and the clicking of computer keys drew her into the room. Toby and Cilla sat in front of the monitor at her double pedestal desk. Cilla must have let Toby in through the screened porch, she thought. Though dressed in jeans and a long sleeved T-shirt, Cilla hugged her arms as though the air conditioning were chilling her. Her eyes were a tad too bright, almost feverish looking.

They looked up in unison when she entered. "I forget how computer literate kids are today. Are you having any luck?" Laney asked, not able to tear her eyes away from Cilla.

Toby had just clicked on an Internet site and they were waiting for it to come up. "Not yet," he said. "Most of the antique instrument sites don't have graphics. It's hard to picture an instrument without—whoa, Cilla! Will you clap your baby blues on that!" Toby exclaimed, jumping forward in his seat.

As a graphic gradually appeared in a large box, Cilla's eyes widened, her face suddenly animated. "Toby, that's it!" she yelped, nodding at the computer screen and grabbing the brass ring artifact off the desk at the same time. "A surveying compass! See, the description says it's six and a half inches across." She measured the diameter of the ring with a ruler that Toby had brought from the carriage house. "The same size as ours! And there is this thing," Cilla said, pointing at the monitor and with her other hand, slipping the long brass piece with slits out of a brown paper bag next to the keyboard.

Laney read the small print under the colored picture. "They call that a 'sight vane.' There's supposed to be two of them—one on either side of the compass."

Cilla put the ruler to the metal. "Seven inches. Not quite as long as the one in the photo. It says they were connected to a fifteen inch compass plate with screws." Her eyes were suddenly sparkling like sunlit blue pools.

"These have to be parts from a plain compass. It looks just like it," Toby said, as he printed out the web page. "Uh-oh," he said as he read on. "This artifact is from the mid-eighteenth century. Dr. Gage will be pissed . . . er . . . mad."

Cilla grabbed the printout and read. " 'They used a surveyor's compass to measure angles in respect to compass bearings . . .' Say, maybe this compass belonged to that skeleton you unearthed."

"It was found in the same level," Toby said.

"You told me Dr. Gage thought he was Caucasian," Cilla added and scrunched her mouth in thought. "I did a paper on the settling of Kentucky when I was a freshman. Surveyors were a dime a dozen in the second half of the eighteenth century."

"Well, I'm going to leave you two archaeologists to your digging and start some dinner. Toby, you're welcome to join us," Laney said, happy that Cilla seemed so animated over their research.

8

Toby continued to surf the Net to see if he could find anymore information on surveying instruments but only came up with one other photo of a more sophisticated model—an 1830's compass complete with a tripod and wooden carrying case. Toby shut down the computer and swiveled the desk chair so that he could better see Cilla, who had fallen asleep on the tan leather sofa when he had gotten lost in cyberspace. He watched her fine blond lashes flutter against her cheeks. Kinda like butterflies, he thought. Whoa man. Where did that soppy image come from?

But he sure wanted to kiss that soft mouth—ever since the first day of the dig.

Cilla stirred and her eyes opened. When she caught him giving her the once over, she pushed herself upright. "I must have drifted off. I didn't get much sleep this weekend."

"You shoulda been here instead of Washington. A lot of excitement at the dig."

Cilla stretched, exposing her tight midriff above her jeans. Her small breasts strained against the tight T-shirt. "I wish I had stayed with you guys. I was totally bored out of my skull. Eugene—he's my mom's boyfriend—wouldn't let me do kakka. What about you? How come you're staying here? Don't you live in Hickory?"

"Yeah, but I wanted to camp with the rest of the crew. I thought it would be like being a real archaeologist. As it turned out, Dr. Gage let me bunk with him. I'm learning a hell of a lot."

Cilla's eyes suddenly darkened and she shivered like a cloud had passed over the sun. "I might stay here next weekend," she said.

"You going with that guy?"

"Luke?"

"If that's the creep that picks you up every Friday."

Cilla shot him a look.

"Dr. Gage told me about your dad. That must have cut the heart out of ya," Toby said.

Cilla swallowed and stared at her hands.

"Say . . . I didn't mean to bring you down. It's just that I know what it's like not to have a dad."

Cilla glanced up.

"My dad died when I was a baby," Toby said, "but at least I never got to know him."

Cilla's brows connected in sudden empathy. "I didn't know. Your mom . . . did she ever—"

"Marry again? No," he said sharply. He didn't want to talk about her.

"Where do you live?"

"In that tent out there."

"No, I meant . . . before the dig." She smiled, exposing straight white teeth and a darting dimple at the corner of her mouth. So seldom did she smile, he hadn't noticed it before.

He shrugged. "Where ever."

"You don't live with your mom?"

"Used to when I was a kid. Now I either stay at a friend's place or in an efficiency that mom uses when she's between jobs."

"Cool. What she do?"

"She's a live-in. Takes care of sick or old people," he said with a cynical tone. He wished she'd drop the subject.

She looked at him curiously. "I take it you two don't get along."

"You got it."

"You going to college?"

He frowned. "If I can dig up the money. You?"

"Yeah . . . no . . . Mom wants me to."

"What do you want?"

"Maybe I'll get married after high school."

"God, Cilla. You're just a kid. Why would you do that?" He thought of her with Luke and felt sick.

She shrugged. "Your mom, is she working now?"

His mother again. He wished she'd leave it. "Yeah. She's taking care of some guy who busted his leg."

9

"Woman, why would you pick me up in the heap of scrap that almost caused my demise three months ago? My God, your own insurance adjuster declared it brain dead," Shar Hamilton roared at Laney as they approached the 1989 Nissan. "What kind of friend are you, anyway?"

Laney, used to Shar's verbal abuse of her mode of transportation, ignored her friend's tirade, flipped open the trunk and began the lengthy operation of stowing Shar's luggage. Indeed, three months before, she *had* put her friend in peril. How many times had she chastised herself since then? Afterwards, at her own expense, the automobile had been fully repaired, given two new coats of white paint, and despite Shar's disrespectful eulogy, was brought back from the dead. Laney loved the car, except when she braked on a hill. Then she wished that it had automatic transmission.

Shar was still ranting as they climbed into the Whooptie, the name Laney's late sister had ironically given to the car. Just days after Cara's death, Laney learned that her sister had willed her the beat-up Nissan and Stoney Creek Bed & Breakfast on a two hundred and fifty acre horse farm.

Whopping her head on the frame of the door, Shar crammed her willowy frame into the front seat—her knees pressing painfully against her travel bag and a suspicious looking purple tote that began to shudder and emit muted odd sounds as soon as Shar crunched the door shut.

"What have you got there, girl?" Laney asked uneasily, as they

pulled out of Blue Grass Airport parking. She braced herself for anything from a king cobra to a vibrator.

Shar fluttered her gray eyes at Laney indignantly, reached into the
tote and extracted a ball of tabby fur surrounding two copper eyes.
"Judy said she'd house-sit my Westie, but drew the line when I wanted to leave the kitten too." Judy was Shar's co-worker at *Three Rivers
Magazine*. "So . . . here we are," she crooned, nuzzling the hot little
creature.

Laney turned the air to high. "How did you ever get him by security?"

"I put the bag on the conveyor belt and flirted with the security
officer as it passed through."

"Shar, that's an x-ray machine!"

"Oh-my-God, I forgot. That won't hurt him, will it?"

"You'll have to ask a vet that one. Just be glad it wasn't a microwave.
Why didn't you put him in a cat carrier?"

"Woman, last April when I flew to Florida with Malcolm, he went
baggage. A Doberman came on the plane with him and he was para-
noid for days . . . wouldn't let me out of his sight." Shar snuggled the
half-grown kitten.

Laney thought maybe that wasn't really the case, that the kitten was
just spoiled and loved clinging to her—hence the name Shar and
Malcolm had given him—"Kudzu." The kitten was the son of Gray's
cat, Puccini. Shar had acquired the tabby when he had been left on
Gray's doorstep three months before.

"You're allowed to board with small animals if you put them in an
approved pet carrier. But purple totes definitely don't qualify," Laney
said.

"That's a relief. I'll have to purchase one before I go back. Now,
before we get to Hickory, fill me in on this wench that's taking care of
Malcolm." Shar stretched Kudzu out on her long thighs and scratched
his belly until Laney heard his motor engage.

"Shar, maybe I was just imagining Ivy's overindulgence. I suppose
it's just part of her job. After all, Malcolm does deserve a bit of pam-
pering."

"Then, by God, *I* shall be the pamperer, " Shar said and gravely
added, "What's she look like?"

The kitten purred. Laney agonized in silence.

"That good, huh?"

"You'll see soon enough."

As they traveled, Laney filled Shar in on the progress at the dig and Cilla's problem with Eugene.

"Humph. Why Eugene doesn't leave the disciplining to Tina is beyond me. Kids expect limits from a parent and will accept it more readily. Down the road, Eugene could take some of the responsibility after Cilla accepts him."

"You sound like you know what you're talking about. Something you haven't told me?"

"Me? Woman, I never had any kids, nor did any of my three husbands—at least any they told me about. I just read it in a book somewhere and it just made sense to me."

"I think I'll pass your gems of wisdom on to Tina."

"Couldn't hurt."

Laney parked the car in the Finish Line Restaurant's parking lot just off Main Street. The eating spot was the place to go in Hickory for breakfast, lunch or dinner. Before entering the restaurant, Shar granted the kitten a rushed pit stop in a half-barrel of geraniums.

Laney's friend, Jesse Mills, met them at the door and squealed with the joy of seeing Shar again. Jesse, working the day shift on Monday, was dressed in her usual uniform, a turquoise jockey shirt tucked into slim black slacks. Her shiny brown bob bounced below the matching cap that shaded her bright gray eyes. Shar gobbled her up in a smothering embrace and the two of them prated simultaneously, both asking questions, neither listening to each other's answers. They were Laney's dearest friends and only three months before, they had been instrumental in helping her discover the truth behind a plot of murder, blackmail and betrayal. Laney stood back while the love for her friends washed over her. She wished that Gray were there to share her reminiscences.

As though reading her thoughts, Shar asked, "Now, what's with you and Gray? Not once has his name crossed your lips," Shar said, hooking her arm through Laney's while Jesse led them to a table in front of a window overlooking Main Street.

"Out with it, woman," Shar reiterated, after ordering their lunch. Kudzu lay beneath the table concealed inside Shar's tote. She tapped her glossy scarlet nails in a skittish rhythm while she waited for Laney's reply and the glass of milk that she had ordered with her lunch. Laney was eager to see how she was going to manage the tabby's mid-day feeding undetected.

The clicking nails finally got to Laney.

"I think Gray's jealous," Laney blurted.

Shar's dimpled chin rose, her head tilted, and she raised a brow. "Must be Bucko."

"His name is Bucky," Laney corrected. She frowned. "How did you know?"

"I no sooner got off the plane when I heard 'Bucko said this' and 'Bucko did that.' "

"His name is Bucky! . . . wait just a minute, Shar . . . what are you implying?" Laney sucked in her breath and then lowered her voice to a whisper. "I haven't done anything to make Gray feel threatened." She glared at her friend, trying to look as convincing as she could.

"Maybe not," Shar said, with doubt in her eyes. "But what about Bucko?"

Laney decided to leave the name alone. She shrugged at Shar's question.

"No leers, ogles or winks? No tweaks, tickles, or lingering touches while Gray's around?"

"Shar, enough!" Laney said, feeling a rush of blood to her face as she remembered. At that moment, Jesse brought their lunches. Shortly after Jesse vanished, so did an ashtray of milk—into the tote.

Plates of abalone tuna and green grape salad on a fresh tomato with mugs of chilled soup made them pause in their discussion while they did justice to their lunches.

"What does Gray do?" Shar asked, licking a melon soup mustache off her upper lip. She blinked as the mid-day sun streamed through the mini blinds transforming her strawberry blond pixie into a luminary.

"He retreats and pouts . . . doesn't talk about it."

"At least he doesn't punch Bucko out. I can remember when—"

"God forbid—" A muffled ring stopped Laney in mid sentence and she foraged in her bag and came up with her cell phone.

"Cilla . . . is something—" Laney listened with growing alarm at the hysterical teenager. Her lunch pitched and tossed, then plummeted.

"I'll be there in a few minutes," Laney said, and clicked off. In a frenzy, she was on her feet, gathering up her bag. She tossed a twenty on the table.

"Shar, they've shut down the dig," Laney said with a dry mouth.

"Bucky's been attacked by Indians."

Laney dragged Shar to her feet. Neither heard the snickers as a trail of milk followed them out the door.

10

The mini-bus in the drive sported North Carolina plates. It was empty. Perched on the fence like a row of birds from a Hitchcock movie, fifteen people—Laney counted them—were firmly established with feet planted on the middle plank and arms braced for balance along the upper rail like a braid of human rickrack.

As Laney slowed and braked next to the bus, Cilla, Toby, and Bucky, followed by the rest of the crew, stormed the Whooptie. Laney opened the door and a blast of hot air took her breath. Everyone seemed to be talking at once.

Bucky gestured a time-out and there was instant quiet. "Laney," he said gravely. "This is going to take a word from you."

"From me? . . .wh . . .what can I say? Why are they here?" she sputtered. Shar, with Kudzu under her arm, sidled up to her.

"Look, this is a Native American protest group bussed in from North Carolina. Someone informed them about the dig. They think it's illegal," Bucky said.

"Illegal? Bucky, you told me—"

"I didn't lie to you, Laney. Come over here in the shade and I'll spell it out." His warm, firm arm encircled her waist and he talked quietly to her as he guided her to the big maple.

Ten minutes later, Laney was ready. As she approached the fence, the group of people dropped to the ground and linked arms, barring her way. Most of the individuals were obviously of Native American descent. Laney instantly recognized Orenda Griffin, the woman who had canceled her bed and breakfast reservation on Friday.

"Do you have a spokesperson?" Laney called.

Orenda stepped forward. So *she's* the culprit, Laney surmised.

"This is private land," Laney stated quietly. "You have no right on this property without my permission," she added gently.

Orenda stretched to her full height, which still wasn't a great stature. Her brown eyes, almost black, flashed angrily. "This is a Native American cemetery," she stated. "The remains unearthed here are protected by the Native American Graves Protection and Repatriation Act," she retorted with a withering stare.

"Mrs. Griffin," Laney answered, "the law only pertains to Indian burials on federal or tribal lands. This is private property."

"I'm Native American," Orenda spat, correcting Laney's nomenclature. "And the law extends to federally funded university excavations." Orenda was shouting now.

Bucky stepped forward. "Mrs. Griffin, Parker Webb University is funded exclusively by private funds."

Silence ensued at Bucky's announcement. A young man holding a red blanket suddenly broke ranks, climbed through the rails and jumped into the excavation. He proceeded to cover the exposed skeleton lying on its support of dirt.

Straightening, he stood arrogantly next to the vermilion covering. "How would you like to have your grandfather's skull sitting on a shelf in some university or museum?" he cried.

Laney answered, "The bones in question are not those of a Native American. They've tentatively been identified as those of a white man who lived over two hundred years ago."

"Grave robber!" a woman yelled.

They mean business, Laney thought. She felt helpless, unsure. She chewed on her lip.

Bucky took over.

"The purpose of this dig is not to plunder graves. We are learning about what early American's ate . . . how they lived . . . how they died."

The crewmembers moved closer, riveted on Bucky's words.

"Kentucky has always been pictured as the 'Dark and Bloody Ground.' But Native Americans didn't come to Kentucky only to hunt and fight. More and more, through artifacts and excavations, we're finding that they, like the pioneer unearthed here—wanted the same things we did—food, shelter, and peace of mind."

He starred directly into Orenda's eyes. The woman swallowed and looked away.

He regained her attention by addressing her. "Mrs. Griffin, only by learning about our cultural similarities, can we learn to tolerate our differences."

Laney listened with growing admiration. He should be a politician, she thought, noting his confident demeanor, his forceful presentation. And for the first time since she had arrived home to find the site under siege, she felt that the situation was under control—Bucky's control.

It was late afternoon before the last protester climbed into the minibus and the doors closed. With a grating of gears, the vehicle backed into the circle drive, turned and shuddered down the lane.

Under the maple tree, Laney gave a great sigh of relief. The crew intermittently creaked to their feet as though Laney's breath was the signal that the conflict was finally resolved.

Two heated hours of confrontation had resulted in a tentative resolution with concessions on both sides. The group calling themselves Native Americans Against Desecration realized that since the university was not a facility receiving federal funds, the Native American Grave Protection and Repatriation Act didn't have jurisdiction over the private dig. But they did know that any unpleasant media attention could cause Parker Webb University embarrassment.

In exchange for a promise that the group would no longer delay the progress of the dig, Bucky invited the members of the group to observe the excavation process and promised to treat any discoveries sensitively. Although it was unlikely that a particular tribe would be determined to be the descendants of any remains found, Bucky still agreed—with Laney's approval—that any remains found would be returned to the site and buried after all research was completed. He also proposed to ask the anthropology department of Parker Webb to establish an annual scholarship fund for a Native American who was interested in taking up archaeology or anthropology as his field of study.

Bucky, Cam and Bonnie wandered back toward the site to cover up for the day. Laney looked around for Shar and realized that both she and the Whooptie were gone.

"Aunt Laney," Cilla breathed behind her. Laney turned. "Shar did-n't want to bother you. She said to tell you that she was driving the Whooptie to Mr. Lamont's. She said she'd be back by dinnertime."

"Well, I guess she was anxious to see Malcolm. I didn't expect to have this . . . Cilla? For heavens sake, child, whatever are you doing in that turtleneck?"

The teen's face was fiery with heat. As though she had just run through a cloudburst, sweaty wisps of hair hung limply about her face and her lips were outlined in white. Even as Laney watched, dark circles of wetness were spreading under her arms and over her breasts.

"Sunday, I grabbed long-sleeved T-shirts by mistake," she explained in a fluster. "I'll remember to get the short this weekend."

Laney was momentarily distracted by Toby who was coming off the front porch with Blackberry on a leash. The dog, still not used to being confined, pulled at the restraint.

"Toby and I are taking turns walking her," Cilla said, breathing hard. "It's all right, isn't it? . . . I mean, that I let Toby into the house?"

"Sure, I appreciate the help."

"After dinner, we're going to hit the public library for some research. Okay?"

Laney nodded and Cilla ran to catch up with Toby and Blackberry. My, look at her, she thought to herself. Cilla's steps seemed lighter, almost buoyant as she scampered across the yard. Laney wondered what Luke would think if he saw Cilla and Toby together. And she suddenly thought about Gray with his sulky departure a couple of days before.

11

Ivy readjusted the fan on the end table so that Malcolm received the full cooling effect. That she deliberately directed the flow so that it just missed including her was not lost to Shar.

The little baggage, Shar thought, as Ivy smoothed the gleaming white sheet over Mal's elevated leg for the third time since Shar had arrived. Ivy turned at the foot of the bed and crossed in front of Shar's chair to scoot the bed tray closer to the bed. It held a glass with a flexible straw, a sweating silver pitcher of ice water, and a covered plate of freshly baked chocolate chip cookies. The aroma was driving Shar crazy. I'll roll over and grow moss before I'll let her see me devour one of those, she agonized.

"Thank you, Ivy. I think that's it for a while," Malcolm said, looking a bit embarrassed by all the to-do. "I can't think of a thing you haven't thought of."

"Humph," Shar said under her breath. I bet the trollop has thought of things you'd never dream of.

"If you don't mind, then, I'll prepare Ms. Hamilton's room," she said, drifting toward the door. Shar caught the faintest whiff of lilacs as Ivy skirted her chair, her navy uniform swishing like silk. At the door, she paused, tilted her head, and smiled—assuming the position a hair too long. Finally breaking the pose, Ivy swept out of the room.

As soon as the door closed behind her, Malcolm clasped Shar's hand and drew her to him. She bussed him good and proper, making his glasses steam.

"Damn it, Shar. I hate this. I mean, being confined like this while you're here. Laney shouldn't have informed you," Malcolm protested when Shar eventually broke the connection to breathe. He wiped his spectacles with the edge of the sheet.

"Hush. This is where I want to be and look what I've brought to cheer you up." Shar snatched up the soggy purple tote, extracted the sleepy kitten and placed him on Malcolm's stomach.

"Kudzu! . . . my goodness, has he grown!" he said, fondling the little tabby who sniffed at his goatee then padded down the sheet to the little hollow between Mal's legs. After a couple of orbits, he curled into a gray ball and promptly purred himself back to sleep.

"I've missed you, lass," he said, pulling Shar towards him again.

The phone interrupted what Shar had hoped might get out of hand.

"Would you get that?" Mal asked at the third ring, pointing to the phone on the deep windowsill behind Shar's chair. She did, and a vaguely familiar female voice asked for Ivy Hart.

"It's for Poi . . . Ivy," Shar said. "I'll go find her."

After searching the kitchen and living room, and calling out Ivy's name to no avail, she climbed the walnut staircase that rose gracefully from the entrance foyer. Standing in the upper hall, she could hear water running through an open door to her right. She poked in her head and called to Ivy again. When she still didn't get an answer, she walked across the soft rose carpeting and was about to knock on the bathroom door when she heard the water cut off. The door abruptly opened.

"Ivy, there is a phone call for you," Shar said breathlessly from her climb up the stairs.

"Thank you," Ivy said, looking startled to see Shar in her bedroom. She moved to the nightstand next to a handsome cherry sleigh bed. The Lamont tartan throw that Shar swore had been on a chair in the library when she arrived, was folded neatly over the curved footboard of the bed. As Ivy reached for the phone, her hand froze above the receiver. Cocking her head toward Shar, Ivy's eyes hooded unexpectedly and their twin orbs of blue ice pierced Shar's composure so deeply, she stepped backwards as though the woman had landed a blow.

"Shut the door as you leave," was Ivy's frozen dismissal.

Wanting to slam the door behind her, instead, Shar closed it unsteadily and quickly dropped to her knees.

12

Blackberry was barking at the front door. Laney, about to fix a toddy for herself, replaced the lid on the ice bucket and hurried into the hall. From the basement, she heard the water pump cut off as Cilla finished her shower upstairs.

Through the screen, she saw Gray pace the front porch. His cat was wrapped around one arm and a box of chocolates melted away in the other. Instead of his usual blood spattered overalls, he had spruced up in clean khakis, a sunny yellow oxford cloth button-down, and penny loafers minus socks. His tan face shone from a fresh shave. In spite of herself, Laney's heart leaped.

"Can't seem to last more than a couple of days," he said, with chagrin, adding, "Got off the big pieces." He risked a smile while polishing a shoe on the back of his pants.

The boyish gesture did it. She held the door wide to let him enter, trying her best to appear merciless. The past two days had been tough on her as well. He must have caught her slight vacillation as he passed, for he suddenly dropped Puccini and the chocolates to the Persian rug and crushed her to him.

He smelled of after-shave, soap and pure maleness. Laney drank it in with great gulping kisses—his mouth smothering her breath, his tongue sweeping deep and a hand grasping her bottom.

"Hmm," someone said behind them. "Think I need a bucket of water?"

Could only be Shar, Laney determined as they pulled apart. Heat crept to her hairline. Gray cleared his throat and studied his shoes.

"Look, I'll go back out to the car and come back in," Shar called through the screen and did an about-face. Laney and Gray watched as half way down the path, she evidently changed her mind and swung over towards the dig. Shar's marathon legs, covered to below the knees in a pair of hot pink pedal pushers, ate up the yard. Above her purple halter top and wrapped about her long neck like a furry scarf, Kudzu hung on for dear life.

Laney fixed Gray a bourbon and water and a Bloody Mary for herself at the credenza bar. Gray, his body behind her, his arms around her waist, nuzzled her neck as she worked.

"Gray, we need to talk about this," Laney said, twisting about and handing him his drink. But at that moment, Cilla, followed by Blackberry, bounced down the staircase and skipped down the hall to the kitchen. Laney was relieved that Cilla hadn't seen the two of them a few minutes before.

"Toby invited me for hamburgers on the grill with the crew. Okay?" Cilla asked when she drifted into the parlor sucking on a bottle of pop.

"Sure," Laney said, noting that she had another long sleeve shirt on. This one, however, was a lightweight white cotton blouse. She had curled her hair and it hung from two red barrettes in pearly waves down her back. Laney's eyes traveled down her body to her chino shorts that gapped at the waistline and made her brown legs appear spindly. All this physical work must be making her lose weight, Laney thought.

As Cilla ran out, Shar crashed in and slammed the paneled door behind her.

"Mind if I turn on the air?" she asked, adjusting the thermostat in the hall. "If I'd known Kentucky was this hot, I would have gone to Death Valley for my vacation. At least the hottest temp ever recorded there was only 134 degrees. Malcolm's AC won't be operational for a couple more days."

"How *is* Malcolm?" Gray asked, sitting in a wing chair.

"He's just hunky-dory. Poison Ivy sees to that," Shar said, dropping Kudzu in Gray's lap and fixing a Bloody for herself.

Laney laughed.

"You won't laugh after I tell you what I heard," Shar said.

"What?" Laney said.

"Did you tell Gray about the pow-wow this afternoon?" Shar asked.

"I haven't had the chance," Laney said.

"Let me," Shar said, plopping on the red damask sofa next to Laney. Her silver thistle earrings danced. "Bucko and his crew had to stop the dig this afternoon while a tribe of Indians held them hostage." Laney caught the smirk on Gray's face at Shar's ridicule of Bucky's name.

"That's not exactly accurate, Gray," Laney said, interrupting Shar's colorful description. "A Native American group from North Carolina protested the dig."

"Anyway, they ended up smoking the peace pipe," Shar went on after sipping at her drink. "But guess who sent the smoke signals to the group in the first place?"

Laney groaned. "Orenda Griffin, the spokesperson who had canceled her reservations here—no pun intended," Laney said giggling in spite of herself at Shar's disrespectful travesty and her own complicity.

"Wro-o-ng," Shar said. "Poison Ivy. I heard her on the phone talking to Orenda just before I left Malcolm's. From the conversation, I gathered she knew the woman and got her to call in the braves. Then, when Orenda apparently told her the dig was going to continue, Poison Ivy went on the warpath. Never heard such language."

"Surely, not that gentle lady—" Gray began.

"Why would Ivy want to stop the dig?" Laney interrupted.

"Maybe she's Native American, herself," Gray said.

"Yeah . . . sure," Shar said. "Not with those ice blue peepers and skin as white as hoarfrost."

"Now Shar," Gray said. "She still could be of Native American ancestry or just be a sympathizer."

"Right . . . ." Shar said, sarcastically. "Whatever you say, Gray. But I just hope that for the future of Bucko's dig, Ivy's son doesn't feel the same way about this dig as she does."

"Ivy has a son?" Laney asked, sitting forward in her seat.

"None other than Toby Hart, Bucko's outstanding field school teenager," Shar answered.

"Our Toby?" Laney exclaimed incredulously. "How in heaven did you find all this out in the short time you were there?" Laney asked.

"The phone rang while I was talking with Mal in the library. The caller—Orenda, I later realized—asked to speak with Ivy Hart. I tracked her down in her room—my room, I might add, according to Malcolm. When she came out of the head and saw me, she sent me packing with a look that would freeze the balls off the devil himself— but not before I saw a photo of Toby on her night stand. It wasn't hard to put two and two together."

"But how did you hear the conversation?" Laney asked.

Shar grinned.

"Shar, you didn't?" Laney said.

"Ear-to-the-keyhole. Works like a charm."

Puccini meandered into the room and Kudzu shot from Gray's lap to Shar's. Puccini only yawned and flopped onto the carpet. Stretched out toe to tail he was twice the length of his son, Kudzu.

Laney jumped from the sofa to refresh her drink, grabbing Gray's on route. "Bucky certainly can't afford to have anymore surprises at the dig," Laney said, glancing at Gray after mentioning Bucky's name. She didn't miss his jaw muscles drawing in sharply. The two of us need to have a little talk soon, she thought.

13

Two moths fluttered at the yellow overhead porch light. Cilla couldn't imagine why bugs could be attracted to light in all that heat. Toby kicked off on the wicker swing, creating the tiniest breath of air on her face. If only she didn't have to wear a long-sleeved shirt, she thought. When she had sneaked out of the house Saturday night to be with Luke, he had promised her that he would never hurt her again. *If only he means it this time.* Cilla rolled up her sleeves—but not so high that Toby could see the bruises. *It really was her fault, anyway. She had come on to Toby a little. It was hard not to. He was so cute and easy to talk to.* She looked out across the yard to the darkness beyond the porch.

Toby remarked lazily, "Looks like everyone is asleep."

She and Toby had been talking about the dig on the front porch for over an hour.

"I'll probably stay up for another couple of hours reading some of this junk." He nodded at the stack of books on the wicker coffee table.

"Won't you keep Dr. Gage awake?"

"Naw. I'll use my flashlight. He sleeps like the dead, anyway."

"Sounds like you've done this before."

"Sometimes I wake up in the middle of the night and can't go back to sleep," he said, uneasiness crossing his face.

Cilla wondered why but didn't want to pry. "Sure is a lot of material to go through. But I'll take half of the books. I can't wait to get started."

"You know, Cilla, this is like finding a needle in a haystack. The information may not even be in these books, or anywhere for that matter."

"Yeah, but won't it be cool if we could give Bones a name?"

"Cilla, this is stupid. No way. Too many surveyors back then . . . so few historical records," Toby said pessimistically.

"It will be fun trying though. Don't forget to make a copy of the notes on Bones that Dr. Gage is preparing . . . and thanks for the sundae after the library," Cilla said, looking straight into Toby's eyes for the first time.

He stared back and even when she finally averted her eyes, she knew he was still looking. Something inside her teetered on the brink when she felt him leaning toward her. Then he did it. He kissed her on the mouth like she had never been kissed—softly, like a whisper, sweetly, like she was someone really special.

His arm wrapped around her.

"Oh," she winced, and drew away.

"What is it?" Toby said in alarm.

"Nothing, really. I . . . I fell . . . this weekend at home. It'll be all right," she said. But as he withdrew his arm, she thought she saw more than just concern in his eyes. For an instant, she could have sworn that her pain had frightened him.

14

Laney rode her bike to the mailbox and was on her way back to the house with a basket full of bills when she heard Gray's opera-belching Jeep behind her. She moved to the side of the lane and skidded to a stop.

"Goin' my way, honey?" he quipped.

"Sure, big fellow. I'll race you to the house. Loser fixes lunch," she called as she outmaneuvered the Jeep and continued in the center of the lane so that Gray couldn't pass her.

"No fair," Gray shouted, following her into the house and down the hall while she sorted through the mail. One by one, she studied them. With a long face, she dumped them onto the kitchen desk, except one that she held up. "Damn, my SASE." She ripped it open, scanned the rejection form letter, then tossed it into the trash.

"Still haven't heard from the publishing house that requested chapters, huh?"

"Let's not talk about it. In fact, let's go see what's going on at the dig before you have to make lunch," she said, boring a forefinger into his gut.

Sensing her forced cheerfulness, Gray snatched her finger and brought it to his mouth. His lips crept to her palm.

"I love you, you know," he said huskily.

"I know," she said and lifted her mouth to his. God, kissing his soft mouth was like touching velvet with her lips, she thought. How she loved his kisses.

Gray cleared his throat. "Let's get this over with," he said, leading her back down the hall. Blackberry, anticipating an outing, wagged a black and white tail at the front door. Laney snagged Blackberry's leash off the hall table and snapped it to her collar.

Members of the crew were scattered about the yard eating their lunches. Laney spotted Cilla and Toby in front of a tent. Laney waved and Toby, who was sprawled in the brown grass writing in his note-book, waved back. Laney didn't see Bucky among the crewmembers. Gray, his arm around her shoulders, gathered her closer as they walked toward the site while Blackberry strained at the leash.

Laney tied the collie to the lowest rail and she and Gray climbed the fence and perched on the top rail, peering at the progress that had been made.

Most of the stones in the southwest quadrant had been removed, leaving the skeleton, a faceless, unnamed specter, lying on his pedestal of earth. Now that the dirt had been removed from around the bones, Laney could see that several rib bones were broken—evidently crushed by the weight of the stones that had covered them. Bucky had told Laney that the range of accuracy for dating bones in the historical era would most likely be plus or minus one or two hundred years—point-less if the skeleton was only a couple of hundred years old. But being thorough in his research, he had sent off a bone sample to be carbon dated, anyway. He believed that identifying the age of artifacts found in the same level or in association with the remains—in this case, the compass—would more accurately date the skeleton.

Laney's eyes traveled diagonally from the skeleton across the center of the dig and settled on the northeast quadrant where most of the morning's clearing had taken place. A canopy lay in the grass, ready to be erected over the area after lunch. All of the largest surface stones had been removed from the quadrant, and under the scorching mid-day sun, it looked as desolate as the surface of the moon.

Just outside the grid, inches from where the grass of the pasture began, a gasp of a breeze dropped down between two small stones and stirred up a tiny dust whirlwind. It dispersed into the air like a puff of smoke.

"Look at that, will you," Laney said, pointing.

"First breath of air we've had in two weeks," Gray answered.

"Not the breeze, silly," she said. "That brown thing. It looks like burlap."

"What, you say!" a voice exclaimed behind them.

Laney swiveled on the rail as Cam grasped the top plank and vaulted the fence, landing as lightly as a cat on the dry turf surrounding the site. He immediately dropped to a crouch and his eyes riveted on the material in question.

"Blast!" he exploded in rage. "Gage will go off if this site was used for a trash dump."

Hearing Cam's clamor, the crewmembers began rushing over, some still carrying apples or half-eaten sandwiches.

The assistant crew chief removed two small rocks and an area of sod, exposing a large rock slab. The burlap peeked from beneath one corner. The slab encroached onto the grid area about a foot.

Toby and Cliff joined Cam and inched the stone away until the material was uncovered.

"It *is* a burlap bag," Laney said, watching Cam grow more incensed by the second.

"Looks like it's been in the ground for a long time," Gray said. "Too cheap to pay your trash bill, Laney?" He nudged Laney in the ribs.

"Funny, Gray," she said.

Cam was not amused. With a scowl as dark as a thundercloud, he pulled a penknife from his pocket. Dropping to one knee he made quick short cuts in the burlap.

Taking hold of the cut edges of the bag, he spread it wide. The members of the crew, who had converged at the fencing, strained forward to see, their inquisitive faces grouped like a bouquet of posies.

Cam gasped and his body recoiled. He sprawled in the dust, the color in his face draining away like someone had pulled a plug.

A general cry arose from Toby and Cliff who also had seen the contents clearly. The others at the fence mumbled.

"What?"

"What is it?"

"Dr. Dalton, tell us."

Cam struggled to his feet, for a moment blocking Laney's view of the contents of the sack.

But Laney had seen the shriveled form, the tiny shrunken head. And like a brand burned into the flesh, Laney knew that the leathery and withered doll-like shape lying between the folds of the dusty jute bag would be forever engraved into her memory.

Her ears buzzing, Laney cried out. The sky began to spin as the burning sun seared a path to her brain.

"Laney," Gray shouted, his hand missing as he tried to prevent her from falling off the rail. As she slipped into unconsciousness, her body slumped forward into Cam's and Toby's arms.

Laney's eyes fluttered and snapped open. Gray, on his knees cradling her head in his lap, called her name softly.

"Laney, thank God," he said. "You'll be all right in a moment or two. You've had a terrible shock. We all have."

She immediately recalled the whole gruesome scene and felt the nausea grip her throat and uncontrolled dizziness begin again. She swallowed and shook her head. Wrenching herself free of Gray's arms, she sat up. At her feet, Cilla sat in the grass on her knees, a relieved expression spreading across her pale features when she saw that Laney wasn't going to die. Behind Cilla, Toby and the rest of the crew stood in anxious groups staring at her, and above, sparrows sang in the branches of the maple tree.

How could they, Laney thought. "Where's Cam?" she mumbled, looking around the yard. Her mouth was cottony.

"He's inside calling the police," Gray answered, wincing that he had to tell her.

"Gray, this isn't happening again?"

He didn't have to answer her. They both had seen the wrinkled, contracted remains.

"Gray, I want to go inside . . . please," she murmured, struggling to her feet. Gray and Cilla guided her toward the porch.

"Cilla, is Blackberry still tied to the fence?" Laney asked, as the three of them stepped into the cool hallway.

"I'll get her," Cilla said and bounded out the door.

Gray led her into the parlor and eased her into the Morris chair. He lifted her feet so that they rested on the ottoman. Seeing her shiver, he covered her with a soft throw, tucking it firmly around her shoulders.

"You're shocky. I'll be right back," he said and disappeared down the hall to the kitchen to get her a glass of water.

She was drinking the liquid in weak sips when Bucky exploded into the foyer. He stormed into the parlor with powerful strides that shook the floor. Laney had never seen him like this. He kept running his fingers through his hair with such great sweeping movements that she was afraid he would rip the curls out by the roots.

"Laney . . . Cam called the police . . . they're . . . on the way," Bucky said, his mouth in a kind of spasm. He stepped to the credenza and poured three fingers of bourbon into a tall glass and drank it down. He fixed another and did the same. Without another word, he strode out the door.

Gray knelt next to her and took her cold hands in his. He blew his hot breath on them.

"Gray . . . an infant," she sobbed.

"Shush . . . don't." His words faded as the sirens grew louder.

15

Laney hadn't moved. Gray let her be, hoping that rest would fortify her for whatever lay ahead. But he knew she didn't sleep. Frightened brown eyes stared at him from above the throw as though imploring him to make it all go away. Every freckle on her face showed through her pallid skin like some terrible pox had stricken her. He bent and held her body close, his lips against her reddish brown hair.

She suddenly pushed him away and got to her feet. "Gray, I have to see . . . ," she said.

He couldn't stop her from dashing through the door onto the porch where she pulled up short when she saw all the vehicles parked along the lane in front of the site—three St. Clair County patrol cars, a state police vehicle, and a blue mini-van that belonged to Patrick Wasson of the *Hickory Times.* Gray grabbed Laney's hand as she stepped off the porch and started across the brown grass.

Cilla, with Blackberry in tow, ran to Laney. Toby wasn't far behind her.

"We're not allowed near the site," Cilla said excitedly.

From where he was standing, Gray saw that the area had already been cordoned off with yellow crime tape.

A Commonwealth of Kentucky vehicle with State Medical Examiner printed on the side pulled up behind the mini-van, and a man and a woman got out. After pausing to speak briefly with the state policeman, the woman climbed through the fence. She squatted next to the jute bag.

Karen Thompson, Gray thought. He remembered seeing the forensic anthropologist on a channel twenty-seven newscast when she had supervised the exhuming of a John Doe thought to be a woman's missing relative. DNA testing of the remains positively identified the man as the brother of the woman.

The young man accompanying Dr. Thompson immediately began taking photos of the scene.

Standing next to his squad car, the St. Clair County sheriff, Gordon Powell, was questioning Cam while deputy Freddie Rudd took notes. Gordon looked up and motioned to Laney and Gray to come over.

"God, do I have to do this?" Laney asked Gray.

"It shouldn't take long. You only saw it for an instant," Gray said to Laney. Her expression remained anxious, as though his words had melted in the heat before reaching her ears.

"I'm sorry for this," Gordon said, as they approached. He turned back to Cam and dismissed him with a brief, "That's all, Dr. Dalton." Cam forced a smile at Laney, then walked toward the camp where the rest of the crew sat scattered beneath the maple tree.

Although it must have been ninety-five degrees in the sun, Gordon's shirt and pants looked as fresh and crisp as though they had just been starched and ironed. In contrast, dark brown wet marks stained Freddie's beige uniform wherever it touched his meaty frame. Gray could hear his labored breathing and couldn't miss the empty candy wrapper peeking out of his pants pocket.

"Just a couple questions, Laney," Gordon said. "Do you mind, Doc? You'll be next."

Gray walked back to where Cilla and Toby stood, but stationed himself so that he could see Laney's face. Her eyes were wide with the intense emotion of the situation but she answered his questions nervously.

All of a sudden, a stricken expression darted across Laney's face, and Gray knew Gordon had hit a nerve. She swayed and Gray read her lips. There was no doubt what she uttered in answer to Gordon's question—"No." With that, she turned and walked away unsteadily, but not to him. She rushed straight by him to the house—her face ashen, her eyes filled with fear.

Tempted as he was to follow Laney inside, he instead took her place at the patrol car. Freddie had opened the rear door and was seated with both legs on the ground. His face looked as though he had fallen asleep on the beach.

When Gordon asked Gray how the infant had been discovered, he related detail by horrible detail. Gray was sure Laney had been asked similar questions.

"One last question, Doc. Do you have any idea who the mother of this baby could be?" Gordon asked, thumbing over his shoulder. And instantly, Gray realized that was the question that had shaken Laney to the core.

16

"Shar, she won't talk to me," Gray complained, wearing a path across the parlor carpet. He had just finished giving Laney's friend the diminutive rundown of the day's occurrences. Shar hadn't said one word since his tirade had begun. In fact, the only movements she had made were short, swift ones to her mouth from the hand that held the Bloody Mary.

"What did you expect, Gray?" Shar said, finally breaking her silence. "It's just too much. It's only been three months since the tape episode."

"Damn it, Shar. I know what she went through . . . what we all went through, for that matter. More the reason to try to help Laney handle this. But it's something more . . . something Gordon asked her."

"What do you think it was?"

"Has to be the same question he asked me. He wanted to know if I had any idea who the mother of the infant could be."

"Graham Prescott, are you saying that Laney might know who this baby belonged to?" Some of Shar's Bloody sloshed onto the front of her white tube halter that barely covered her meager bosom. She grimaced and rubbed it in with her thumb.

"If her reaction was any indication of—"

"Where is she?" Shar broke in.

"Her bedroom."

"Give me one more shot in the arm," Shar demanded, holding out her glass.

Shar burst into the room and advanced upon the bed where Laney lay curled about a goose down pillow. Laney's still, white face stared blankly through unruly clouds of flaming hair like an eye of a hurricane

"Woman, get a grip," Shar demanded, giving Laney's butt a slap.

As though shot from a cannon, Laney slammed the pillow into Shar's face, totally catching her off guard and knocking her away from the bed. With astonishing quickness, Laney grabbed Shar's wrist and shoved her onto the bed. Laney roughly pressed her friend to the mattress, straddled her stomach, and pinned Shar's arms with her knees. All the while, Laney's eyes—twin eruptions of fire—promised more violence.

"Now that's more like it," Shar laughed guardedly, secretly worrying that her unexpected slap may have created a monster.

But the flames in Laney's eyes were quickly quenched and she rolled off her friend. She sat on the edge of the bed picking at the blue ribbons that were woven through the rumpled gray spread. "It's Cara's baby," she whispered, her eyes continuing to darken as though some inner light was being extinguished.

Shar wasn't sure she had heard correctly.

"Did you say Cara's? . . . Your sister's baby?" a voice asked from behind them. Both women's heads turned simultaneously toward Gray standing in the doorway.

His legs were anchored wide, his hands tucked under his armpits in his familiar diffident gesture.

"Gray, come in," Shar invited, although Laney's expression wasn't very welcoming.

"Laney," Gray began, crossing to Laney and staring down into her colorless face. "You don't know that!"

"This was Cara's house for seven years before she left it to me," she said, jumping to her feet and shoving Gray aside as she stormed to the window. Shar bounced off the bed and followed her.

The window faced west and Shar's eyes traveled with Laney's across the yard to the fence in front of the site. The official vehicles were still there and Bucky and his crew still milled around the yard.

"Why would you think she would conceal a birth?" Shar asked her quietly, her arm encircling Laney's waist.

"Ask Gray," Laney said. Shar detected sarcasm in her tone and at the same time, something stirred Shar's memory.

Shar looked back at him. By his hurt expression, Shar knew he had caught Laney's snideness.

Gray inhaled sharply and his jaws tightened. "I think Laney is referring to her sister's abortion while I was dating her eight years ago. Cara had told Laney it was my child. It was not. Laney has known the truth for over a year. Isn't that right, Laney?" Gray's eyes narrowed as he confronted her.

Laney lowered her eyes. "I'm sorry. I had no right. . . ."

Shar's memory raced fast forward and caught up just as Gray finished his explanation. Laney had told her the story shortly after her sister died. It was apparent that Laney still had some unresolved issues about Gray and Cara's relationship, Shar thought.

A small sob escaped Laney's lips. Shar pulled her into an awkward embrace and she felt a hot tear fall on her bare shoulder.

"Just because Cara once had an abortion, doesn't mean she would have hidden a birth," Gray said. "Anyway, Gordon believes this infant was full term. Wouldn't you have known if Cara were pregnant?"

"I'm not so sure," Laney said. "Cara was plump. She could have hidden it easily." It was evident that Laney had already pondered the situation. "Anyway, I was living in Pittsburgh all those years. There were several times that a year passed between my visits."

"Surely Cara's husband, Joe, or your mother would have suspected," Shar added, then remembered reading just recently of a girl, her pregnancy unknown to her classmates, who had given birth in the restroom during a prom and actually danced afterwards.

Laney crossed to the fireplace. She lifted a bisque doll from the white wicker rocker. Shar recalled that Laney had bought the doll because it had the same heart shaped face, golden hair and clear blue eyes of her sister. Cara had died before Laney had the chance to give it to her.

"Aunt Laney," Cilla called from the doorway. "Luke's here and he's taking me home." Her skin, drawn tight over her fine cheekbones, appeared almost transparent. Shar noted how thin she seemed and wondered how she could tolerate the long-sleeved plaid blouse that was tied under her breasts.

"What about the dig?" Gray asked.

"Dr. Gage said it's been put on hold . . . the cops and crime tape and stuff," Cilla answered.

Laney nodded. Shar thought she was relieved that Cilla was leaving.

Shar helped Cilla lug a box of library books and a small suitcase out to Luke's truck. Luke sat in the driver's seat, impatiently tapping his fingers against the steering wheel, his eyes glued on Toby who was watching from the camp area.

Luke's rather disposed to idleness, Shar thought as he glanced at them through the side mirror while they slid the box and luggage into the bed of the pickup. She also thought he could do with a shampoo. His greasy yellow ponytail reminded her of the straw muck Aaron forked out of horse stalls.

"Cilla," Bucky boomed from behind them. Although Shar was six feet tall herself, the man loomed over her. He winked at Shar, then turned to the teenager.

"Hopefully, this delay won't be much longer so don't plan to be gone more than a day. And keep up the research. Who knows, maybe you and our man, Toby, will identify our surveyor over there. Did Toby give you a copy of my notes?"

"Yes, sir," Cilla said, patting the purse on her hip. The strap crossed over her chest like a bandoleer.

Luke checked out the horn, making them all jump, and Cilla rushed to the passenger door. She tossed an embarrassed wave and jumped inside. When Luke scratched off, Cilla needed a two handed grip to wrench the door shut. The truck spun out, barely missing the beige Oldsmobile that Shar had borrowed from Malcolm.

"Cilla needs to watch that one," Bucky snarled. "I think the 'green eyed monster' has the son of a bitch around the throat."

"Who's the other swain?" Shar asked.

"Toby Hart," Bucky said, nodding at the young man that was eating up the brown turf towards them. A puff of dust accompanied every stride.

Ah yes, Shar thought when he reached them. Poison Ivy's teenage offspring. Now that I know he belongs to her, I can see the resemblance. He has the same blue eyes and lashes to die for.

"Dr. Gage, the sheriff wants you . . . ASAP," the boy blurted gasping for breath.

"Goddamn it, I wish they'd get that bag of bones out of here so we can get on with the dig," he said, and stormed toward the site.

Toby blinked at Bucky's insensitivity. Shar was struck dumb.

17

Ⅰt wasn't like Luke to be so quiet, Cilla thought. He had driven all the way to Mason County without uttering a single word—driven fast, whined gears like some race car driver at the Indianapolis 500.

"Luke, please slow down. You're scaring me," Cilla said for the fifth time, knowing that each time she said it, it just seemed to urge him to go faster. But she just couldn't help herself from saying it. This time, she was surprised when he did as she asked. He slowed, then suddenly turned right onto a familiar gravel road. She knew where they were going.

"Luke, honey. Grandma is expecting me. My mom's at a festival in Louisville."

Luke still didn't speak. He followed the gravel road that forked to the right and braked in a cloud of dust next to a windowless greenhouse.

Behind the greenhouse, Luke's dad leased a large strawberry and pumpkin patch alongside a field of young evergreens from Garvin Mullins. Luke's job after school, weekends, and during the summer months was to keep the crops weeded and sprayed. He and his father, Sam, lived on another farm on the outskirts of Washington where their garden center was located.

The home place on this farm had burned some time in the fifties, leaving a greenhouse and a twenty-foot high grain bin next to part of a feed barn. Firemen had managed to save half of the barn when a spark from the house had set it on fire. The bin was used for feeding the few head of cattle that belonged to the farm's owner, but most of the grain was sold. Cilla could see three cows wallowing in a muddy pond behind the bin. Garvin and his son, Steve, lived in a small tenant house on the back of the farm.

"Let's see it," Luke said.

"See what, Luke?" She was frightened. She'd seen that look before.

"Whadda you think? The note," he said with control, but his hand shot out like a rubber band and grabbed the purse strap. A quick yank and it snapped. Pulling the bag into his lap, he unbuckled the fastener and dumped the contents onto the seat of the truck between them.

"Luke," she cried, "you have no right."

He grabbed up the only folded sheet of notebook paper among her things.

"That dig guy said the jerk gave ya a note. That gives me the right." He unfolded it and scanned the sheet.

"It's only Dr. Gage's notes on that skeleton they dug up," Cilla said, praying that Toby hadn't added anything to it. She hadn't had a chance to read it.

"What's this, then . . . huh?" he said, taking the sheet of paper and palming it into her face.

She shoved his hand away, beginning to cry. She could not understand why she always cried when she was angry.

" 'Don't forget Monday,' " he read. "What's happening Monday, Cilla? You fixing to go out with that jerk?" Luke wadded the note and threw it on the dash.

"That's the day the crew is cooking a jambalaya dinner and Aunt Laney and I are invited." She lied. Even though the dinner was planned, she knew that the Monday Toby was referring to had passed. It was the night he had kissed her.

She couldn't believe it, but the answer seemed to have satisfied him because he was smiling.

Then he hit her—a solid blow with his fist to her stomach that took her breath. He hit her again. She tried to call out but her mouth wouldn't work.

She grappled with the door handle but his hand grasped hold of her hair in a vise grip and he pulled hard. A clump came out in his fist. Again she felt the scream in her throat but as she gasped for air, only a strangling wheeze escaped her lips.

"I ain't gonna have it, Cil. You comin on to that jerk like some bitch in heat," he snarled.

Every second was an hour. She groaned, her abdomen throbbing with endless erupting fire. Managing a sucking breath, she struggled to straighten her body, finally collapsing into sobs as little by little, the pain subsided to a tolerable level. Desperate and frightened, she tried to pull her wits together, to say something, anything to prevent him from hitting her again. She knew there was no use denying his accusation. He wouldn't believe her anyway. Instead, she pleaded, "You said you'd never hit me again," she cried into her hands. "Luke, you promised. . . ."

"It's your fault, Cil," he whined, slowly getting his rage under control.

"Maybe we should just . . . you know . . . break up," Cilla ventured, untying the knot in her shirt above her bruised and swollen midriff. She wiped her eyes with the ends of the shirttail.

She didn't know whether Luke was remorseful or that maybe he had just spotted her breast as she pulled up the tails of her blouse, but he suddenly grabbed her to him. Through wet kisses and caresses, she heard him murmur, "Cil, I'm sorry. I don't know why I do it . . . hurt ya, I mean. I'll never again. This time I mean it. Please, Cil."

She hurt so badly, but she just couldn't exist without him. Maybe this time it would be different. Through the open window, she could hear the whine of the drier fans in the grain bin. Luke pressed her down onto the torn vinyl seat and unzipped her shorts. She must be going crazy. She let him.

18

"Wake up, Toby," the voice said as a strong hand violently shook his arm. "You're dreaming a bad one."

"Don't . . . !" Toby cried out as he startled awake.

"Man, that must have been some night terror," Bucky said, patting Toby's arm in the dark. A click and the flash of the lantern lit up his face. Bucky's eyes were shiny black marbles staring at him inside the small tent. Toby jerked upright. He felt the dampness of the sleeping bag beneath him and smelled his own sweat.

"Shit, Dr. Gage, I'm sorry I woke you," he said groggily, his heart still hammering like a piston.

He hadn't had the nightmare for almost a year. He didn't know why it had suddenly returned with its suffocating fear that if he didn't hide, he would die. In his dream, he would sometimes slip into a closet behind clothes that hung heavily on his shoulders, other times under a bed among shoes that smelled like dirty feet, all the while, fearful that if he would so much as breathe, he would be found.

Bucky smiled in the eerie blue-white light. "Used to have nightmares when I was a kid, too. Outgrew them. Now, I only have sweet dreams of soft women with big hooters," he said with a laugh, winking and punching Toby's arm. "Now, let's get some shuteye." Bucky clicked off the light. "Tomorrow, I hope to get this dig back on schedule."

Bucky rustled around getting settled on his air mattress. It wasn't but a few seconds until Toby heard the even respiration of sleep coming from the professor's side of the tent. His own breathing quieted.

Soon, the crickets and other creatures of the night drowned out all other sounds. As he lay staring into the darkness, Toby worried that the dig might never get back on schedule again. He had seen Gordon Powell and Karen Thompson with their heads together while the forensic anthropologist pointed here and there on the little form. Finally, when they had collected the tiny remains, they'd left the farm, leaving only the yellow crime tape encircling the excavation. Sheriff Powell had promised Bucky he would get back with him tomorrow.

Toby punched his pillow and buried his face into its damp softness. Hearing the strident cry of a screech owl, he shivered. At the same instant, he wondered if it had been the discovery of the infant that had triggered his haunting dream to return.

19

"**I**'m telling you, Mal, the woman hates Kudzu's guts," Shar said, pulling the sheet up over him after helping him to the bathroom and back to the bed.

"Shar, you must be mistaken," Malcolm gasped, out of breath after hopping the distance on his good leg. Shar readjusted his pillow, then reached down and lifted the kitten onto the bed. The tabby found his favorite little cranny between Malcolm's legs and nestled in.

"Like hell. She torments the little guy. Just this morning, I saw her take a swipe at him with the broom. He somersaulted across the kitchen floor like he was on the damned U. S. gymnastics team. 'Accident,' she said. Later, she whisked his saucer of milk away in mid lick and poured it down the sink. When she caught me watching her, she said she thought he was finished."

"Sharlene, her behavior is exemplary around me. She's a well-disposed lady . . . nothing she won't do to make me more comfortable."

"Well-disposed, my eyeball," Shar said under her breath while she turned the oscillating fan on the bedside table on high. "The bitch thinks that if she makes me miserable enough, I just may grab up my little dickens and march right out the door. In your dreams, wench."

"Did you say something, Sharlene?"

"Not me. How much longer will she be here, Mal? You'll get your walking cast tomorrow. And I can do for you until you get used to your crutches."

"I think I'll keep her on as long as she's willing to stay. The woman can cook, Sharlene. Did you taste her Scotch eggs this morning?

Outstanding."

As though she were listening to Malcolm's accolades just outside the door, Ivy appeared with a pitcher of lemonade and three glasses on a tray. "Anything else I can do for you," she asked, directing the question to Malcolm as she placed the tray on the bed table next to Shar. She lowered the speed on the fan and smoothed Malcolm's sheet as she circled the bed to the other side. When she neared the window, Shar saw her glance outside.

"Excuse me," Ivy said in a tight voice and quickly walked out of the room. Shar dashed around to the window and saw Toby Hart standing by a side entrance that led to the kitchen. As she watched, Ivy stepped off the small stoop and approached Toby. She reached into her apron pocket and retrieved an envelope as she spoke to her son. She held it pressed against her chest with two hands while Toby remained in avid conversation with her. Suddenly, Ivy's hand flew to her mouth just as Toby snatched the envelope away and jammed it into his short's pocket. Ivy backed away, turned and rushed back into the house. Toby shrugged and walked toward the front of the house where he had parked his truck.

"I wonder what that was all about," Shar said to Malcolm as she poured two glasses of lemonade.

"What's that, my dear?" he said.

Before she could answer, Ivy stepped into the room. Blue spidery veins webbed the opalescent skin beneath her eyes. Shar offered her a glass of lemonade and Ivy grasped it with tremulous fingers and took a long draft. As she drank, Ivy looked over her tumbler at Shar. Their eyes fused for a long moment, but Ivy's normally steely eyes wobbled—a barely discernible motion. As Ivy pulled her mouth from the glass, she glanced down at Kudzu on the bed between Malcolm's legs. In a quick, fluid motion, Ivy extended her hand holding the glass as though she wanted Shar to place it on the tray. Shar reached for it but an instant before her fingers grasped the tumbler, Ivy released it.

Down it fell—tumbler, ice, and lemonade—right onto Kudzu, all comfortable and snug in his little hollow without a care in the world. Abruptly, he exploded in a thrashing, grappling frenzy. By Malcolm's violent reaction, Shar envisioned the kitten's needle-sharp claws tearing into the warm private area that the kitten definitely had more knowledge of than she.

Malcolm, his face as red as the blood that the cat must have drawn, shot upright in his bed. Behind his spectacles, brown bug-eyes threatened to pop right out of their sockets. "God all mighty . . . blessed Mary, Mother of God . . . get the little bastard off of me," he howled.

Ivy smiled.

20

"The baggage did it on purpose," Shar said, whisking Laney's Bloody out of her hand, draining the glass and handing it back to her as she shoved her way into the foyer.

"Couldn't it have been an accident?" Laney suggested, following her friend into the parlor where Shar stirred up two more drinks at the credenza. Inside the purple tote that Shar had parked on the oriental rug, two kitten ears appeared.

"No way! Those sulfurous blue eyes of hers gave her away. She was upset about something and she knew I knew it. Then she looked down at Kudzu and knew instantly what she wanted to do. It was almost like she did it to divert my attention."

"What about Malcolm? Does he believe she dropped the glass on purpose, too?" Laney asked, taking one of the drinks from Shar.

"Woman, men are so goddamned stupid," she said with exasperation. "After Ivy practically threw herself on a funeral pyre in remorse, what else could he do but assure her that it was just an unfortunate accident? 'No fault of yours, my dear,' if I may quote the little worm."

Laney laughed as Shar laid her drink on the marble topped center table and ran out onto the porch. A moment later, Laney heard a thud at the front door.

"Are you sure this won't be an imposition," Shar asked, dragging a suitcase over the threshold. "I'll gladly sleep on the library sofa if you don't have room."

Shar turned, handed the cab driver—a bald little fellow with crooked teeth and a bright smile—a handful of cash. "Thank you, you sweet thing," she said and dismissed him with a wave.

"Shar, honest . . . I have plenty of room. The Harneys and Brice McIlvaine are only here for one more night and as for Cilla, I haven't a clue when she'll return if, in fact, she does at all," Laney said, closing the door behind Shar. "But I do have a concern. Won't Ivy interpret your departure as a sign of victory?" Laney asked, as she dropped onto the sofa.

"Bite your tongue, woman!" Shar retorted as once again she took up her drink. "I have not—and may I emphasize—*not* been defeated. I am merely regrouping . . . changing tactics, so to speak. When I find out more about this scheming snake in the grass, I'll go in for the kill."

"What about Malcolm. You're leaving him in her clutches. Aren't you afraid that she'll seduce him?" Laney laughed.

"After Kudzu's full frontal attack? I . . . don't . . . think . . . so." She swept Kudzu out of the tote and kissed his little black nose.

"What do you think Ivy was so troubled about?"

"It's a given . . . whatever was in that envelope. When Toby snatched it away, it set her off." Shar looked out the front window. "Speaking of trouble, you'll be unhappy to know that the sheriff of St. Clair County just pulled up."

Gordon stood behind the center table as though he were about to begin a lecture. A spiral-bound notebook bulging with notes and a ballpoint pen jammed through its coil lay on the marble surface.

"I wanted you to hear where we stand in the investigation," Gordon said to Laney and Shar. Laney sat with her hands balled into fists and Shar kept glancing at her.

Gordon thrust his stalwart chest outwards and took a breath. "Karen Thompson called me this afternoon and gave me a preliminary on the infant remains." He was conscious of Laney's resolute facial expression as he continued. "The infant is a neonate."

"Neonate . . . what's that?" Shar asked. Kudzu, curled in her lap, purred.

"I'll explain. A neonate is a term for a newborn, usually a child that is less than four weeks old. In this case, Karen believes that the child in question had just been delivered when it was disposed of."

"How did she determine that, Gordon," Laney said.

"At the site, she showed me how the head was strangely bulbous in shape and that the teeth hadn't erupted yet. Also another clue, the mandible—the jaw—wasn't fused. The remains appeared to be the size and length of a newborn. The autopsy showed that the end of the knees were separate—the epiphyses, Karen called them. They get larger as the child grows and slowly unite with the rest of the femurs. The burlap bag provided a quick means of moisture escape and the infant mummified rather than decomposed." Gordon saw Laney's face blanch but the next question also came from her.

"Can they tell how long ago the infant was born?" Laney was holding her breath while waiting for his reply.

"It's hard to determine from the condition of remains. The best way to tell when the infant died would be to date the bag that the baby was buried in. Jute, of course, has been around for centuries, although Karen believes that the bag is fairly recent. It may take a while to date it."

"I assume that the infant was stillborn and perhaps the mother tried to conceal the birth," Shar said, her gaze darting sideways to Laney.

Gordon was strangely silent.

"I can't remember how many times I've read about someone finding a baby in a restroom or dumpster," Shar's voice crackled in the uneasy silence.

Gordon lifted his notebook and turned the pages with nervous fingers until he found one that was book marked with a folded, legal pad sheet of paper. Several loose notes slipped to the table. He cleared his throat as he scanned the yellow sheet, "Dr. Karen Thompson, who you know is forensic anthropologist for the State Medical Examiner's office, believes that this infant sustained a paramortem fracture of the frontal bone."

"What in the hell does paramortem mean?" Shar asked.

"The trauma occurred at or around the time of death," he said.

The two women looked puzzled until with one word, Gordon spelled it out: "Homicide."

Shar gasped. But Laney's reaction stunned him. She recoiled in horror and cried out as though his word was a quick, violent blow to her body. Then as Karen's opinion penetrated deeper into her consciousness, Laney's color bled away, her body convulsed and her hands trembled on the way to her mouth.

"God, no!" she said in a high, hysterical voice. She struggled to control the quavering. "How . . . how does she know this? There must be some mistake."

"Laney, I must admit I've had very little experience with trauma in mummified remains," Gordon began. "I usually deal with recent trauma. But at the scene, Karen indicated to me that she suspected foul play. She showed me where the skull had been crushed just above the eye orbit. Also there was a compound fracture of the left humerus—the upper arm bone."

A groan came from Shar.

"But couldn't that have been caused by the weight of the stones on the infant?" Laney persisted.

"I asked Karen the same question," Gordon said.

"Well?" Laney said.

"Did you ever break a dead twig, Laney?" Gordon asked.

"Huh?"

"Did you?"

"Well . . . yes, I suppose. . . ."

"How about a green twig off a living tree?"

"What are you driving at, Gordon?" Laney asked impatiently.

"Please answer and I will explain," Gordon pressed.

"Yes, of course . . . at some time or other," she said.

"Laney, forensic science has become very sophisticated. Technology can now determine if bones were fractured before or after death. Picture the skull as a hard-boiled egg that's been broken. There are edges of bone, same as in a broken arm. In bones that have been crushed at or around the time of death, through time, the edges age the same—are the same color as the rest of the bone. Like the edges of a dead twig when you break it. If the break in the bone happens after death, the edges are a different color from the rest of the bone. Don't ask me any more details than that. I just don't know all the techniques involved. But, in this case, Karen is convinced that the infant's skull fracture was the cause of death."

"Oh, God—," Laney began.

"This is an ongoing investigation," Gordon continued. "And until we can establish who the mother of the infant was, we would like you to keep this information confidential."

This time, Laney's reaction was subtler but not lost to Gordon. She paled, her expression tightening. The tiniest spasm crossed her face.

As Gordon approached his patrol car, Bucky corralled him in the yard.

"Sheriff," he said in his powerful voice, "when can I resume my excavation? This delay is costing PWU by the minute and these students have taken six weeks out of their summer for graduate work and credit."

Gordon steeled himself. "I'm afraid the site will be off limits until further notice," he said cautiously, noting Bucky's darkening expression as he spoke the words. "It could be a few days or even a week or more before we are satisfied that all evidence has been collected at the scene."

"But the remains were found mostly outside the excavation. We'll postpone digging in the nearest quadrant," he offered.

"Sorry."

Bucky exploded. "You can't do this," he raged, fingers raking cornrows through his ringlets.

"I can and I will," Gordon said sarcastically, already tired of the man's arrogance.

Bucky rose to his full height and hovered over Gordon as though his menacing presence alone could persuade Gordon to reconsider. Gordon never flinched, his gray-green eyes pulsed a hot warning to back off. With a final leer that would bring most people to their knees, the professor reeled and thundered across the yard.

21

"Maybe it's for the best," Laney commented to Bucky as she chopped carrots for a salad in the largest stainless steel bowl she owned. She and Bucky were preparing a farewell dinner in the carriage house for the crew who were flying back to Louisiana the following morning. After a day full of ambivalence and high-colored emotion, Bucky had finally decided to cancel the dig when Gordon reported that Karen Thompson had denied access to the site indefinitely.

"For the best?" Bucky exclaimed loudly. "We were just beginning to collect data when that confounded bag showed up. After the cops finish sifting through the site, there will never again be undisturbed, layered deposits of artifacts that can give us the chronological sequence of this burial episode," Bucky explained while he placed Styrofoam bowls, plastic utensils and paper napkins along the short side of a sheet of plywood stretched over two saw-horses. The all-purpose surface served for artifact sorting and doubled for dining for the crew. On one corner, the skeleton of Bones was stacked in a haphazard pile. Teetering on top of the heap of bones, the skull with its eerie vacant eye sockets seemed to be smiling its toothy grin at Laney as she worked.

It had taken several days for the crew to dismantle the camp, label and box the few artifacts and record data.

"At least Gordon allowed you to collect the bones before he shut down the site," Laney said, as she scattered sliced green olives over the finished salad.

"While practically under armed guard," Bucky snorted. "He wouldn't even allow me to sift through the pedestal of dirt for anymore arti-facts that might be associated with Bones's burial."

"But he promised he would try to leave that area undisturbed, if possible," Laney said, wiping sweat off her brow with her forearm.

"That's the only reason why I'm staying on for awhile longer," Bucky said. "Maybe in a few days, he'll let me back in. But if they take too long, I'm outta here, too."

"How are you going to get all the tents home?"

"Cam and Bonnie are going to drop the crew off at the airport in the morning and then take some of their gear home in their mini-van when they leave later in the day. When I go, I'll take the rest of the stuff, and what artifacts there are, back in my Blazer."

Bucky opened the refrigerator door and retrieved a great bowl of peeled shrimp and Laney replaced it with the salad bowl. It took up the entire bottom shelf.

"Where's Gray?" Bucky asked, with just a hint of a smile. "I thought he was coming to the dinner."

"He had an unexpected meeting. He may be by later."

A muscle rippled through Bucky's cheek. "I'd better check the jam-balaya," he said, swooping out the door to the kitchen garden. Laney followed.

Between the house and the garage, two large heavy kettles simmered on the barrel grill. Bucky snatched the long handled spoon and oven mitts from Toby and opened the first lid. The aroma of onion, garlic, smoked sausage, chicken, rice and potatoes pulled at Laney's mouth, making her insides growl. After testing the rice and potatoes for done-ness, Bucky scooped up half of the large plump shrimp and dropped them into the pot. With another splash of dry white wine and a bru-tal shake of cayenne pepper, he stirred the mixture and replaced the lid. He repeated the procedure with the other pot.

"Your hair is the same color," he said, motioning with the can of red pepper before setting it down.

"So everyone reminds me," Laney said.

"You should wear it loose about your head instead of in a braid," he said, his usually turbulent eyes suddenly settling softly on her face.

"In this humidity? It would popple and lift me off the ground," Laney giggled self-consciously, but she was secretly flattered that he admired her hair.

Laney looked up at the sound of a vehicle in the drive and presently heard the voices of the crew as they scrambled from the van. Cam and Bonnie had taken them to a movie in Lexington and all were unaware of the special dinner their last evening in Kentucky.

"I thought the dinner was canceled," Bonnie exclaimed as she lifted the lid on the nearest kettle. "Dr. Gage, not your Cajun jambalaya! . . . Hey, you guys," she called to the rest of the members of the dig, "someone call the fire department. This will set your taste buds on fire."

"Say, there's a pony keg of beer!" Polly yelled, at the same time the sounds of Cajun–South African music from Paul Simon's *Graceland* tape drifted from the screened porch where Toby had plugged in his boom box.

With a long handled fork, Bucky speared a rosy shrimp from the pot and offered it to Laney. He ran his tongue slowly over his lips while the morsel scorched its way through her mouth. To avoid his salaciousness, she turned away from him and fanned her lips as though the only heat she felt were there. Quickly, she poured herself a beer from the freshly tapped keg and escaped to the serene coolness of the parlor. As she fled, she heard his chuckle. "Damn him," she said. She covered her ears with her hands. But the sounds of voices and music still trickled through the thick stone walls. Abruptly, and unbidden as though just below the surface of her brain, the vision of the mummified baby reclaimed her thoughts. How could she party when a baby had been murdered and buried on this very farm? "Cara's child?" she asked herself out loud.

"Woman, get real," a voice said harshly from the doorway. Shar, holding Kudzu in one arm and with the other poised on her hip, glared at her. Fire-engine red shorts barely peeked from below her oversized royal blue tee. A Hamilton blue and red plaid tie cinched in her tiny waist. "I never met your sister, but you told me enough about her that I feel that I knew her. I would have liked her. The girl who once risked her life on the freeway to try to save a turtle from being crunched by the wheels of a semi cared about life."

"But her abortion eight years ago. . . ."

"Laney, some people just don't believe that abortion is murder. Some think a fetus is not a viable child until born or in the last trimester when the child might possibly live on its own. I don't care to try to judge that issue, myself. The Supreme Court is still trying to sort it out . . . even after Roe versus Wade. But I'll bet my sweet Kudzu that if it was Cara's baby in that field, she sure as hell wasn't the one who killed it."

Laney threw her arms around Shar. Kudzu mewed and jumped to the floor. "Oh, thank you, dear friend. You don't know how I needed to hear that." She forced a smile.

"You know, there's one way they can determine if it was Cara's baby or not," Shar said, leading Laney to the sofa where they both sat down. Shar kicked off her slip-on sneakers, exposing royal purple toenails.

"DNA testing?"

"Yes, that's one way," Shar said, wiggling her bony toes.

"There's another?"

"You bet! You could find out whose baby it was."

"Oh, no you don't!"

"Think about it, woman. If the forensic anthropologist decides to test those bones, the next step will be to compare the infant's DNA to a member of your family . . . your mother . . . you. Maybe they'll even exhume Cara's body."

Laney shot to her feet. "No way! I won't allow it!"

"You could get a head start on the police by doing a little snooping on your own. What could it hurt?"

"I wouldn't know where to start."

"Sure you would. Just think of other women who lived on this farm besides Cara," Shar said, stroking the purring Kudzu who had found his way back to her lap by clawing up the front of the sofa.

"I can only think of one. Melby Burns."

"The mother of Cara's farm manager?" Shar asked, her jaw dropping an inch.

"She lived here until her husband, Cory, died about eight years ago. She ran off with some guy a few days after her husband's funeral."

"See, I told you." Shar said. "Maybe it was *her* baby."

"Doesn't seem likely. Too old." Laney sipped at her beer. "Wait. I do believe there was a daughter though. I think her name was Sandy or Sandra . . . something like that. She also lived in the cottage until she married some time before her father died."

"Maybe she had an out-of-wedlock child," Shar said excitedly. "Where did she move to?"

"I have no idea," Laney said, "and have no idea how to find out."

"Call your mom. She knows everything about everybody."

Laney glanced at her watch. "She'll be here for dinner. I'll ask her then. But that's as far as I'll go with this, Shar. I really don't need this right now." She snatched the sleeping Kudzu from Shar and buried her face into his soft fur.

"Ask me what?" a familiar voice said. Laney shifted on the sofa and smiled at her mother who had let herself in through the screened porch. She stood at the pocket doors that separated the dining room from the parlor.

Shar scrambled over the back of the sofa, her derriere briefly jutting, her bare feet finding the floor effortlessly. "Maddy!" she squealed. "I wondered if I would get to see you. I called several times and stopped by the dock twice." Her long arms wrapped around Maddy's slight body like octopus tentacles and lifted her off the carpet. Maddy's white sailor hat sailed to the floor and cedar-colored hair burst about her face like a fast growing chi-chia doll.

"Mother," Laney said, "we wanted to know if you knew where Melby Burns's daughter lives."

Shar released her grip, grabbed Maddy's hand and guided her to the green Morris chair. Shar sank back into the sofa.

"Funny you should ask. I was talkin with Gwen Jessop just last week about her," Maddy said. "Gwen's a cousin to Melby. Works at Human Resources. You know . . . the gal with the bird legs—"

"Mother," Laney interrupted, "I know perfectly well who you mean. About Melby's daughter. . . ." Laney could hear the impatience in her words.

Maddy frowned and rubbed her right eye and continued, "According to Gwen, Melby married that fellow she ran away with years ago. His name's Emmett Randell."

"Mother . . . her daughter . . . ," Laney said abruptly.

"Cassandra?"

"That's her name," Laney said. "Where is she living these days? I want to talk to her."

"What in heavens for?"

Laney glanced at Shar, silently asking her if she thought she should tell her mother about the remains found on the farm. Kudzu made his way back to Shar's lap.

Seeing her friend's shrug, Laney decided to go ahead. "Mother, something terrible happened here on the farm."

Maddy raised a hand. "Gordon told me all about it. The news is all over. A baby was found buried on the farm."

Maddy rubbed her eye again anxiously.

God, Laney thought. What if Mother knew that the medical examiner believed the child had been murdered. Murdered. Laney shuddered.

Maddy stared at her hands and picked at a nail. "Do you think it was Cara's, too?"

Laney was surprised at Maddy's frankness. "Mother, wouldn't you, Joe, or someone have detected a pregnancy?"

"Honey, you don't have to convince me. I can't believe Cara could have carried a child to term without me knowin. It's just that people are beginnin to talk. Rose told me what's goin around town."

Laney knew that Rose Cohen, a local shopkeeper and close friend of Maddy's heard all the gossip first. "Actually, Shar and I were wondering if perhaps it was Cassandra's child . . . when she lived here as a teenager," Laney said.

Maddy paused before speaking. Then her tone was grim. "According to Gwen, Melby is expectin her first grandbaby any day now. Because of a congenital condition, Cassandra can't have children and is adoptin a little boy."

22

"Sure knocked that theory all to hell," Shar said as she, Laney and Maddy stepped inside the carriage house. Bucky stood at the plywood table ladling steaming jambalaya into oversized soup bowls that Laney had provided as Toby slid a tray with three crisp baguettes out of the oven. The battered range had been donated by Rose Cohen and it was a toss-up which apparatus was the crankiest—the chipped porcelain stove or Toby's white pick-up that carted it there. The crew mingled about the room chatting. Everyone seemed in high spirits, Laney thought, but she couldn't seem to shake the gloom.

"Woman, don't let this set you back," Shar said, glancing back toward the screened porch where she had left Kudzu in the care of Blackberry. The two animals had picked up their friendship of three months before. "We're not going to let this go. It had to have been someone's baby. Maybe—"

"Aunt Laney," a youthful voice shouted and a pigtailed youngster of about ten years with eyes the color of hyacinths and a mouthful of silver braces, plummeted into her body. As she hugged Aggie, Cilla and their mother, Tina, wandered into the carriage house through the open garage doors. Cilla flashed a strained smile and hurried away toward Toby who was standing in line to claim his meal. Toby beamed when he spotted her and pulled her in line ahead of him. Laney noted that an oversized white tee with sleeves that reached her elbows had replaced the long-sleeved shirt that she had worn when she left the farm. A baseball cap covered her platinum hair.

"Tina, how good to see you," Maddy said as the four of them made their way to the dwindling chow line.

"It's only been three months but it seems like years since Laney and I visited you in that darling little village right outside of Maysville," Shar said. "I understand that you and some Eugene fellow are thinking about getting hitched." Laney felt Aggie's hand tighten around hers. She also noticed that Tina seemed distracted and kept glancing over to Cilla and Toby who were in animated conversation.

"At least she still knows how to talk," Tina said sarcastically, nodding toward Cilla. "I can't seem to get a word out of her at home."

Laney shot a look to the couple. "The two of them seem to have hit it off. They were doing some research together before this latest gruesome discovery," Laney said. Tina barely shook her head, her eyes flashing to her youngest daughter.

"When are you plannin to tie the knot, honey?" Maddy asked.

"When Eugene and Cilla stop locking horns," she said as Aggie suddenly released Laney's hand and wandered over to where her sister and Toby were carrying their bowls of jambalaya to a couple of card tables set up at the end of the plywood for the overflow. "I think she resents that I'm planning to marry so soon after her father's death."

"How's Aggie about it?" Shar asked, finally reaching the table and lifting her steaming bowl with both hands. Maddy left them to pass baskets of bread and serve the salad on foam plates. Bucky passed around pitchers of beer while Toby pulled himself away from Cilla long enough to fill soda pop orders from the number two galvanized tub full of ice that was usually used for Blackberry's baths.

"Aggie likes Eugene, but then she's younger and likes all his attention and the activities he plans. But I think Cilla wishes he would drop off the earth so she could do whatever she wants," Tina said.

The three of them found places together at the big table, climbed over the picnic benches with their meals and sat down.

"Can I sit with you?" a tearful Aggie said, sidling up to Laney on the bench.

"Why sure, honey," Laney said. "What's the matter?" The child leaned against Laney's arm and didn't answer.

"I'll get your supper," Tina said, jumping to her feet.

When she was gone, Aggie lifted her head, looked at Laney and said, "Cilla doesn't like me anymore. She doesn't want me for a sister." Hot tears cascaded down her cheeks.

"Aggie, that isn't true. She's just going through a hard time right now."

"Cilla's different now. Sometimes she cries when she thinks no one hears. An . . . and she's always mad. She calls Eugene bad words behind his back." Aggie sank into silence as her mother returned.

Aggie picked at her supper. Even when Bucky spread newspapers over the table and sliced a ripe green watermelon that had been chilled in the tub along with the pop, she refused to eat hers. Shar slurped away at her wedge, spitting shiny black seeds onto the newsprint until she directed a glistening oval at Aggie and it caught her smack on the corner of her mouth. Aggie looked up and caught the smirk on Shar's face, peeled the seed away and tossed it back at Shar. That's all the encouragement Shar needed—the battle was on.

Confined at first to just the two of them, like a contagion, it spread around the tables until watermelon seeds spewed in every direction. The crew couldn't devour the melon fast enough to supply ammunition, so a few scooped up handfuls from the newspaper and fired at each other. Even Cilla, who at first was appalled that her sister was engaging in such juvenile behavior, spat one back at Toby who had smacked one against her cheek. Bucky connected with a volley at Laney and she let fly with a piece of rind that plopped into his blond curls. Cheers and screams of laughter split the evening as the crew aimed and ducked, shot seeds from slippery finger pinches and catapulted them from greasy soupspoons. Maddy got into the row and peppered Tina. Tina landed a perfect strike on Maddy's right breast that brought tears of laughter when Maddy stared down at the glistening oval hung up on her white polo shirt. When there was not a seed left on the table, the satiated crew, flushed with fraternal goodwill, slowly dispersed to the kitchen garden where they began dancing under the glow of torch lamps.

23

In a spurt of good will brought on by the watermelon fight, Cilla, who earlier had been unusually rude to her sister, introduced Aggie around to the crew. When Toby bowed low and asked Aggie to dance to a lively Dixieland number, her braces glinted in the flickering torch-light as they marched around the garden. The crew followed behind, strutting and singing along to "When the Saints Go Marching In."

Finally, pleading that they had a long drive back to Washington, Tina, with Aggie in reluctant tow, left the party at ten. Shortly after, Maddy said her goodbyes, kissed her daughter and was gone.

The soft romantic music of Nat King Cole and his daughter singing "Unforgettable" drifted out from the screened porch and when Laney heard the slam of the screen door and saw Toby take Cilla in his arms for a slow dance, she knew that he had been the one to change the tape. At the end of a second song, Cam and Bonnie wandered off to their tent with most of the rest of the crew straggling behind, know-ing that they had to be up early for their flight in the morning.

"To the swimming hole," Bucky cried suddenly, sailing a paper plate across the garden at Laney and Shar who were helping him clean up.

Shar dropped the garbage bag and sprinted for the house while Toby rushed toward his tent to put on his swimming trunks.

"I don't think I'll go," Cilla said. "I'm not much for swimming in creeks and stuff."

"C'mon, Cilla. It'll be fun," Laney said, putting her arm around her shoulders and leading her toward the house.

"I didn't bring my suit," Cilla protested.

"I've got an extra that will probably fit you. Not much to it, as I remember. I bought it in the Keys in a weak moment during my skinny days," Laney said, remembering the skimpy orange bikini she'd never had the nerve to wear.

Bucky, in the bed of Toby's pickup, shouted over the roaring crackle from his rusty muffler, "Let's go!"

Reaching the house, Laney grabbed the protesting Cilla by the hand and yanked her inside.

Toby parked his truck with his load of hot and sweaty partygoers about halfway down the ramp to the creek. The nearly full moon flooded the riffle with a bright, blue-white eeriness. Water barely trickled into the deep pool to the right of the crossing. Through the years, farmers had hauled rock to the site so that they could access their land on the other side of the creek. As the roadbed slowly built up the barrier, it had formed the swimming hole.

Shar was the first one out of the bed of truck. She wore a chartreuse thong swimsuit that glowed in the dark and her feet were tucked into sneaker slip-ons. The thistle tattoo on her right buttock shimmied as she strode down the rocky causeway in the moonlight. Twice since moving from Mal's house, Shar had accompanied some of the crew for a refreshing dip. Without hesitation, she approached the edge and plunged headfirst into the dark water. After surfacing quickly, she called, "C'mon you guys, last one in is a toad." Her moonlit face bobbed among ripples, her pixie-cut hair plastered to her head.

Laney tugged at the bodice of her old standby black maillot and slid off the tailgate onto the gravel. She stared at her dirty lace-up tennis shoes that made her feet look as long as Michael Jordan's. Feeling Bucky's eyes on her, she was sure she looked as graceless as the black snakebird that lived on the creek.

"Cilla, I'll race you," she said, wanting to get into the water as quickly as possible.

Cilla remained huddled on the wheel well of the truck bed. "You go on," she said. She still wore the baseball cap and oversized tee that she had on earlier, but Laney could see the outline of the orange bikini underneath. She also wore sneakers to protect her feet from any unknown hazard on the bottom of the creek.

Bucky, in fringed blue-jean cut-offs, leaped over the side of the bed and disappeared in the bushes. He had drunk great quantities of beer throughout the evening and Laney assumed he had to relieve himself. Toby, in white boxers, dived into the pool. Shar squealed and subsequently disappeared as he pulled her under the water. Laney eased herself in and wasn't surprised how tepid the water had become from the days of endless sunshine and high temperatures. Treading water, she turned to face the truck and was happy to see Cilla scoot off the tailgate and strip off the baseball cap and tee. She dropped them onto the rocks and quickly lowered herself into the water. She swam a good distance from the others and shouted, "This is cool. I wish I had done this before now."

A splash and tidal wave just off the bank announced Bucky's shortcut entrance into the pool. Emerging directly in front of Laney, he whirled his head, fanning water from his locks onto her. "You need a rope swing over this swimming hole," he gasped spurting water from his mouth. "If Toby and I get a chance, we'll anchor one on that sycamore branch up there," he said, pointing to a ghostly white limb hovering high over the water. As she stared upward, she felt his hands abruptly grasp her waist and pull her to him and down under the dark water. Crushed in his strong arms, his face close to hers, she felt soft bubbles from his mouth froth with hers and instinctively, her palms pressed against his hard body. Her fingers lingered, ever so briefly, on his silken, flowing chest hair. Below, their bodies touched and his nakedness, defined against her thigh, made her gasp. The sound gurgled and echoed in her ears like sonar and his arms tightened. She thought that he would kiss her but instead, he thrust her high out of the water and into the air. She plunged backward into the pool as his mocking laugh rolled up the creek. Surfacing, she sputtered water from her mouth and she saw that another vehicle had pulled up at an angle behind Toby's truck, the lights beaming out over the swimmers.

"Oh-my-God. Gray!" she said in a raspy whisper.

He jumped out of his restored 1958 Buick and made his way down the ramp. From the car's window, Pavarotti's powerful tenor voice singing "Nessun dorma!" rent the night. It wasn't until Bucky swam to the crossing—and to Laney's horror—lifted himself onto the rocks with a powerful thrust of his arms, that she realized the possible consequences of Gray's unexpected appearance. Bucky, his back to the swimmers but in full frontal display facing Gray, stood with hands on his hips and legs spread wide in a defiant pose. If Gray had seen Bucky pull her beneath the dark water, the gesture could only be interpreted as a not-so-subtle statement of superiority, Laney thought with dismay. She heard Shar giggle nervously as she treaded water close to Laney and whispered. "Woman, look at those buns."

Cilla! Laney spun her head. But the teen was at the far edge of the pool in deep conversation with Toby. Hopefully, Laney prayed, the two of them were so full of each other that they were unaware of the tableau unfolding in front of them.

Bucky abruptly swept by Gray and disappeared into the bushes— evidently to get dressed. The fun of the late night dip suddenly over, Laney, with Shar splashing behind her, made her way to the rocks. Gray, his expression unreadable in the shadow created by the white light of his car's headlights behind him, didn't offer them a hand up.

Shar climbed the ramp toward Toby's truck as the boy made his way toward the crossing. Cilla lingered mid glistening rings of water. When Toby arrived dripping on the rocks, Gray turned abruptly and the two of them climbed the ramp. Toby jumped into his truck and Gray continued walking toward his Buick. Laney waited for Cilla.

Cilla neared the edge of the crossing and called to Laney, "Would you get my towel?"

As Laney climbed the grade, she heard the scrambling splash as Cilla left the water. Shar met Laney halfway down with towel in hand and accompanied her back to where Cilla, not waiting to dry off, was frantically struggling to pull her T-shirt over her wet body.

"My God! Cilla!" Laney choked as Shar's fingers instantaneously clamped a vise around Laney's arm, her nails digging painfully.

"Your stomach . . . what? . . . what could have done that?" Shar barely whispered.

Laney stepped aside so that her shadow would not block her view and Gray's headlights caught the injury clearly.

Like some kind of gruesome tattoo gone wrong, a hideous swollen discoloration spread across Cilla's abdomen. Framed above and below by the orange bikini, her abdomen appeared malignantly distorted. Laney wondered if she might have internal injuries. "Oh God," Laney could only whisper, her mouth suddenly dry with fear for Cilla.

Cilla, the tee finally clearing her head, saw the horror in their eyes and quickly twisted from the light and managed to pull the shirt over her middle. But Laney grabbed her shoulders and turned her body so that she faced her once again.

"What's happened to you?" she demanded. At the same instant, without the baseball cap covering Cilla's hair, Laney saw the raw, bald spot in her scalp from where a clump of hair had been ripped. "Jesus, Cilla, you have to tell me! Who did this to you?" Laney demanded, certain that this injury was no accident.

"I can't!" she said.

"You must," said Shar.

Toby's truck roared to life, his muffler popping, drowning out the opera-gushing Buick behind him. He blinked his lights on and off in a playful rhythm suggesting to Laney that he hadn't seen Cilla's injury. When Gray backed off the crossing with his tires throwing gravel and an angry clashing of gears, she was sure he hadn't noticed either.

"Are you coming?" Bucky called from the bed of Toby's truck.

"In a minute," Laney yelled, her eyes not leaving Cilla. "Cilla, tell me," she said forcefully.

"No," Cilla said, then hesitated as though she knew that Laney wasn't going to give up on this. "If I tell . . . you won't . . . I mean . . . tell anyone, will you?" Cilla pleaded, as Toby's pulsing strobes turned the night surreal.

"I can't promise that," Laney said, disgusted that Cilla would try to protect whoever did this to her.

"I think I know," Shar said.

Laney's eyes snapped to her friend.

"It's that boyfriend of hers . . . Luke."

Fear flooded Cilla's face. "No . . . you're wrong . . . he'd never. He loves me. Promise me . . . or . . . or I'm outta here."

Laney saw cold vehemence in Cilla's face—unshakable resolution.

"All right . . . who, Cilla?" Laney said, her mouth a flame spitting sparks into the night.

"Eugene . . . it's Eugene," Cilla blurted.

Later that night when the moon glared yellow through the humidity like a steamy globule of molten gold and Laney finally slid between cool sheets, she was aware that she hadn't thought about the field of stones for several hours. But she also realized that the cause for her shift of focus was just as disturbing as the unearthing of infant remains.

24

The morning sun once again shot hot and hazy through Laney's window. She opened her eyes, gritty with sleep. Lucky that she had slept at all, she thought wearily as, in an instant, she recalled the execrable revelation at the swimming hole.

"Woman," Shar called from just outside her door. Laney groaned and flipped onto her side, burying her head into the down pillow as though sleep could wrench her away from it all.

"Woman," her friend repeated, only louder now as she burst into her bedroom. Laney felt the bed jiggle as Shar bounced her rear on the mattress next to her body. "We have to talk to Cilla."

Laney pushed herself upright, tucked a second pillow behind her head and yawned. She forced a smile when two copper eyes peeked out from one of Shar's robe pockets.

"We tried last night, but she was in such a state, I was afraid she'd take off if we pushed it. Shar, do you think that there's any possibility that Cilla is telling the truth? . . . that Eugene did that to her?"

"Get real. Laney. You've seen that boyfriend of hers. Creep from the get-go."

"But why would Cilla accuse someone of such a horrible thing if he didn't do it?"

"To protect Luke the puke," Shar said. "What is his last name, anyway?"

"Tucker . . . and please don't rhyme it."

Shar grinned evilly. "What are you going to do?" she asked as Kudzu crept out of the pocket and lowered himself rear first to the floor, his little claws snagging the sheet as he descended.

"Tell Tina about Cilla's accusation and also our suspicions about Luke."

"Wrong. Cilla will bolt . . . or worse, run off with the creep. She thinks she's in love with him."

"She's not in love. Obsessed is the word. He has some kind of emotional control over her if she would stick around after what he did to her. And I don't think this is the first time he's hurt her."

"When—?"

"Shar . . . the turtlenecks and long sleeves in this weather. It all connects now. I read up on abuse when Mother went through a similar problem with my stepfather. And from what I've read, it only escalates."

"You're in a dilemma, Laney. If you tell Tina what Cilla said, it could cause all kinds of problems between Tina and Eugene. Could even bust them up. If you tell her you think Luke hit her daughter, I know Tina. She'll lock Cilla in her room and swallow the key. Then the first chance Cilla gets, she'll run away like she threatened last night . . . probably right into Luke's puny arms."

"How about we hold off for a few days until we can get Cilla to see the light. Meanwhile, we'll keep her away from Luke *and* Eugene—on the off-chance it is Eugene."

"What about Aggie? You going to leave her near Eugene if there's even the slightest chance Cilla was telling the truth?"

"I'll invite her here for a few days. That will take care of any immediate threat."

"Do you think that between the two of us, we can keep Cilla away from Luke?" Shar said, sweeping the kitten into her arms.

"It'll be difficult—to say the least," Laney said. "I, for one, won't allow him back on the farm. And I'll pass the word to Aaron to be on the lookout for Luke's truck."

"Well, I have all the time in the world to play watchdog. Malcolm sure isn't tearing down the door like I thought he would."

"He can hardly play Romeo beneath your window with a broken leg."

"Woman, he didn't break his arm. Not a single phone call since I left. Poison Ivy is on the move—itching to get him," she said with a bitter snort. "I just know it."

There was a soft knock on the door. "Aunt Laney?"

"Come in, Cilla," Laney said.

The door opened slowly and Cilla stepped into the room. Her face was pale below the baseball cap, her eyes swollen from the emotional scene the night before. Another oversized tee fell to her hips. Her hand on the doorknob trembled as she spoke. "Dr. Dalton is ready to take the crew to the airport. I thought maybe you wanted to say goodbye."

Laney swung out of bed and grabbed her robe. "I certainly do," she said, sliding her feet into green slippers.

"After breakfast, Toby and I want to go to the library. Okay?" Cilla asked timidly, as though she was afraid that Laney would refuse to allow her to go. Laney glanced at Shar.

"It just so happens that I have some research I have to do there too," Shar said. "Mind me tagging along?"

Cilla hesitated, then smiled. "Sure. I'll start breakfast," she said closing the door behind her.

"Thanks, Shar. I don't think Toby likes Luke any better than we do, but I still would feel better if you went along. I'm afraid I just don't trust Cilla."

Shar snuggled Kudzu. "When I was a teen, nothing could keep me away from a guy if I wanted to see him. One time when I was grounded, I sneaked out a basement window, partied all night, and crawled back under the sheets just as the sun came up. No one was even aware I had gone. I could find the damnedest ways to disappear."

Laney didn't know just how prophetic Shar's words would become.

25

The Hickory-St. Clair County Library stood on the corner of Fifth Street and Carver, four blocks from the county courthouse. The three-story red brick building had been built with Andrew Carnegie funds in the 1920's. Through the years, renovations to the handsome structure had created a black hole for grants and tax money, some apportioned to keep up with computer technology, but most to keep out the rain. Shar, Toby and Cilla, arms loaded with the books checked out on their first visit, ducked under scaffolding in place for the latest fiscal project—tuck-pointing.

As much as Toby enjoyed Shar, he was secretly glad when she inquired at the desk on the second floor for the location of the genealogy section and disappeared down a dark hallway. He and Cilla quickly found a table far enough away from the front desk to allow for some quiet conversation and stacked their books as a sound shield at one end.

Within minutes, they had added several other historical volumes and biographies.

"Damn. I left Dr. Gage's field notebook in the truck," Toby said, getting to his feet and starting for the stairs.

"Wait," Cilla called in a loud whisper. She opened her purse and removed a wrinkled sheet of paper that Toby recognized as the site notes Bucky had given her the day the infant remains were found and that she had taken home to Washington. Cilla blinked nervously as she smoothed it out.

"Did you use that to blow your nose?" Toby joked when he saw the paper's condition.

Cilla didn't answer and seemed jumpy. She kept looking towards the elevator.

"Let's see what we've got," he said.

"To be honest, Toby, I haven't done much reading on this," she said, nodding at her stack of books she had taken to Washington.

"Well, I burned the midnight oil several times and so far I haven't found any surveyor that got lost in Kentucky and was never found. He showed Cilla a list he had made of Kentucky pioneers and surveyors, their dates of death and where they were believed buried. "You were right, Cilla, there were slews of surveyors besides the most famous one, Daniel Boone. Some, like John Floyd, were killed by Indians, but their place of death and burial site is known."

"Look at this cute little green book, Toby." Cilla's dimpled smile warmed him inside. He wished she would smile more often.

"*The Discovery, Settlement, and Present State of Kentucke,*" he read on the spine.

Cilla opened the book to the title page. "It's by a John Filson," she said and flipped to a series of primitive maps of Kentucky in the eighteenth century.

"Who was he?" Toby asked, noting that the book contained chapters about the climate, trade, soil and inhabitants of early Kentucky. A sizable appendix about the adventures of Daniel Boone took up half of the book.

Cilla's eyes scanned the introduction written by William H. Masterson, who had been a Professor of History and Dean of Humanities at Rice University. "Masterson says Filson moved to Kentucky in 1782 or 83 and taught at Transylvania College in Lexington," she said.

"I knew Kentucky was still part of Virginia back then but not that Transylvania was already there," Toby said.

"I think it was the first college west of the Allegheny Mountains," she said.

"Aren't you smart," Toby said, lightly elbowing her in the ribs.

She tried to hide it but pain blipped across her pale blue eyes like an EKG then flattened as she exhaled.

What in the hell was going on, Toby thought. The porch! It had happened before on the porch. His mouth opened, ready to ask the words when he stopped dead. Suddenly, he remembered something about the midnight swim. Cilla pulling her tee down over her body in the moonlight. His flashing headlights on Shar and Laney. Shock on their faces. He had wondered.

Cilla continued to read silently from the Filson book but Toby couldn't concentrate any longer.

Shar suddenly reappeared from the archives. "Do you have a name for Bones yet?" she asked, sitting next to Cilla.

"We might," Cilla said, her smile claiming her face. She showed Shar the little Filson book. "Seems John Filson was in Kentucky surveying roads about the right time—in the seventeen-eighties. He wrote this book and drew maps."

Shar followed Cilla's finger as it moved across the text. "Toby," Cilla said excitedly, "Filson disappeared in October 1788, and it says right here that he was reported either killed or captured by Indians. But no one ever witnessed his death. Nobody ever found his body." Her face was alight with the thought that perhaps this was the clue they were hoping for.

Toby, who had been reticent through Cilla's account, suddenly grabbed the book and swore, "Shit, Cilla, can't you read?"

Mary Neuman frowned at him from behind the front desk. Toby lowered his eyes knowing his anger was directed at someone who wasn't even there. He murmured an apology to Cilla and squeezed her hand.

"Cilla, look at Dr. Gage's notes," he whispered as he pointed to the rumpled information sheet in front of him. "Bones was over six foot tall. Filson is referred to as a 'little schoolteacher' in this book." He underlined the passage with his fingernail. "Another thing, Filson was thirty years old when he traveled to Kentucky in 1783. He disappeared in 1788—that made him thirty-five. According to Bucky, Bones was near fifty."

"Bummer," Cilla said, obviously crestfallen.

"Don't give up," Shar said as she patted a stack of Kentucky history books. "Check out some biographies of some better known pioneers. Sometimes names are mentioned in reference." She stood. "Persevere," she proclaimed, lifting one long sneakered foot onto the seat of her heavy oak chair and rolling her eyes skyward. With her hand slapped over her bosom, she delivered in a worldly voice, "Failure after perseverance is much grander than never to have a striving good enough to be called a failure." Cilla giggled but Ms. Neuman dressed Shar down with a Darth Vader scowl.

Shar turned her head toward the librarian and announced supremely, "George Eliot—English novelist."

As Cilla dug into a biography of George Rogers Clark, and Shar made copies of reference material she had found in the genealogy room, Toby tried to concentrate on the Boone section of the Filson book, but it was no use. Ask her, dumb ass, he upbraided himself silently but immediately rejected the idea. No, she would only deny it. Anyway, he already knew. Just as sure as anything, someone was beating up on Cilla. And like he didn't know who—yeah, sure. And like hell, he'd ever let him do it again.

26

"Laney, I'm sure Aggie would have loved to spend some time at the farm but she's at my sister's in Ripley, Ohio, across the river," Tina said over the phone. "Margaret picked her up this morning for a two day visit. The girls go every summer. This is the first year Cilla's missed since I don't know when."

"Well, Aggie had such fun last night and I thought—" Laney said.

"She did, didn't she? Toby is such a nice young man. If only. . . ." Tina's voice faded. "Anyway, tell Cilla that there were three hang-ups on the answering machine when I got home last night. I know the calls were from Luke. He never *will* leave a message. He called again this morning. This time he asked when she was coming home."

Checking up on her, I bet, Laney thought.

"Eugene and I are going to take advantage of the kid-free interlude and go to Doe Run Inn for a couple days. Mother will mind the shop for me. She has the number where we'll be if you have any problems. But I'm certain both my girls are in good hands. We'll stop on the way home. Bye."

As Laney placed the phone in the cradle, she thought of the confrontation with Cilla the night before. God, if Tina suspected that either Eugene or Luke was abusing her daughter, she'd go off. Laney definitely felt guilty about keeping something so serious from Tina, but rationalized it would only be for a couple of days—until Cilla confessed that Luke was the one hurting her and she decided to break off with him for good. Meanwhile, she and Shar wouldn't let Cilla out of their sight.

Kudzu squeezed through the crack in the library door and rubbed against Laney's ankle. "Pussy, do you miss your mommy?" she asked the kitten after scooping him into her lap. He looks more like Puccini every day, she thought, rubbing the small dark M between his copper eyes. Thinking of Gray's cat reminded her of the unhappy ending to their midnight swim when Gray happened upon Bucky swimming in the buff with her. Whatever must Gray think?

She was just about to lift the phone to call him when it rang in her hand. She recognized the soft hello. "Mother," she said into the receiver.

"Honey, I was thinking about our conversation last evenin. You know, about the baby found on the farm and all. There's someone I bet you've never thought about."

Laney's thoughts were brutally brought back to the problem of the infant remains. "Who, mother?" she said irritably.

"Why, Alice Carson, of course! After all, she lived in the house the longest. In fact, her father built the place around the turn of the century," Maddy said.

"Mother, that's impossible. She would be too old to have a child."

"You said Gordon doesn't know how long ago the baby died. It might have been twenty years ago, for all we know."

Laney thought about the woman who along with her husband, Paul, had sold the farm to Cara and Joe seven years before and moved away right after the sale. Laney remembered the last time she had seen Alice before she moved to Pittsburgh. She recalled a woman who seemed much older than her husband, and Cara had remarked to her how, when she closed on the farm, Alice Carson had appeared ancient in contrast to her husband. She also recalled that Cara had compared Paul to a vigorous Howard Hughes. Her stomach tightened and she scolded herself that she was imagining that Cara and Paul Carson . . . She dispelled the image away with a shake of her head. "Mother, where did the Carsons move to after the sale?"

"Somewhere warm, I believe. Florida . . . maybe Georgia. Honey, my memory just isn't what it used to be. But there's a box in the attic from when Cara and Joe took possession of the farm. Maybe there's a clue in there. Cara and I threw anything the Carsons left behind in a wooden box and stored it in the attic. There's even some horse paraphernalia that we found in the tack room. It should be somewhere under the eaves in that second room if Joe didn't throw it out. I know for certain, Cara didn't. That sister of yours hung on to everythin she ever owned."

"I'll check the first chance I get," Laney said, feeling a bit ill over her runaway thoughts. She cut the call short and immediately dialed Gray at the clinic. Natine Sullivan answered on the second ring.

"Sorry, Laney, you just missed him. He had an emergency out at Taylor Ridge Farm."

"At Malcolm's? Oh my, I hope it's nothing serious," Laney said, her stomach contracting like a fist.

"Something about an Angus bull . . . you can get him on his cell phone or I can beep him," Natine said.

"No . . . not if it's an emergency," Laney said. "I'll talk to him later."

Laney rang off. Poor Malcolm, she thought, hearing the grandfather's clock in the hall chime three times and at the same moment, voices on the front porch. They're back, Laney thought with some relief as she recognized Cilla's soft tones. Maybe this is as good a time as any to talk to her about Luke. She took a deep breath and opened the door.

27

Gray bent over the huge animal, his stethoscope buried in the thick black hair of the bull's chest. He moved it to the right, then left, listening for some sign of life from the creature.

Nothing.

Malcolm, his body supported by wooden crutches, strained forward so he could better see into the pen inside the newly built show barn. "Don't tell me we've lost him," he cried to the vet. Standing next to him, Malcolm's farm manager, Grover Smith, noisily sucked in his breath. Grover, better known as Smitty, swept thick fingers through cropped coffee-colored hair and the knuckles of his other hand tightened about the pen's top rail.

Gray glanced up. Malcolm's brown eyes, magnified by his thick glasses, were immense. His goatee glistened with beads of sweat as though sprayed with mist.

A couple of agonal gasps from the bull drew Gray's eyes downward. The animal's mouth frothed and he took a final puffing intake of air then lay still. Gray touched a dilated fixed pupil with his finger and cursed. The bull's left back leg jumped.

"Gray, look—" Malcolm said, in a dither.

"Just a reflex, Malcolm. I'm afraid he's gone," Gray said, getting to his feet, not anxious to look at Malcolm. The last few times he had seen the Scotsman, he had seemed withdrawn, not himself. This definitely would not help his mood.

"How could that be?" asked Smitty, shaking his head as though he could negate the cruel fact with his distraught gesture.

Gray walked to the steel trough attached to the pen. "When did the animal last eat?" Gray asked, running his hand across the surface of the metal and inspecting the residue on his palm. He swept his hand over it again and picked at something.

"Smitty?" Malcolm looked over at his manager. The young man's face had paled and moisture wetted his upper lip.

"Mr. La . . . Lamont, Jake was sound as a bell just forty-five minutes ago," he stammered. "I fed him myself. As usual, he was at the trough before I finished dumping the feed."

"Gray," Malcolm said. "My animals only get the very best feed. We grind it ourselves. Corn, cottonseed hulls, and oats. I invite you to check out our feed pen." Malcolm pointed with a crutch to the small enclosure at the end of the barn.

Gray donned a rubber glove and bent once more over the beast. Again and again he ran a finger through the bull's mouth, inspecting the residue each time. "Hmm," he murmured, getting to his feet and showing Malcolm and Smitty.

"What is that?" Malcolm asked.

"A needle," Gray said, concentrating on the gray-green particle.

"An evergreen?" Malcolm said, his mouth parting.

"You've got it," Gray said. "Taxus. I'd bet my life on it."

"Taxus?" Malcolm said incredulously .

"Your garden variety yew. I just want to know how your bull got hold of it," Gray said.

"We have no taxus on the farm," Malcolm said, alarm written all over his face. "All shrubbery is either boxwood, barberry, or Leyland cypress."

"I think you'd better call Gordon," Gray said, removing the glove carefully from his hand so that he didn't disturb the evergreen needles stuck in the bull's saliva.

"Gordon Powell?" asked Malcolm as he hobbled out of the pen. Smitty followed, unsteadily, deeply stricken by the tragic death of the prized animal under his care.

Gray laid the glove carefully on a bale of straw just outside the pen before answering. "The one and only sheriff of St. Clair County. I think your bull has been poisoned." At that moment, Gray's beeper went off and he loped to his truck to call the number on his cell phone. Not once thinking of his new Andrea Bocelli CD that he had bought only that morning, he left for his second emergency call of the day. Puccini stretched and smiled his cat grin.

Malcolm and Smitty stood just outside the feed pen in the show barn. The planked pen was about twelve foot square and five feet high with a hinged wooden entrance door facing the inside corridor near the end of the show barn. Gordon had refused to allow them in the small space for fear of disturbing any clues. But as far as Gordon could see, nothing seemed out of place.

A giant storage bin divided into three sections stretched along one wall, its hinged wooden lid propped open. Gordon peered in. The first compartment held ground corn mixed with tiny bits of pink cobs. The second section held what looked like little gray tuffs of cottonseed hulls. Gordon wasn't sure what was in the third box. Oats, he assumed.

Against another wall were several metal and plastic garbage cans labeled with the names of various nutritious ingredients such as Pro Pallet, Show Tina, and soy bean meal. All had lids.

Gordon studied the contents of a wooden mixing trough attached to an adjacent wall and resting on three sturdy legs. A green, quart sized scoop was lying on the surface of the sweet smelling feed.

It wasn't too hard to spot. "Malcolm, I hate to tell you this but Gray seems to have been correct. Someone dumped taxus cuttings into your mixing trough." Gordon carried a handful of the feed to the doorway.

"Look at that, would you?" Smitty said, "those green needles mixed in with the grain."

Gordon dropped the feed back into the trough and began inspecting the white buckets sitting around. Which bucket did you feed Jake with?" he asked Smitty.

"I think the one closest to the trough there," he said. Gordon looked carefully at the residue on the bucket. He saw a couple of needles sticking to the sides.

Gordon returned to the trough and scooped a couple of handfuls of the grain into a plastic bag and twisted a tie.

"How could such a little amount be so lethal?" Malcolm asked.

"Personally, Malcolm, I hadn't any idea that yews were so toxic

either. Doc said that a cup in a bucket of feed could put an animal
down."

Smitty's voice suddenly raised an octave. "Sheriff, I mixed this feed
this morning and the three bulls were fine after eating."

"Which means that someone dumped the taxus and mixed it
through after the morning feeding," Gordon said.

"But why didn't I notice it? It's not hard to spot," Smitty said, flailing his arms in growing agitation.

"Not hard to spot if you're looking for it, Smitty. You said it yourself. You fed the bulls from this trough this morning. No reason to
suspect anything," Gordon said.

"Can you imagine if you had gone on and fed the other two show
bulls with this mixture?" Malcolm said while glancing over the partition at the remaining animals. He did a little hop on his good leg and
almost lost his balance. Smitty grabbed an arm.

"There are times when the pens are full," Smitty said, "before our
big sale in the spring. These three bulls were only penned because of
prepping for the St. Clair County Fair next month." He wiped sweat
from his forehead with a navy handkerchief pulled from a pocket in
his blue jeans.

"So you feed them twice a day?" Gordon asked as he spotted
Freddie approaching them from the other end of the barn.

"Morning and afternoon. Jake was snorting around so I went ahead
and fed him a little early like I always do. I sort of liked that one. He
was smart. I mean . . . he seemed to know that if he caused a little
commotion, I would feed him first. Afterwards, I pulled my pickup
over to the other barn across the yard to load up some hay for the
heifers in the first pasture because there isn't much grass out there.
Drought's taken care of that. When I drove back here to drop off a few
bales and feed the other two bulls, I saw Jake foaming-like 'round the
mouth. He staggered a bit. Next he fell to his knees and I called
Doctor Prescott, pronto. Jake was down before he ever got here. If it
was the feed, I never seen the likes of anything so fast."

Freddie had reached the trio of men and was huffing from the exer-
tion, his face the color of a sunset. "Sheriff, look what I found just
outside the barn." He held the spiral of an orange notebook with two
forefingers. "Think it's important?"

"Everything at a scene is important until proven not to be,"
Gordon said. "Get any prints on the scoop and the notebook." His

eyes caught some printing on a white label in the center of the cover. "McVey Cemetery—St. Clair County, Kentucky." No doubt about it, Gordon thought. It must belong to someone at the stone gravesite at Stoney Creek Farm.

28

The quickest way to the attic was to climb the back staircase just outside Laney's bedroom. After reaching the landing, Laney, Blackberry, Cilla, Kudzu, and a reluctant Shar who didn't much care for dark and dusty places where "crawly critters" might abide, climbed two more steps to a second landing. Behind a partition wall, a narrow paneled door was hidden. The door was always kept shut to prevent the escape of heat in the summer and cold in the winter into the upstairs.

When Laney shouldered the door open, the heat of the attic smacked her and took her breath.

"Woman, I forgot to tell you that I get faint when hot," Shar said, fanning herself with long fluttering fingers. Well . . . er . . . most of the time," she said, swatting Laney on the behind. Laney wiggled her butt and Cilla giggled.

After climbing the narrow steps into the gloom, Laney felt for the wall switch. The dull yellow light from a cheap ceiling fixture lit up most of the room, but left the corners in shadows.

Laney recalled the few times she had been in the attic. The first time had been when she'd stored her things from her Pittsburgh move. The first Christmas on the farm, she had dragged her decorations along with some of Cara's, back downstairs. Gray had helped her both times. Thinking of Gray, she promised herself she would call him the first chance she got. She wondered about the emergency at Malcolm's.

"This room looks like it might have been used for servant quarters at one time," Shar said, her body hunched to keep from brushing against cobwebs. She pointed to a dresser and folding cot. Popping her head into a little room built into a corner, she immediately jumped back. "Ugh, stinky bathroom."

Laney opened a door that led into the second attic room. When she pulled the cord on the hanging light bulb, it flashed, popped and went out. "Damn."

"The light from the window should be enough, Aunt Laney. What are we looking for anyway?" Cilla asked in a whiny voice that bordered on surly.

Seems anxious to be gone, Laney thought. Bet she suspects that I'm going to ask her about the abuse again, and her suspicions are right on the money. The first chance I get.

"Answer the question, woman. I'm exuding something and it ain't pretty." Shar's face was crimson from the heat. Kudzu began to explore.

Laney's own hair was corkscrewing at the hairline. "I'm trying to find out where Alice and Paul Carson moved after they sold this farm to Cara and Joe. Mother said that I might find the answer in a box of stuff they left behind."

"We've sure got our work cut out for us," Shar said, stepping gingerly around mouse droppings. She grabbed at a dowel rod protruding from the nearest cardboard box and a confederate flag unfurled. "The South shall rise again," she proclaimed. "Your sister was some pack rat."

"Speaking of rats," Laney said, "I think Kudzu is doing a bit of ratting, himself."

Laney pointed toward the eaves where she had caught a flash of barred tail moving behind a large carton.

Blackberry, dropped to her belly in a puddle of light formed by sunshine streaming through a small square window facing west. Dust motes danced in the sun. The Border collie began to pant and drops of saliva wetted the planked floor between her front legs.

The three women were drawn to the dust covered glass. Far below, Laney could see Bucky and Toby helping Bonnie and Cam load their van for the trip back home to New Orleans. All the tents had been dismantled, except the small triangle of blue canvas that was Bucky's. Laney rubbed her palm across the glass so they could see more clearly.

Just then, Toby's head jerked upward and he let go of one corner of the site screen he was loading into the rear of the van. Laney gave a start of surprise when he suddenly stormed toward a pick-up that had just parked behind Cam's van in the drive. Even from her high vantage point, Laney could see rage distorting Toby's features. Instantly, Laney recognized the vehicle and the skinny fellow that hopped out of the cab.

"Oh my God. Luke!" Laney gasped.

Cilla shoved Laney aside. "Toby! . . . No!" Cilla exclaimed as though Toby could hear her at the attic window. Her hand clawed at the wavy glass as Toby swung before anyone could stop him. Luke dropped like a stone. As Toby crouched over him, silent screams escaped Luke's mouth. Covering his face with both hands, Luke writhed and dug his cowboy boots into the dry grass, fighting to get away from Toby's continuous blows. Grabbing Toby's arm, Bucky pulled him off and when Luke moved his hands from his face, blood streamed from his nose.

Suddenly, Laney's farm manager appeared out of nowhere. Yanking Luke to his feet, Aaron dragged him back to his Ford and shoved him into the front seat. Retracing his steps, Aaron picked up Luke's baseball cap and threw it into the bed of the truck.

Toby struggled in Bucky's arms, still trying to get at Luke who had started up the engine of his truck.

Cilla spun away from the window and started for the stairs.

"Going somewhere?" Shar asked, her slender body suddenly filling the door opening like an instant blow-up doll, arms crossed and sneakers nailed to the poplar boards.

"Shar, please!" Cilla cried, trying to squeeze by.

"Not on your life," Shar said, her arms abruptly flying outward, barring any chance of exit.

"Cilla, Luke's gone," Laney yelled from the window. "He's left the farm."

Cilla burst into tears—great heaving sobs. Her anguish tore into Laney's heart.

Laney crossed the room, Cilla's cries mingling with the creaking boards underfoot. When Laney enveloped her in her arms, Cilla moaned and shivered like a bleak and wintry wind before twisting away.

"Don't touch me. You just don't understand!" she screamed. She shoved at Shar who grunted but stood like a rock, blocking her way. She tugged frantically at Shar's arm, trying to dislodge it from the door frame.

"Girl, it's no use," Shar said. "You can't slip by me. Only way out of here is through that window there, but you'd better have wings and hips like a worm."

Cilla pounded her fists against Shar's fingers, then pried at them until tears came to Shar's eyes and Laney pulled Cilla away. The girl collapsed onto the dusty floor, sharing the rectangle of sun with Blackberry. She covered her face in her hands while the dog nosed her fingers.

"Is this the only way you know, Cilla?" Laney asked "Brute force? Luke's way? Why don't you show *me* your power! Punch me, Cilla! Pull out clumps of my hair! Maybe choke me, kick me? Demand that I do as you say, Cilla, like Luke does."

"He loves me," Cilla blubbered. "He says I'm special."

"You're not special to him, Cilla—you're only the object of his control. He wants to have absolute power over you."

"He doesn't. . . ."

"He doesn't call you incessantly, checking on you, wanting to know your every move? Where you're going? Who you're talking to? Toby. Does he know about Toby, Cilla? I bet he does. Perhaps the gut bruise and hair yank was about Toby."

Cilla's face showed that Laney had hit home but still she resisted. "No . . . you're wrong. Luke didn't hurt me." She hugged her body and trembled. "It was Eugene . . . I told you last night."

"Bullshit!" Laney said, the profanity spilling from her mouth no matter how hard she tried to hold it back.

The language seemed to have shocked the child. Cilla's mouth parted, but just for an instant.

"This is stupid," Cilla began. "You guys won't believe me."

"Maybe if you told the truth," Laney said while trying to remember everything she had read about abusive behavior—the insecurities, jealousies, possible alcohol or drug abuse, anger. But it was Shar who said the magic words.

"He will kill you, Cilla," she said, her arms dropping to her side.

Leave it to Shar to get to the crux of the matter, Laney thought.

Cilla's head jerked upward. She gaped in stunned silence.

"Just as sure as anything, he will kill you . . . or hurt you badly. Don't you read the newspapers? Watch the news? Cemeteries are full of people like you. Hospitals, too," Shar went on.

"Luke wouldn't," Cilla said, glaring at Shar.

"He has."

Silence. Then, "It's my fault. I make him mad."

Finally, an implicit admission of Luke's guilt, Laney thought.

"What'd you do—shoot his mother?" Shar asked.

"He has no mother."

"Aw, Cilla. That's no reason," Laney said.

"His mother . . . she deserted him when he was a baby," Cilla said.

"Made it tough, perhaps. But he has a father . . . and always a choice," Shar said.

"His father hits him. I've seen him."

"Abuse is learned behavior. What if you and Luke had a child?" Laney suggested.

"I'm not pregnant!" Cilla yelled.

Thank God, Laney thought. "And if you were?"

"I'd never hit my baby."

"Luke?"

The suggestion stunned Cilla. Silence pulsed through the attic. Cilla shivered and moaned deep. She raised her eyes to Laney's. "Aunt Laney, I'd totally die if—" she managed.

"Honey, if abuse is all you've ever known, it goes on and on. Like generations on welfare."

"He said he'll change."

"Bet he's said that before." Shar curled a lip.

"I can't break up with him. He needs me. Said he'd kill himself."

"Emotional blackmail garbage," Laney said with control although she wanted to scream the words. "Bet he tells you he has to have sex too . . . it's what guys need . . . that he'll get another girl if you don't comply."

Laney watched the pretty mouth tighten with each haunting phrase. Cilla shook her head frantically. In the shaft of the sun, her hair was pure gold. She had combed bangs over the sore spot. Cilla sighed. "Aunt Laney, I have to think. Please . . . I can't stand. . . ." Her eyes pleaded the next words. "You won't tell Mother about . . . you know . . . what I said about Eugene. I shouldn't have." She began to cry again and mumbled, "Sometimes Eugene's a jerk—you know— wants to be cool but tries too hard. But he's never hit me."

"I won't tell your mother," Laney said. "But you have to promise me that you won't see Luke."

Cilla didn't answer.

"I have to have your word on that."

"But he's hurt," she whined.

"Just his feelings. He drove away under his own power, girl," Shar said.

"Why did Toby punch him?" Cilla asked weakly.

"I'd say Toby figured out that Luke hurt you and was just giving him what was coming to him."

Cilla smoothed Blackberry's ears and stood shakily, her face flushed with emotion and the heat of the attic. "Aunt Laney, can I go to my room. I promise I won't try to see Luke . . . but I can't promise you I won't talk to him on the phone."

I guess that's the best I can hope for right now, Laney thought, suddenly wrung out. Laney pulled a rigid Cilla into her arms and was reminded of better times before it all had happened, when Cilla was still innocent and untouched, when she still gave spontaneous hugs and experienced pleasure where she found it.

The child's wet face found the hollow under Laney's chin and Cilla breathed, "Aunt Laney, I can't help that I love him."

"Oh but you can," Laney answered. "When your self-respect empowers you and you finally realize that no one has the right to hurt you. God, how can I get through to you before it's too late?"

29

Laney didn't know how long she gazed out of the attic window after Shar accompanied Cilla downstairs, but shadows had lengthened in the yard when Cam and Bonnie finally climbed into the van to begin the long drive home to Louisiana. When Cam shook Bucky's hand through the opened window, Laney felt guilty for not seeing them off but remembered that she had bid them all a hasty goodbye that morning when the couple had taken the crew to the airport.

After the van pulled away, Bucky stood talking with Toby for a minute or so, then strode toward his tent and ducked inside. He must be going to take a nap, Laney thought as he zipped the screen closed.

Toby remained standing in the yard, his hands in back pockets, his mouth in a frown.

Then, as though he felt her watching him, his eyes riveted on the attic window where she stood. Laney managed a tiny wave, then turned to the task she had originally climbed to the attic to do.

Stirring up dust and an occasional spider web, she pushed and shoved cartons aside to get to the far dark corner under the eaves where her mother had said the Carson box was located. Several cardboard containers labeled "tax records" reminded her that Cara's things really ought to be gone through and discarded. When she broke a path to the corner, she tugged at a wooden box with cracked leather handles at either end. Kudzu ran from behind it with something small and gray in his mouth.

"Need help?" asked a voice from the doorway.

Laney straightened, bumping her head on a rafter. "Why, Toby, how? . . . Great . . . I can use a bit of grunt." Kudzu ran by him and disappeared into the gloom of the front room, the morsel wiggling.

Thick sinewy arms rippled as Toby slid the box toward the center of the room and then lifted it to his shoulder with broad hands. Laney recalled how those same powerful limbs had thrashed Luke over and over in the yard. And she wondered how badly Luke was hurt.

"Where do you want it?" Toby asked.

"Under the window," Laney pointed.

"Kinda heavy. What's in it?" Toby asked, setting it on the floor with a thud. The orange-gold rays of the evening sun slid over the sill onto the box.

"That's what I intend to find out."

Laney squatted and unhooked the clasp holding the top in place. The two of them shoved the lid back against the wall.

A blanket lay folded over the contents. It emitted strong odors of must. She sneezed.

As she lifted it away, she realized it wasn't just a blanket, but a red horse blanket that was trimmed in black grosgrain ribbon. She shook it open. By its size, the covering was obviously meant for a weanling or yearling. She was caught by the beautiful farm crest on one end of the blanket. A large golden C encircled a smaller red P against an oval ground of jet black. A golden wreath outlined it all. Against the rich ruby color of the fabric, the woven emblem was beautiful.

Toby's hand shot out and impulsively fingered the raised lettering, his touch a caress. "Oh," escaped involuntarily from his lips.

"The initials must stand for Paul Carson," Laney murmured. "Beautiful, isn't it?"

Toby was silent, his face unreadable.

Laney laid the blanket aside and lifted a crushed wide-brim hat. She punched it out, shaped the felt and set it jauntily on her head. The same initialed crest embossed the band, front and center. She posed and fluttered her eyes at Toby. Reaching for a packet of letters and papers secured with a rubber band, she felt Toby's eyes still upon her.

No wonder the box was so heavy, she thought as she sorted through an assortment of bridles, hoof picks, mane and tail combs that lay scattered among tools obviously meant for one who could shoe horses—horseshoe nails, metal shoes and a hammer.

Toby couldn't take his eyes off the hat.

Uncomfortable under his gaze, she dropped the hat back into the box and grasped the bundle of correspondence. "I believe I'll look at these downstairs," she said. Again he fingered the crest before placing the blanket into the box and closing the lid. She stood, but Toby remained on his knees. "Toby, are you coming?" she asked.

"Yeah . . . sure," he said, slowly getting to his feet. His eyes finally focused on hers. "Uh . . . the reason I came up . . . I guessed you saw that," he said thumbing at the window behind him.

"Yes, I did. Cilla saw it too."

"Don't care who saw. He had it coming."

"You know?"

"About Cilla? . . . yeah." His body jerked in a sudden spasm. "He hurt her bad, huh?"

"Yes."

Toby kicked the wooden box. "For Chrissake, why does she keep seeing the stupid jerk?"

"We've talked. She's promised not to see him."

"Don't bet on it."

"I won't."

Concern turning to viciousness flashed in his eyes. "Don't sweat it. I'll watch out for her."

"Thank you," she whispered, but even with his words, she still felt uneasy.

30

Laney wasn't expecting to see either Bucky or Gordon at her door, but they stood there together. Gordon, as though straight out of a John Wayne movie, shifted the weight of his holster belt with his thumbs. Bucky, not waiting for an invitation, shoved right by her into the hallway.

"Where is he?" Bucky said, his mouth cruel.

Hearing the commotion, Cilla, Toby, and Shar rushed out of the library.

Seeing Toby, Bucky lunged at him. He grabbed a handful of T-shirt and yelled, "You promised not to let it out of your sight!" His curls were gold flames about his fiery face.

"Hold on there," Gordon said, stepping between them.

"What?" Toby asked. He was bewildered.

"My field notebook!" Bucky shouted.

Gordon interrupted with a quick explanation. "Toby, one of Malcolm's prize bulls was poisoned and Dr. Gage's notebook was found near the scene. The professor said he loaned it to you this morning. Is that true?"

Toby's face grew pale. "Yeah . . . I mean . . . I was doing research at the library. He said I could take it."

"And did you?" Gordon asked.

"Yeah, I mean I took it . . . but I left it in my pickup."

"Was it there when you got back to the truck?" Gordon asked.

"I guess so. I don't remember. I . . . I was so pissed off over the damage to my truck."

"What—?" Gordon began.

"Don't remember?" Bucky thundered, interrupting Gordon.

"Enough of that," Gordon admonished Bucky. "Toby, think hard, son. Do you recall seeing the notebook after your trip to the library?"

The boy looked around frantically. His eyes darted back and forth from Bucky to Gordon. "I just can't remember."

Cilla's tiny voice broke in, "When we got back to the truck, someone had tossed a cigarette butt through the window while we were gone and it had burned a track on the vinyl seat cover. Toby was so mad, we didn't even think about the notebook."

"Sheriff Powell, I went along on that research trip and I remember seeing the book on the dash when we got in his truck here at the farm," Shar said, "but I don't recall seeing it when we climbed back in his truck."

"You lock your truck, son?" Gordon pressed.

"I never . . . I mean . . . no."

Laney thought back through the day. She had seen both Bucky and Toby early that morning when Cam and Bonnie had left to drive the crew to the airport. Bucky had left shortly afterwards—to do some errands in town, so he had said. Toby, Cilla and Shar drove to the library right after breakfast and she didn't see them again until they got back after lunch—about one o'clock. That's when Cilla, Shar and she had gone to the attic. She didn't know what time Bucky returned from town, only that he and Toby were in the yard when she saw the confrontation with Luke—Luke!

"Look, the diagnostic lab is going to do a post-mortem on that bull in the morning to confirm that poisoning diagnosis of Doc's. I'm going to have to get back to you two after that," Gordon said. "But it sure is odd that the professor's notebook ended up out at Taylor Ridge."

With the threatening statement, he left, Bucky practically climbing his heels. The door crashed behind him.

Toby was shaken as he and Cilla went back to their research in the library. Laney and Shar retreated to the kitchen where Laney began frantically slicing mushrooms and water chestnuts on the butcher-block table in the center of the kitchen. She added them to diced, cooked chicken. Shar chopped vegetables for a salad—her only specialty.

While Laney whisked sour cream into a sauce made with chicken broth, she worked in silence, her mind flitting back and forth from the emergency at Malcolm's, the mummified infant and Cilla. She began to grate cheese into the sauce.

"Woman, are you sure you want cheese in there?" Shar asked.

Laney looked into the bowl. "Whoops, cheese goes over the dish after its cooked," she said, dropping the chunk of cheese and the grater onto the butcher block. She collapsed onto a stool. "Shar, so much stuff going on. Is it somehow related?"

"Woman, what are you talking about?"

"You know—the bull poisoning, the stolen notebook, the infant remains, and Cilla."

"Woman, you bonkers or what?" Her mouth pursed into a thinking pucker. "Bull, book, baby, battered. Bull, book, baby, battered." She circled the butcher-block table, repeating the litany like a witch from Macbeth. "Bull, book, baby, battered." She pulled up. "Nope, no connection." Shar punctuated the remark with a flourish of the paring knife.

"Look, I admit, the infant remains may be a separate episode, but there has to be a connection between the dead bull and the displaced notebook. Toby had possession of the notebook, later found at Malcolm's near the dead bull. Remember earlier today when Toby punched out Luke? There's no love lost between those two. Luke throws Toby black looks every time he comes to the farm. Jealous. Maybe Luke stole the notebook and tossed a cigarette into Toby's truck while all of you were in the library, poisoned the bull out at Malcolm's and planted the notebook nearby so that Toby would get the blame. Remember, Toby's mother lives there."

"Like I forgot about the noxious weed. She probably killed the beast herself."

Laney glared at her friend. "Get real," she said, as she lined a large greased dish with crushed crackers and added the chicken mixture.

"I'm telling you, woman. She has an evil streak running through her like a dybbuk."

"What, pray tell, is a dybbuk?"

"The wandering soul of a dead person that gets inside a living person and controls what they do. It's based on Jewish folklore."

"Now I know you've gone and lost it."

"Well I don't really believe that crap. Anyway, Poison Ivy doesn't need a dybbuk to control what she does. She thinks up vicious things to do all by herself. Don't forget what she did to my Kudzu."

Hearing his name, the kitten scampered out of the pantry and streaked to Shar. Laney wondered what had become of the mouse he had caught in the attic.

Laney looked up and smiled at Shar as she poured the sauce over the chicken mixture. She covered the top with cracker crumbs, dotted it with butter and shoved it into the oven. She set the timer. "There, now we have time for a toddy. You can help me go through these papers, too," she said, sitting at the breakfast table overlooking the kitchen garden and the carriage house beyond. Heat lightning flashed in the southern sky. She thought she heard a distant rumble. Shar bounded out of the room to fix the bloodies at the bar in the parlor.

Laney stared aimlessly out the window. It felt odd not seeing at least a few members of the crew milling about. She sighed. She missed Gray.

The portable phone next to her hand rang and when she put it to her ear, her heart leaped when she heard Gray's soft voice. He was at Malcolm's trying to console him about the loss of his prize bull. He asked about her day, what she was doing as though that was the reason for his call. Idly and cautiously he felt her out, and she knew her perfunctory answers weren't what he needed to hear. All he wanted to know was that everything was once more right between them. So she said the words and he sighed, his relief evident. She invited him for dinner and told him to ask Malcolm.

Laney powered off as Shar swooped into the room. She held a tumbler in each hand and sipped from one that was threatening to overflow. She placed them on the table. There were more flashes in the sky but closer now.

"Guess who's coming to dinner?" Laney asked, squeezing the lime wedge over her drink.

"Gray," Shar said, sitting down and stirring her drink with a long, pink-nailed forefinger. With her other hand, she fondled Kudzu in her lap.

"Close."

Shar's head snapped up. "Who?" Kudzu jumped to the floor.

"Gray, and some gimpy Scotsman—"

"Mal? Mal's coming here?" she squealed, and was long gone down the back hallway and up to her room to change before Laney could finish her guest list.

" . . . and a woman named Ivy."

31

Laney lifted the bundle. The old, crackled rubber band around the papers snapped as she began to slide it away. The papers spilled to the tabletop.

Why in the world did Cara and Mother save all this stuff, Laney thought as she shifted through the papers? A bill for grain and salt blocks from Brumfield's in Lexington, Jockey Club application forms, brochures for stallion seasons. She stopped when she found an ultrasound photo of a mare's early pregnancy—the fetus a tiny black hole in a white fan-shaped swish. She had seen lots of these in the two springs that she'd been breeding mares. She remembered Unreasonable's scan the year before and how excited she had been when the old mare had gotten in foal. Now, her foal romped with Maria, a nurse mare acquired after Unreasonable's death.

Her fingers moved rapidly through the pile. "Mostly junk mail—but what do we have here?" she said, lifting an envelope and scanning the return address.

Warm arms embraced her from behind and she jumped. The smell of shaving cream and soap nudged her senses. She turned her head and the warm familiar lips smothered hers. She tasted sweetness, peppermint, maleness. It seemed like forever since she'd sampled it. She felt Blackberry, who had slipped in with Gray, begin to quiver in fear against her legs as outside, the wind picked up.

"I let myself in with my key," Gray said, slipping into the chair Shar had vacated. "What's so interesting about that envelope?" His hand crept around her shoulders and he leaned until his face found his favorite hollow on her neck. She writhed with pleasure, then tensed as she remembered the unresolved jealousy issue. They had to talk, but not now.

"It's Paul Carson's," she said.

"What are you doing with it?"

"I'm trying to find out where he moved after he and Alice sold the farm to Cara and Joe."

"Oh, I get it. You're back on the mother of the infant's trail, aren't you? Dammit, Laney! Why don't you let the authorities handle this? You have no need to get involved again." Gray jumped up, yanking his arm away.

"Come on, Gray. Maybe if I'm the first one to find out who the mother is, the police won't probe into Cara's past again." She stared at the return address on the envelope. *Bank of Georgetown, Georgetown, Kentucky.* Directly beneath, the words jumped at her: *Trust Department.* The envelope was addressed to Mr. Paul Carson on Hickory Pike, Hickory, Kentucky—her address now.

There was a clattering in the back hallway, and Shar burst into the kitchen. She wore a sleeveless Hamilton blue and red plaid sundress that was cut low in front and just barely covered her fanny in back. Gold thistles dangled from her earlobes. "Well, where is he?" she asked.

"If you mean Malcolm, he'll be here directly," Gray answered.

Trying to divert the conversation away from what she was sure was coming next, Laney began to give out orders. "Shar, you set the table and I'll get some of Mother's goodies out of the freezer for dessert." She jumped from her chair and stacked Paul Carson's mail on the built-in desk in the kitchen. The diversion didn't throw Shar off the scent.

"Wait . . . just . . . one . . . minute," Shar said. "Malcolm can't drive. How's he getting here?"

Laney winced.

"Ivy's bringing him," Gray said innocently.

Shar's head jerked back as though Gray had hauled off and hit her. She blinked. "Poison . . . is . . . coming here?" Shar stammered.

Gray looked at Laney in bewilderment. "Laney, what in hell—"

"Gray, you knew that there was a problem between the two women. I suppose I should have reminded you before I told you to invite Malcolm. When you got back on the phone and told me you had invited Ivy too, the dirty deed was already done. I guess you couldn't very well have uninvited her."

"I knew there was some friction there but when I asked Malcolm, Ivy was standing right there," Gray said.

"Friction? . . . like a couple pieces of number 200 sandpaper rubbing together," Laney said.

"If you think I'm going to break bread with that wanton you're out of your skull," Shar said. "Malcolm or no Malcolm." With that, she stomped to the doorway of the hallway, then suddenly banked like an aircraft hitting turbulence until she again faced Laney and Gray.

"On second thought," she said with a wicked leer, "I'd love to have dinner with Ms. Ivy Hart." A clap of thunder punctuated the remark.

Oh-my-God, Laney thought. But Shar just smiled, her gray eyes shining like stainless steel in the sun. Laney heard Shar humming "Auld Lang Syne" as she began to set the table. Outside, the first rain in over a month pelted the window.

32

Malcolm was genuinely delighted to see Shar again. Leaning heavily on his wooden crutches, his lips formed a generous bow as Ivy guided him through the front door. Not lost to Laney was how under narrow lids, Shar's eyes guilefully slid to Ivy and stayed glued to the woman as she glided down the hall, through the kitchen and into the breakfast room. She left a heavy scent of lilacs in her wake.

Instead of her usual dour uniform, Ivy wore a summer dress of ice blue that mirrored the color of her eyes. Laney gave Ivy an uneasy once over. The bodice of her dress, smocked with elastic and barely containing her swollen bosom, met a full skirt of gauzy material that floated about her hips and seduced her shapely legs as she walked. Her diminutive feet were tucked into high-heeled cloth sandals that matched the color of her dress. Still parted in the middle, but released from its severe bun, Ivy's brown hair hung in lustrous waves about her flawless ivory features. Laney shot a glance at Shar. Was that uncertainty clouding her friend's face? She's met her match with this one, Laney thought with discomfort.

Once in the breakfast alcove, everyone fussed to get Malcolm settled comfortably at the round table.

Toby and Cilla had chosen to eat on trays in the library while they continued their research. Toby had barely nodded to his mother when they loaded their plates in the kitchen and he lost no time escaping down the hallway.

The wind drove the rain against the house in heavy waves, the lights dimming twice. Laney lit the candles in the hurricane globes on the table. She carried an oil lamp to the library for Toby and Cilla. When she returned, Laney saw lights go on in the carriage house through sheets of water streaming down the window. Bucky's taken refuge there from the storm, she thought. I bet he's heating up leftover jambalaya for dinner. Maybe I should have invited . . . she glanced at Gray to her left. No, not tonight.

Malcolm sat next to Shar, his back turned slightly away since his leg was propped awkwardly on a pillow on the chair next to him. Ivy, sitting next to his footrest, occasionally patted his little pink toes peeking out from his walking cast.

If Laney had any doubt that Shar had lost her resolution to do whatever she'd planned, it slowly faded in the next few minutes. Every time Ivy touched Malcolm, Shar's eyelids narrowed until there were only gashes covering stony pits. Ivy answered her glare by leaning to her left, plumping the pillow under Malcolm's foot, her bulging cleavage distracting and goading Shar until the room seemed to crackle with anxious expectation.

Ivy's dance of seduction wasn't lost on Gray. He kept trying to distract the women with aimless banter but sweat broke out on his forehead as Ivy smiled alluringly at Malcolm and abruptly left her seat. She reached around Malcolm, her breasts pressing against his shoulder as she caught his napkin before it slipped to the floor and slowly smoothed it lovingly over his lap.

Fearing the worst, Laney had only hoped to get through the first course. But it wasn't to be.

All at once, Shar laid down her salad fork, the clink of metal against porcelain more frightening than the crash of thunder that followed. The lights flickered and went out. Candlelight cast a ghoulish glow on the five faces.

"Ivy, Malcolm was truly impressed with your Scottish treats. Family recipes, I assume?" Shar remarked.

Shar's comment seemed innocuous enough, although Laney thought it tainted with a frosty undertone.

Reluctantly, Ivy's eyes fluttered away from Malcolm. "Why . . . yes."

"Wonderful," Malcolm mumbled through a mouthful of green salad while reaching for the roll on his butter plate.

"The Scotch shortbread, your mother's recipe?" Shar asked Ivy.

"No, my grandmother's . . . ," Ivy began, then hesitated. She snatched up Malcolm's roll.

"Yes?" Shar urged.

"Malcolm, would you like me to butter your roll?" Ivy said, plunging his knife into the tub of butter.

"You were saying, Ivy . . . something about your grandmother," Shar said.

"Well, yes. She . . . was from Scotland."

"You don't mean it," Malcolm said, suddenly interested. "What part of Scotland?" he asked.

"I . . . I can't remember," Ivy stammered.

Where's Shar going with this, Laney wondered.

"What was your grandmother's maiden name?" Shar asked a little too sweetly.

"I don't remember." Ivy mumbled uncomfortably, then took a long draft of her ice water.

"You don't remember your grandmother's maiden name? How odd!" Shar said wickedly. "I bet Toby knows."

Gray jumped to his feet. "I need to freshen my drink. I'll ask him while I'm up. Anyone else need anything?"

Shar handed Gray her glass. "Fix me a bloody, will you?" Her eyes glowed bright with anticipation as he disappeared down the hall.

Laney took the interlude to serve the casserole. She circled the table, her hands covered in oven mittens. Ivy's hand trembled as she spooned the bubbling mixture onto Malcolm's plate and then her own. Laney placed the casserole on a trivet and after scooping an ample portion for Gray, she served herself and sat down.

Gray returned to the table. "Well, Ivy, Toby was surprised that you had forgotten your grandmother's maiden name. It's Campbell. In fact—and I don't profess to know anything about these matters—according to what you told your son, you may be a direct descendent of Sir Colin Campbell, who lived during the seventeenth century," He said, handing Shar her drink. "Didn't know the chap myself, but surely that calls for a toast." Gray held up his glass.

A curious whining sound came from Malcolm as he drew in his breath. Apprehensive eyes swung to his face. He blanched to a clay-like gray and jerked upright in his chair, his leg crashing to the floor. Pain slashed Malcolm's features as though struck by a sword, and he struggled to his feet. Balancing on his good leg, he leaned forward and swiped hard at Gray's glass held high. The tumbler of bourbon and water dashed against the wall.

"My goodness," a startled Laney gasped as the glass shattered.

"Never!" Malcolm shouted. "Never in my presence shall someone toast that bloody limb of Satan!" The color that had so quickly drained from his face gushed back, purpling his skin.

Ivy, her perfect features disfigured with fear, scrambled to her feet and ran from the room.

Shar swung her own glass to her mouth and drank greedily. Above the rim, her eyes danced.

33

"Unbelievable, Shar Hamilton," Laney said later when the storm both outside and in had abated.

The electricity had been restored and the two of them had just begun loading the dishwasher. They were alone in the kitchen except for Kudzu whom Shar had let out of the pantry as soon as Ivy had left.

Ivy had dashed from the house and raced away in her car, leaving Malcolm behind. Gray offered to drive Malcolm home after Shar had calmed her fiancé. Gray promised to get him settled for the night and to even remain overnight at the house, if needed. Shar begged in vain to do the administering, but Gray and Malcolm both agreed that a second confrontation with Ivy was unwise.

"Woman, I'm not proud of what I did, but the hussy had it coming. Did you see the way she—"

"I did. So did Gray. Unconscionable behavior. It made me blush," Laney said.

"Anything makes you blush," Shar answered.

"How did you know she had Scottish roots and all?"

"When you told me her mother had taught her how to make Scotch shortbread—that was my first clue. A little snippet of info from Jesse that Ivy's grandmother was a Campbell by birth and some serious snooping at the library earlier today really wrapped it up. Being a Hamilton myself and up on clan history, I already knew the Campbells and the Lamonts had been feuding for centuries. The Campbells were held responsible for the loss of much of the original Lamont lands, not to mention a massacre of one hundred Lamonts in some Scottish churchyard in 1646. The Lamonts weren't blameless in the centuries of plundering and killing, and I'm sure Malcolm knows this. But poor Toby inadvertently hit a nerve when he just repeated what his mother had told him about his ancestry. How would he have known how Malcolm felt about this Sir Colin Campbell, one of the ringleaders in the bloodbath?"

"Did *you* know about Sir Colin?"

"Not until today when I read about him. I had hoped that when Malcolm learned Ivy came from Campbell stock, it would dampen his infatuation for her. But when Toby dropped the bomb that Poison's family might be traced back to Sir Colin Campbell himself, that cinched it."

"What do you think Ivy will do?" Laney asked.

"It doesn't really matter," Shar said. "Malcolm and I are back on track, that's what's important. Looks as though you and Gray are, too," she said, flicking soapsuds at Laney as she washed the casserole dish.

"We are, but we still have the jealousy issue to deal with and he's having a fit about me getting involved in the investigation of the infant remains."

"Did you find out anything in the papers you discovered in the attic?"

"Not really, unless you want to consider an envelope from the trust department of the Bank of Georgetown a clue." Laney retrieved the envelope from the kitchen desk.

"There's a name typed under the return address."

"I assume it's the name of a trust officer. It's postmarked July 1988, a year before Joe and my sister moved here."

"That's using your old noggin, woman."

"Well, I'm going to call the bank in the morning and see if they have an address for Paul Carson." Laney stared at the address. "I wish the letter weren't missing. I'm curious to know whose trust this is."

"Probably was one that Carson's parents set up for him, or . . . one he set up for his own children."

"He had no kids."

"As far as we know," Shar said cryptically.

"As far as we know."

34

"I'm really whipped, Toby. Let's call it a night, okay?" Cilla said.

"But this book on history mysteries is just getting interesting."

"Look at the time. Everyone's gone to bed." Cilla rubbed her eyes, still red and puffy from her crying episode in the attic.

Toby took a quick look up from his book and suddenly realized just how exhausted she appeared. "Only fifteen more minutes, I promise. Can you handle one more chapter in that Harrod bio?" He smiled at her, then his eyes dropped down to his book.

He also was reading about James Harrod, one of the first Kentucky settlers. Toby was engrossed in the chapter on his disappearance. In Harrod's younger days, even before Daniel Boone, Harrod had explored and surveyed much of the territory before it had been made a state and eventually he had established the town of Harrodsburg.

Toby finished a paragraph. Jeez, another surveyor. What else is new? He read on.

In 1792, the same year Kentucky achieved statehood, Harrod donned his broad-brimmed beaver hat, trousers, linen hunting shirt trimmed with silver buttons and left his wife and seven-year-old daughter to go on a hunting trip with two other men. They were thought to have gone up the Kentucky River. He was never heard of again, no body was ever found. The book gave three possibilities for what happened to Harrod: that he just took off because of marital problems and maybe lived with the Indians, that he was killed by one of the other two men in his hunting party, or that he just disappeared and later died in an accident in the woods.

"Say Cilla, check this out," Toby said. "This guy really fits!" Toby read the passages to her.

A bit reticent from her earlier disappointment at the library over John Filson, Cilla didn't seem too excited at first. "How tall was he?" she asked, recalling Filson, the "little schoolteacher."

"That's the best clue so far," Toby said. "Harrod was a rough and tough guy about six feet tall—and listen to this." He read a couple more passages to Cilla and looked at her. "See, no one knows exactly the year he was born but most believe he was about forty-six when he died. Bingo dingo! That's close to the age that Bucky figures Bones bit the dust."

Cilla giggled and her dimple appeared briefly at the corner of her mouth. He loved it. Damn, back to the project.

They both read silently until Cilla said, "Toby, can you detect healed fractures on a skeleton? Harrod got thrown from his horse a couple times. Broke his thigh bones in two separate accidents."

Toby dropped his book on the sofa and grabbed Cilla's. The worn spine was beginning to tear away from the binding. He read the paragraph.

"You're totally amazing, Cilla. This is our next project! . . . Study Bones's bones," he said gleefully, then abruptly frowned. "But I don't recall Dr. Gage mentioning anything in his notebook about healed fractures."

"Maybe you just overlooked it. I wish we had that notebook. I wonder when the sheriff will return it," Cilla said.

"Before I see Dr. Gage again, I hope. Did you ever see anyone so ticked?"

"Who do you think swiped it?"

Toby paused before answering. "The same jerk who left the cigarette calling card in my truck," he snapped.

Wrinkles formed across Cilla's brow. "No way. Luke wouldn't do that, Toby."

Back off, he thought. Best let her figure it out herself. But in his mind, it was a no-brainer. The jerk saw his truck parked at the library and lifted the notebook off the dash, thinking it was his. After tossing the hot butt, he drove to Mr. Lamont's, snuffed the bull and planted the notebook so the cops would think he was responsible for its croaking. If he'd known all that before he'd gotten his hands on Luke in the yard, he would've . . . His mouth watered with the thought of it and for the first time he thought about his thirty-eight revolver at the apartment in his bedside drawer. He couldn't believe the picture he was conjuring in his mind. He was out at Mason's farm target-shooting and instead of the knothole in the hackberry tree, Luke was the target. Toby had him in the gun sight and was squeezing the trigger slow and steady. . . .

He shook the image away and focused on Cilla. "Cilla, your eyes are crossing," he said, patting her knee, then pulling her to her feet. She lingered as though not wanting to leave him. Not trusting himself, he stepped to the window. "The storm's about over," he said, peering out but fully aware of her next to him. He had difficulty in distinguishing the rain beating against the pane from the exciting syncopation of his heart. Her warm arm brushed his and in the black glass reflection, her head slowly tilted until it barely rested against his shoulder. Then she was gone, the heavy library door clicking shut behind her.

He instantly missed her, as though she had taken something of him away with her. He lingered, not wanting to go to his tent, into the wind, into the rain.

The grandfather clock in the hall chimed twelve. Thank God the day was finally over, he thought. So much had happened—Cilla, her body battered by the rutting jerk, the fight, the stolen notebook, the mystery of Bones and something he wouldn't allow himself to think about—the strange mingling of fear and wonder he had felt in the attic.

35

"Clean as a whistle." Freddie dropped the field notebook on Sheriff Powell's desk. "Someone wiped it down with disinfectant."

"Dammit," Gordon said. "Any unusual residue we can trace down?"

"Lysol. There's a bottle in the show barn at the clean-up sink."

"Shit. What about the scoop?"

"Only Smitty's prints. Whoever did this must have used his hands to mix the taxus in or wiped the scoop clean afterwards. I don't get it. If someone wanted to implicate Toby Hart, why didn't they leave the prints on the notebook alone? Toby's prints would have been on it."

"Stupidity, I bet. Probably didn't think about prints when he grabbed the book, then later at the barn, it occurred to him and he looked around and found the Lysol to get rid of his own prints. Anything on the bull?"

"Just the *Taxus media hicksii*. Very hardy and very common. Got 'em in my front yard."

"How d'you know all that crap?"

"Gardening's my hobby, remember? By the way, no tire marks on the road. No one saw anything unusual." Freddie opened a stick of spearmint gum and folded one into his mouth.

"No nothing." Gordon creaked back in his chair and watched Freddie chew. "What's with the gum?"

"Doctor put me on a diet after I tipped the scales at 250. Said it wouldn't be long before he'd have to send me off to be weighed at the yards."

Gordon chuckled. "I wondered where your usual sausage and egg biscuit was."

"My stomach's eating itself. I wish there was a skin patch for junk food addiction."

Gordon shifted some papers around on his desk. "Have we heard anything from Karen Thompson?"

"Not since we turned over those old gunny sacks we found in the McVey horse barn. Detective Barron breathing down your neck over the murder investigation?"

"Yeah." He didn't mention what Barron was pushing Karen to do.

Deputy Nancy West opened the door a crack and stuck in her head. "Karen's on line one," she said and slammed the door. It shook the courthouse.

Gordon winced, dug in his pocket and threw a ten-dollar bill on the desk. "Freddie, do me a favor. Buy some foam or felt weather stripping and line that door frame before I kill that woman."

Freddie took a final slurp from his coffee and pocketed the bill.

"Morning Karen. Whatcha got?" Gordon said into the phone.

Cracking his gum, Freddie lingered.

After a long interval, Gordon said, "Thanks. Keep in touch, Karen." He stared at the phone a moment before dropping it into its cradle.

The only sound in the dingy office was Freddie's gum.

Gordon wrote something on his calendar desk pad and underlined it three times before speaking. "The burlap that covered the infant had a faded logo on it. It matches the logo on the sacks that hung in the barn at Stoney Creek Farm. They traced them to a sweet feed sack that was used at Hickory Feed Store from 1960 until they stopped making them and the store switched to white plastic in eighty-five."

Freddie thumbed through his notebook. "According to our notes, Joe and Cara Collins moved to the farm in eighty-nine, so . . . if Hickory Feed Company stopped using the burlap four years before, that should take Cara off the hook."

"How d'you figure? It doesn't matter when they stopped making the sacks if we found them still on the farm just last week."

"Are you saying that the baby could have been buried in one of those sacks anytime from 1960 on?"

"Yep."

"Can't Thompson tell how long the child was in the ground?"

"Evidently not. When they turn up mummified remains from centuries ago, all they have to do is carbon date and they can get an approximate time of death—plus or minus a hundred years. But with anything this recent—1960 or later because of when the burlap was manufactured—they can't do that. Makes me wonder."

"What?"

"Why the murderer put the baby into burlap instead of plastic."

"Probably thought burlap would rot faster."

"That's what I would have thought. The faster the sack disintegrates, the quicker the infant does the same."

"But this time, it didn't."

"Slab kept the moisture out and promoted evaporation. Karen said it was most unusual. If the child had been buried in a plastic bag, after a while it would have turned to mush and disintegrated. No one would have recognized any remains as human. The skull would have been reduced to what would look like corn or taco chips, the skeleton, little chicken-wing bones, pebbles and toy jacks."

"Pebbles and jacks?"

"Vertebrae pieces in a infant skeleton resemble a mix of pebbles and tiny jacks."

Freddie paled and swallowed. He cracked his gum for a full minute. "But plastic bags would have been hard to trace. Most are anonymous. No markings."

Gordon thought about the meeting going on in Karen's office as they spoke. "This is going to be a hard one to crack without . . ." He added a fourth line under the three letters he had written on the pad.

"DNA testing," Freddie said.

"You got it."

36

"Finnan haddie and scones it's not, but it's far better breakfast than what I fix for myself," Gray said to Malcolm as he buttered six slices of raisin toast and stacked it on a tray along side an unopened jar of marmalade, two teacups and saucers, sugar bowl, and a couple of apples that rolled around as he carried it all to the table. Just as he was about to scoot into the bench in the breakfast nook across from his friend, the kettle began to whistle. He poured water over Malcolm's teabag and stirred while the boiling water dissolved the instant coffee in his own cup.

"You can't know how I appreciate you spending the night with me. I wasn't so sure I wanted to stay by myself with this leg."

"Guess you could have asked the woman to stay," Gray said with a wink.

"Never in— What in bloody hell!" he said, suddenly interrupted by a great rapping on the kitchen door.

Gray slid from the bench and peeked through the glass in the window. "It's Smitty."

"Well let the man in before he breaks something."

Gray opened the door and a yellow slicker with matching cap slid inside and slammed the door.

"Gray, fix him a spot of tea, would you?" Malcolm asked while stirring sugar into his teacup.

Smitty raised a hand. "None for me, thanks. And I don't look for you to be drinking yours after you hear my news." Through the rainwater dripping from the brim of his hat, Gray saw that Smitty was frightened.

Malcolm dropped his spoon onto his saucer with a clatter.

"I don't know how anyone got into the farm, Mr. Lamont, but it's happened again."

"What's happened, my man. You don't mean—?"

"The same as before. But this time it's three heifers in the pasture next to the feed barn. Dead as doornails."

Malcolm tried to rise but Gray pushed him down with a gentle hand on his shoulder. Malcolm's color threatened a stroke. "No need to kill the messenger, my friend," Gray said. "I'll go with Smitty and call the police from my cell phone."

Gray was surprised, but Malcolm didn't resist and leaned back in his booth and closed his eyes as though by doing so, all of it would vanish. Gray pulled on a pair of Wellingtons that were by the door, and a trench coat from a hook above and followed Smitty out the door.

The rain was down to a drizzle, almost a mist, as they jumped into the blue Dodge farm truck. Smitty had left the motor running.

"They were three of his prize heifers. One, the offspring of Jake who was poisoned. I'm telling you, I'm getting a bit spooked over this," Smitty said. "If it's not safe on this farm, I'm thinking I should move the wife and kids, you know."

They drove into the barnyard between the two barns. The metal show barn where Jake had been poisoned was to their left as Smitty pulled into the hay and straw storage barn directly across from it and stopped. They climbed out of the truck and walked the center aisle toward the yawning entrance on the far side of the barn.

It was easy to see that hay stacked on the right of the aisle was dangerously low—only reaching to Gray's shoulder in most areas, and the bright straw bales on his left that usually touched the rafters, weren't even close. This rain won't help much, Gray thought. Because of the drought, there won't be much hay or straw for sale in the county this winter. Malcolm may have to thin out his herd in the fall.

As they exited the barn and approached the gate to the heifer field, through the drizzle, Gray spotted three huge mounds of black under a tree near the fence.

"Shit," he said. "Malcolm doesn't need this right now. Broken leg, losing his best bull, drought using up all his hay, now losing three more valued animals."

Smitty opened the gate and latched it behind them. "I moved the other heifers to an adjacent pasture," he said, "just in case there was still some taxus around. You might want to check them out. Over there." He pointed to about twenty or so animals in the next field.

Before they had even reached the heifers, Gray noted that the animals were swollen grotesquely, their legs stiffly pointing upwards from the bloat. Unusual, he thought, if they had just died. He dropped to a crouch. No slobber or foam in the closest animal's mouth that had been so evident with Jake. He donned a glove and swept his hand through her mouth. No evidence of taxus needles. God, these Angus had been fine looking specimens. Gray shook his head with the pity of it.

He drew his hand through the heifer's dense hair. It was barely wet. "Must have moved under the tree for shelter during the storm last night." He immediately had a thought. His eyes traveled up the trunk of the maple and he saw it. Unmistakable. The fissure rent the trunk of the tree from as high up as he could see down to where the knurled roots snaked like spokes in a wheel from the trunk hub. "Jesus," he said, as he stood and backed away from the canopy of leaves until he could see most of the tree.

"What?" Smitty said, following Gray into the open.

"Look," Gray pointed to where the tiniest finger of smoke escaped from one of the largest limbs. He was surprised that he hadn't noticed the odor of burning wood before now. "Bolt of lightning, Smitty. The heifers weren't poisoned. They were under the tree when it was struck last night. Must have killed them instantly."

"Holy hell."

"Rather like that, I'd say."

37

"I thought Gray said he would call us and let us know what was going on," Shar said, glaring at Laney.

"I guess he thought it was too late to call."

Laney poured tea from the blue and white teapot that had belonged to her sister. The rain still lashed the window and she couldn't see the carriage house where Toby and Cilla had joined Bucky for breakfast. At seven a.m., Laney had discovered Toby asleep on the beige leather sofa in the library when she'd let Blackberry out. He was embarrassed that he had slept in the house without asking her first, but Laney assured him it was all right, considering the severe storm that had passed through. She hoped that Bucky hadn't jumped all over him again this morning about the notebook.

Shar spooned two heaping tablespoons of honey into her cup. Stirring the viscous mixture, she finally lifted the spoon and licked off the coating of honey like it was a sucker, then dropped it clanking onto her saucer. "I can't stand it. I'm going to call Malcolm whether Poison answers the phone or not," she said and huffed across the breakfast room to the desk. As she reached for the phone, Blackberry began to bark and Kudzu ducked into the pantry. Gray, waggling his house key and tracking water onto the brick floor with Malcolm's Wellingtons, bent and petted the Border collie while holding Puccini in his other arm.

"Well, it's about time, thou sluggish bearer of enlightenment," Shar said with hands on her almost hipless hips.

"Have you ever tried to pull pants off an elephant leg? It was after midnight before I had settled Malcolm in for the night," he said.

"You mean the trollop didn't assist you?"

"She's gone."

"Gone?" Laney asked.

"Gone for good, according to Malcolm," he said.

Shar sat down shakily. "Last night was just too much fun and much too easy. Gone forever? I think not."

"I know so. When we got to Malcolm's, Ivy had moved all her stuff out of the guestroom and not a trace of her remained save several chocolate chip cookies that Malcolm and I personally took care of. He indicated that he wished you would come and stay with him your last few days in Kentucky. He feels very remorseful over the way he treated you."

"He ought to—yielding to the whims of that woman just because she pampered him." Shar's smoky eyes smoldered. "I just won't stand for it!" she fumed. "Maybe I can't cook Scotch eggs, but I can make a Rob Roy that would curl his argyles and I would give him a hell of a roll in the hay if he'd ever let me."

"Shar!"

"Well, it's true," she said contritely.

"How about breakfast before you traipse over to Malcolm's. It may be your last good meal for awhile," Laney said, with a smirk. "Join us, Gray?"

"I grabbed something at Malcolm's before I left," Gray said. "But I'm afraid the poor guy didn't eat any breakfast, himself."

"Your cooking would take anyone's appetite away," Laney said.

"Wish that was the reason. He lost three heifers in that storm last night. They were under the wrong tree at the wrong time when Zeus wielded a thunderbolt."

"Oh, poor Malcolm," Laney said.

"Punishment from the gods for the way he treated me," Shar said.

"Anyway, I have calls all day. But I might stop back later if you'll fix me a toddy." Gray winked at Laney and gave her a kiss goodbye.

Over breakfast, Laney fingered the envelope from the Bank of Georgetown and at eight-thirty, she dialed information for the number.

"Here goes nothing," she told Shar and punched in the numbers.

When a woman answered, Laney asked to be transferred to the trust department.

"May I speak to Jerome Whalen, please," she asked, her finger under the name on the envelope.

"This is he," a friendly voice said.

Surprised that she had reached him so easily, she stammered a little and identified herself. She told Whalen she believed that he had handled some kind of trust department account for a Paul Carson.

An interval of silence followed, then finally, he spoke, "I can't divulge any information on accounts here, ma'am."

"Could you at least tell me where I can reach Paul Carson? It's very important that I speak with him."

"I'm sorry. I don't know how you can contact him. I can't help you." Mumbling another apology, he rang off.

"No luck, I gather," Shar mumbled, her mouth full of Maddy's blueberry muffin.

"That was the oddest call," Laney said, clicking the power button. "I had the distinct feeling he was lying to me. Like he did know how to get in touch with Carson."

"Why would he lie to you?" Shar said, slathering butter onto her last bite.

"Got me. But after you leave, I'm going to call the bank back and speak to someone else. If Jerome Whalen won't tell me how to get in touch with Carson, maybe someone else knows where he's moved."

"Woman, go at it!"

After breakfast, Shar collected her things and Laney drove her to Malcolm's in the recurring rain. After a brief visit with him, Laney returned home, leaving the couple in the den holding hands and staring into each other's glazed-over eyes.

Collecting her mail from the front porch where Aaron had left it, she was jolted by her SASE from the publishing house that had requested chapters of her novel. Expecting another reject, she opened it slowly while she sat on the porch swing. Blackberry ran up on the porch and shook, spraying water over the letter.

"Shazam!" She read the letter a second time. The critical sentence jumped out at her:

Our preliminary evaluation is that the work shows market-
ing potential, and we would like to review the complete manu-
script in order to make a determination about publishing.

Laney squealed and danced around the porch, waving the letter.

"Is this some kind of rain dance? Because if it is, it sure as hell worked and you need to stop," Bucky said as he stepped onto the porch. His curls, drawn tight by the rain, glistened like diamond studded gold. Water streaked his safari jacket.

Laney, with her face flushed with happiness, ran to him with the letter. "Look, Bucky, Hammond Publishing wants to see my complete manuscript."

"Cilla told me you'd written a novel but I had no idea you had sent it to a publisher." Bucky scanned the letter quickly, then hugged her, lifting and spinning her around.

"That's wonderful. It truly is," he said, finally setting her down. He smiled down at her with a look of admiration on his face. She stepped out of his arms, but he abruptly crushed her to him again, his lips covering hers in a kiss that caught her breath in her throat—his arms enfolding her body.

Reeling with astonishment, she pulled her mouth away but not before she felt a rush of heat sweep deep.

"I've wanted to do that for a long time," Bucky said, his breath ragged with desire.

"I . . . Gray is my life," she stammered, wrenching from his arms.

"That kiss makes me think not," he said.

"It . . . was the excitement of my news."

"If you say so," he said, smiling suggestively.

"I do," she said, stooping to retrieve the letter from the floor where it had fallen. Disconcerted, with fluttering hands she collected her purse, keys and the other mail from the swing and headed for the door.

"I am leaving on Saturday," he said, his right brow raised, his tone, mocking and provocative. The taunt quickly softened with his smile. He turned on his heel and stepped off the porch into the rain.

Once inside the safe, dark hallway—the solid door against her back—her heart steadied. But reckless thoughts careened through her mind—Bucky's inviting glances and subtle touches, the midnight swim. She had first thought them all harmless flirtations. But now, with Bucky's kiss, she realized that his playful come-ons had risen to a new and dangerous level. Gray already suspected . . . suspected what? That she and Bucky . . .

It was good that he was leaving.

She lifted the phone from its cradle and the voice said her name. "Laney McVey?"

"Yes," she said, dropping her mail on the library desk.

"This is Jerome Whalen."

"Yes, Mr. Whalen, how—"

"Listen, carefully," he said, his voice edged with tension. "If you want to know about Carson, meet me tonight at eleven at Royal Spring Park in Georgetown." He seemed to struggle to control the quavering. "C . . . come alone. Don't bring anyone or tell anyone about this call." The phone went dead.

"Hello . . . hello," she spoke into nothingness. She replaced the receiver, her own voice cracking. "No . . . no, please don't let this happen," she choked. She sank onto the desk chair, her thoughts scattering like the raindrops on the library window. She furiously gulped air until at last, her head ceased spinning and she could focus on the man's voice. Tight. Strangled. Rising in octave as he spoke. Fear? Laney swallowed dryly, her own pulse quickening.

Think, Laney, she scolded herself while trying to ignore the prickling chill climbing her spine. Why was Whalen in such a state? And why did he call her to set up a meeting about Paul Carson? Her stomach clinched and her face grew hot. "But if Whalen thinks I'm stupid enough to meet some guy I don't know in some dark park, he'd better think again," she snorted.

She licked her dry lips and pumped her right leg like a piston. "I can't deal with this now. It's too much," she said, then abruptly lifted the phone and dialed.

"Shar," she said when her friend answered, "how about going to the outlet mall in Georgetown this evening?"

38

"Well, kiddos. What did you find?" Bucky asked as he burst into the carriage house and kicked the door closed against the rain. He strode to the plywood table where Cilla and Toby had partially reconstructed the skeleton from the pile of bones.

"What do we have here?" he asked, knuckles on his hips, his jacket dripping water.

Toby sat slumped on the bench next to Cilla. He looked up glumly as Bucky stared at Bones.

"Couldn't find any healed fractures? I showed you what they'd look like in *Field Methods in Archaeology*," Bucky said.

In a wooden voice, Toby said, "We think we found a couple but they're on the shin bones, not on the thighs like the biography said."

"Bummer," Cilla uttered. She fingered a portable phone in her lap.

"I can see what you mean," Bucky said. A gust of derisive laughter exploded from his lips.

With a swift maneuver like he was jumping pieces in a checker game, the professor switched the shin and thighbones in the skeleton, threw his head back and convulsed with glee.

Toby saw their mistake immediately.

Although Dr. Gage was certainly enjoying the moment at their expense, Toby didn't care. He bolted off the bench and Cilla squealed.

"It's Harrod! It has to be!" Toby shouted, giving Cilla a high-five. The portable phone clattered to the floor.

"Hold it, you two," Bucky said. "Granted, you have a strong argument that this may be the skeleton of James Harrod but this discovery, alone, is not conclusive."

"But Dr. Gage," Toby protested, "his height, age, the date of the surveying instrument, the healed bone fractures—all point to Harrod."

"You'll have a tough time convincing historians with only that evidence. Their argument would be that it may only be a coincidence," he said. "Your book there, Toby—*History Mysteries* by James C. Klotter. Read it again. Look for more clues in your biographies. Perhaps there is something you've overlooked."

"Maybe the sheriff will let us back into the field," Cilla said, picking up the phone.

"Fat chance!" Bucky said, snorting as though he had just gotten a whiff of garbage. "And even if our expert sheriff finally allows you to sift through the pedestal of dirt that Bones was lying on, it'll be without me. Come Saturday, I'm outta this hellhole."

"He sure has it in for Sheriff Gordon, huh?" Cilla said to Toby after Dr. Gage had mumbled something about going into town for a six-pack of beer and left in a gust of wind, rain and anger.

"Yeah."

"You can't blame him. He had a lot invested in this dig and I don't mean just money. Research papers, prestige, and junk like that."

"I guess that's it. But at least he seems to have forgotten about the field notebook for the moment," Toby said as the portable phone in Cilla's lap rang for the second time since she had brought it over from the house. The first time, Cilla had held the phone to her ear. When after a minute, she had shut off the power button, Toby first thought that there hadn't been anyone on the line. Except for one thing—her eyes had widened and her face had grown ashen as she listened. The jerk, Toby thought.

But this time she spoke into the phone. "I can't talk right now," she said, cupping her hand over the mouthpiece, twisting her head away from Toby. Her back to him, she walked over to the refrigerator, whispering into the phone.

"The jerk again," he said, the words butting against clenched teeth. He reached Cilla in two strides. He snatched the phone from her hand.

"Toby . . . don't!" she said.

He clicked off the power and threw it onto the plywood table. Bones bounced.

As he reached for her hand, she cringed as though he might hit her.

"Jesus, Cilla, I'm not going to hurt you." His hand remained extended until she, with a sigh, slipped her icy fingers into his. He warmed them between his hands. He lifted her palm toward his lips—and froze.

A strangled cry caught in his throat. No mistaking the partially healed, pink scars on her wrist. Two perfect circles. He stared, his gaze lasering into them as though his eyes were the fiery cigarettes tips that had put them there. He groaned.

She saw that he saw and snatched her hand away.

"Why, Cilla?" he choked. "Why do you even talk to him after what he did to you?"

"I have to—"

"You have to? My God, he's a monster . . . some kind of animal." He was shaken by the implied meaning in her remark. "He's threatened you, hasn't he? That first call. I saw what it did to you."

"No, Toby, that wasn't even him," she said defensively.

He studied her face closely. "You don't really expect me to believe that," he said.

"I don't care if you do or not. It wasn't Luke," she said icily. She looked away and chewed on her lip while shifting her feet.

"What is it, Cilla?"

"Maybe it's nothing."

"What? Trust me, Cilla. Tell me."

"The first call . . . it was for Aunt Laney. I listened. I shouldn't have."

"Cilla, we were talking about—"

"It was from some man," she interrupted. "A Jerome Whale . . . Whalen, I think. He told Aunt Laney to meet him at some park in Georgetown tonight at eleven. He was totally freaked. It scared me." She shivered.

Whalen. The name sounded familiar. He wondered if . . . "You don't think she will meet him, do you?"

"I'm not so sure. Remember just this April? . . . the murder she and Shar Hamilton got involved in?"

"I read about it . . . but surely she'd think twice about—"

"Get real, Toby. Especially since this Jerome guy said he could tell her something about the guy that used to live in this house before Aunt Laney's sister lived here."

Paul Carson! The crest in the attic! Again it worried Toby's memory. "Why would she care what Whalen could tell her about Carson?" he asked Cilla.

"She thinks Carson may somehow be connected with the baby that they found at the dig."

"No way! You mean maybe Carson knew about the infant?" He couldn't have, he thought and at the same time wondered why he'd formed an opinion about a man whom he had never met.

"I really haven't a clue, Toby." Cilla straightened Bones's shinbones. "But Aunt Laney's search in the attic must have come up with something and now there's that phone call. It's all totally spooky."

The papers Laney found in the wooden box! They must have given her something to go on, he thought. Toby wondered what Whalen was going to tell her about Carson. How did he know Carson? He made a quick decision. If Laney McVey left the farm tonight, he would follow her.

"Toby . . . Toby?" Cilla repeated. "What are you thinking?"

"About that call." He tossed the thought from his mind. "And speaking of calls, the second one was Luke Tucker, wasn't it?" he asked cautiously. He tried to keep the anger out of his voice and softened his question by taking her hand again. He led her to a window overlooking Stoney Creek. Brown as a chocolate malt, the creek folded and swirled its way downstream toward the dam.

"The rain stopped," she said, as though he hadn't spoken. Toby squinted at the sun slithering in and out of clouds above the trees. Below, raindrops dripped silver and gold from the branches.

"Cilla," he whispered, her name soft as silk on his tongue. She turned her head and gazed up at him with eyes dark with pain. There seemed no other way to end her heavy sadness so he pulled her into his arms and kissed her. She trembled as though she might shatter suddenly into pieces.

Speaking against her lips, he asked her, "How can I help you find the guts to break with him, Cilla? You don't love him."

"How would you know that?" she snapped, her breath hot against his. "Luke was there right after my father killed himself. I was crazy.

He understood."

"You were vulnerable. He took advantage."

"He was the only one who understood what I was going through."

"Luke's words, huh, Cilla?"

She began to cry and tried to pull away from him. He held her as tightly as he dared until she collapsed sobbing against his shoulder.

"Toby, he swears he'll get even if I leave him, he'll hurt my family, himself . . . you," she sobbed. "It would be my fault."

"Stupid threats. You're not responsible for his craziness," Toby said, but inwardly wondered if Luke's jealously could send him over the edge. "You know, Cilla, you gotta have fight in you . . . be tough as old boots and sweat it out. Sure you're scared, so get a restraining order or something to keep the creep away from you."

"I've heard about them."

"Do it, Cilla."

"I'd have to spill the beans to Mom and she'd totally freak if she saw . . . you know."

"*Do* it," he repeated, while picturing Tina Sands going off when she heard what the jerk did to her daughter.

"I can't," she said in a lifeless monotone.

"Can't won't cut it, Cilla."

She drew away and didn't speak for a long time as she made her way back to the window. Her palms jerked to her face. Barely perceptible, her shoulders straightened while her hands fell to her sides and rolled into fists. She spun. Her chin rose and she trembled a tiny smile. "I'll do it."

39

"Woman, we shopped 'til we dropped, closed up the Cracker Barrel Restaurant, and took a night-time walking tour of Georgetown's historic district. So 'fess up. What's the real reason you lured me away from Malcolm tonight?" Shar asked.

She and Laney sat in the Whooptie parked across the street from the courthouse. Earlier, Laney had dropped Cilla off to sit with Malcolm when she'd picked up Shar, but the real reason she had asked Cilla to stay with Malcolm was for her own peace of mind. She didn't want to leave the teen alone at the house.

Laney shifted in her seat, pretending to admire the courthouse through the rear window of the car. Imitation gaslights along the sidewalk lent a soft glow to the façade. "I understand the courthouse was built by a Pittsburgh architect during the Victorian period," Laney said. "It was recently renovated. Look at that brickwork."

Shar shook Laney's arm. "You're beginning to sound like a member of the Scott County Tourism Commission. Enough already. What's up, you crafty witch?" she demanded menacingly.

Laney knew when Shar was at her limit and was surprised that she hadn't pressed her before now. She hated to shop and Shar knew it.

Laney quickly related the disturbing phone call she had received from Whalen and revealed her plan to meet him at Royal Spring Park at eleven o'clock.

Shar made a sound of disgust from the back of her throat. "And you want me to accompany you? Over my dead body, Agatha."

"No, no. He insisted that I come alone. He must know something about Paul Carson. Maybe even something that could connect him with the infant remains. Why else would he ask me to meet him in secret?"

"Laney, you can't meet Jerome the Ripper in a dark park by yourself."

Laney glanced at her watch again. Four minutes to. She had to go. She scrambled in her purse for her cell phone and shoved it at Shar. "If I'm not back here by eleven thirty, call the police."

"No!" Shar cried as Laney bolted from the car.

Laney, hoping that Shar wasn't following her, glanced back at the Whooptie. She scurried across Broadway, which bisected Main, and passed the Den of Antiquities across from Bohannons' Books With a Past. Their colorful sign of oversized books was in shadows.

Main Street was deserted at this hour but Laney kept close to the storefronts and ducked inside the vestibule of the Georgetown Antique Mall when she suddenly saw approaching headlights behind her. The vehicle turned south onto Broadway.

When Laney reached the corner of South Water Street and Main, she stepped onto a small lookout platform at the top of a steep, wooden stairway. Below, the Royal Spring Park was dimly lit by old-fashioned street lamps standing at intervals along a walkway overlooking a narrow stream of water.

Cautiously, Laney descended the steps until she stood at the foot of a vine-covered viaduct that supported a section of Main Street. The sound of water drew her eyes to a pair of arches in the stone. Through these gaping black openings, the water—from Royal Spring—flowed into an inky darkness. Because of the high span and a couple of non-functioning street lamps, part of the park was bathed in shadows, but she could make out a small log cabin. High upon the opposite bank, the public water plant loomed like a fortress against the sky.

Her eyes darted frantically around the park, trying to pick out Whalen in the gloom, but the stone benches and picnic tables that dotted the grassy strip between the cabin and the viaduct were empty and there were no cars in the South Water Street parking lot.

Wait! Was that someone seated at one of the tables? It was, she thought as the unmistakable figure of a man with his back toward her took form in the darkness.

"Mr. Whalen?" she called timidly. The man didn't respond. Perhaps he hadn't heard her, she thought. She stepped onto the soft sod and moved towards him. As she approached the table, her breath quickened and her roaring pulse challenged the sound of rushing water from the spring.

"Mr. Whalen," she repeated, this time a bit louder. She stretched out her arm and touched his back, lightly.

With a sickening wheeze, the man suddenly slumped forward onto the table, his forehead cracking against the hard surface, his arms dangling ape-like at his sides. Laney snapped back and watched in horror as he slowly slouched to his right and slid to the ground. He flopped onto his back, his head lolling, his glassy eyes staring fixedly through slotted eyes like viscid wounds.

At once, a voice shrill with terror exploded out of her. She spun and ran. An eerie whine accompanied her frantic flight up the stairs and she was at the landing before she realized that the sound was coming from her own throat.

Suddenly, a figure stepped out of the darkness and arms closed around her waist in an iron grip. She struck out at the form while another sickening wave of overpowering fear closed over her.

"Quit, woman. It's only me," a familiar voice grunted.

With every bit of energy drained out of her, Laney collapsed in Shar's long arms, mumbling incoherent bits of sentences. "Shar . . . did you see? . . . he's dead . . . Whalen's dead," she choked through dry lips.

"Dead? . . . Whalen's dead? What? . . . how?" Shar stared bug-eyed into Laney's face.

Laney's mind rolled through possibilities like a freight train. "Heart attack, maybe?"

"My God!" Shar blurted.

"Just when I was about to learn—" Laney was suddenly struck mute as an idea formed in her brain.

With a burst of adrenaline, Laney jerked away from Shar's arms and reeled back down the steps. She felt strangely dreamlike.

"Are you crazy? Let's get out of here," Shar whispered, but Laney heard her footsteps behind her on the stairs.

Laney reached the body first. Shar's fingers found her arm and yanked hard. "Laney, what in the hell are you going to do?"

Laney wrenched away and dropped to her knees next to the body.

"Oh God, you're not going to give him mouth to mouth, are you? Woman, he's dead as a dodo. Look at his eyes."

"Don't just stand there. Help me," Laney demanded. "Maybe he was going to give me something, some information, papers, letter. Hell, I don't know," Laney said, furiously searching the side pockets of the man's dark windbreaker.

"You don't even know if he's Whalen," Shar said. "Could be some bum or junkhead hanging out at the park."

"Bums don't wear Hilfiger jackets."

Shar groaned, then crouched beside the man and shoved her hand into one of the pockets of his dark colored slacks.

"Get his wallet, if you can."

"Car keys," Shar said, dangling them from two fingers. She stepped over the man, squatted and searched his other pant pocket. "Nothing." Reaching under him, she tried to work out his billfold. "We're like a couple buzzards picking over road kill," she snapped.

"Shazam! I found an envelope in his shirt pocket," Laney said.

"Laney, a car!" Shar cried, as headlights swung an arc in the parking lot.

"Let's get out of here," Laney said.

"I'm for that," Shar said, already bounding across the grass.

They scrambled up the steps, as car doors slammed and laughter from a couple of teenagers bounced through the park.

Shar and Laney had just reached the Whooptie when a girl's scream rent the night.

40

Aᶠᵗᵉʳ arriving at Taylor Ridge, Laney and Shar looked in on Malcolm in the den. Cilla was curled up on the small sofa asleep. Malcolm, on his back in the hospital bed snored softly, a copy of Robert Burns's poetry and songs upon his chest. His eyeglasses, resting over his mouth, clouded and cleared with each even breath. After taking a moment to read "Remorse," the book-marked poem devoted to the anguish of guilt, Shar moved the book to the bedside table along with his glasses. Shar shot Laney a triumphant smirk that was edged with tension. When Kudzu lifted his barred head and leaped from his hollow, Shar lifted the tabby into her arms. Laney turned out the light and the two women tiptoed from the room.

In the parlor, Shar hastily mixed bloodies at the wet bar. Shar slurped from her glass as she passed the other to Laney. "What do we have, Jessica Fletcher?" she asked shakily as she sat next to Laney on one of the twin Queen Anne settees that faced each other in front of the fireplace. The springs creaked.

The envelope lay on a marble covered coffee table resting in front of them. Laney swigged her drink, trying to postpone what she feared might be a disappointing ending to their night of fear and ran her other hand nervously over the yellow silk upholstery that was wearing thin. As the vodka began to warm her insides, she allowed her eyes to wander over the antiques in the parlor—two Hepplewhite mahogany side chairs, a magnificent bonnet-top highboy against the wall behind a wing chair and a Queen Anne mirror between the unadorned windows. Malcolm had shipped them all from Florida. She kicked off her shoes and twitched her toes through the pile of a small oriental rug under the table.

Enough of this, she told herself and reached for the envelope and ripped it open with a single, almost brutal movement. Her fingers shook as she removed the contents, a single sheet of paper with the letterhead of the Georgetown Bank across the top.

"Laney, the date!" Shar said. "This was written seven years ago."

Heads together, the two of them read:

Ms. Ivy Hart, guardian for Toby Hart
P.O. Box 100
Hickory, Kentucky

Re: Trust/Will, Paul Carson   #50108-0

Dear Ms. Hart:
I would like to introduce myself as the new administrative officer handling your son's trust account.
We have reviewed the trust administration assets of the late Paul Carson, carrying a value of $500,300.00 in income properties, cash and securities.
We expect the total annualized income from these assets to continue to be approximately $30,000 per year, but like in the past, be aware that the amount could fluctuate with the market. As Trustee/Executor of, Mr. Carson's estate, when the boy is eighteen years of age, we will distribute the remainder in full.
As agreed in writing, the name of Toby's father, must continue to remain anonymous.

Very truly yours,
Jerome S. Whalen
Assistant Vice President

"Oh my God! I don't believe it," Shar gasped. "Paul Carson is Toby's father!"

" 'The late Paul Carson' are the key words here, Shar," Laney said, shaken, her mind doing another long distance run. "Carson was deceased when Whalen wrote this letter."

" 'Assets to continue' are more key words. It appears that Carson must have provided for the boy before his death. And very well, too.

Income from over half a mil!" Shar thought out loud, holding the letter and reading it through again.

"I wonder when he set up the trust," Laney said.

"You told me he and Alice had no children. I wonder if his wife knew about his son. And I wonder how Carson met Ivy."

"I'm curious about something else, Shar. Evidently, Whalen wanted me to know about this. Why else did he have the letter on him when he died?" She stared long and hard at the copy.

Laney suddenly jumped back in horror, grasping Shar's arm in alarm.

"Laney, what is it?" Shar said

"Shar! . . . your fingers, the back of your hand! . . . look!" Laney shouted, gripping her wrist and turning her hand back and forth.

Shar let out a strangled cry, "Oh woman! . . . what's that sticky crap? Looks like—"

Laney lifted Shar's hand and gave her fingers a sniff. No mistaking the metal-like odor.

"Laney, say it's not blood! I'll puke."

"Maybe you're injured," Laney said, but not seeing any wound.

Shar snatched her hand away, charged to the wet bar and turned on the tap, gagging and heaving. Her hands trembled as she rubbed them together under the stream of water.

Laney handed her a small stack of paper cocktail napkins to dry her hands.

"Laney, that's the hand I used to try to remove Whalen's wallet from his back pocket. There's no blood when you have a heart attack, is there?"

Laney's felt her facial muscles twitch as she answered, "If he had a heart attack . . ."

Shar's face was ashen and she stared saucer-eyed. "If?"

Her legs no longer able to support her, Laney dropped to the floor in front of the wet bar. Shar shakily retrieved their Bloodies and joined her. "You don't mean what I think you mean!" she said with a hysterical laugh.

"Maybe it wasn't his heart. Maybe someone . . . "

"Don't say it!"

"How else would the blood get there unless it pooled from a wound."

"Wound? . . . like in gunshot?" Shar's face got grayer.

"Or stabbing. I didn't notice anything when I walked up to him, but that part of the park was in shadows and he was wearing a dark jacket." Laney remembered how she had parted Whalen's jacket and removed the letter from his breast pocket. The shirt was light—either powder blue or white—and she definitely hadn't seen any stains. She suddenly recalled Whalen's phone conversation. "Shar, when Whalen called me, he sounded scared out of his gourd."

"You think someone was threatening him?"

"That's what I'm thinking," Laney said, fingering the letter. "Whalen was vice president and trust officer of the bank and the letter says Paul Carson's name must be kept anonymous. Maybe someone was afraid Whalen was about to spill the beans that Carson was Toby's father."

"Divulging confidential information . . . why would he do that?" Shar chewed on a nail, remembered the blood, and wiped her mouth with the back of her hand.

"Shar, first things first. We need to get a police report or at least hear the news to be sure he was murdered."

Shar jumped to her feet and turned on the TV but it was after one a.m. and the local channel news was over.

"Try WHIC radio. I believe they have a nighttime program that plays music until three. They probably break for news."

Shar turned on the power of a small stereo on the bookcase next to the fireplace and turned the dial until she heard music.

"That might be it," Laney said as the soft strains of a love song drifted out of the speakers. The last thing I feel is romantic right now, Laney thought. Laney refreshed their drinks as the song played through. Shar paced in front of the unit.

After a couple of advertisements and the weather report, the announcer said:

"From Georgetown in Scott County. Georgetown police report that the body of a man was found at Royal Spring Park about eleven forty-five last evening. The police believe the man had been stabbed. The body was discovered by two teenagers who reported seeing someone running away from the scene. The victim's identity is being withheld until notification of next of kin."

"Oh-h-h . . . that cinches it," Shar shrieked, clicking the radio off. "Someone ran him through and we have our prints all over the poor sucker . . . and all over the letter, I might add."

"Did you hear what he said—that someone was seen running away?"

"That only means that the butcher must have been there while we were there! Oh! . . . remember, we heard those kids drive up and get out of the car." Shar took another chew from her nail and spat out a tip. "Laney, I think we better call the police. What if the killer saw us take the letter?"

Ignoring her friend, Laney, said, "Shar, if the killer was trying to shut Whalen up, why didn't he search Whalen after he stabbed him?"

"I bet you interrupted him!" Shar croaked, wild-eyed. "Dammit, woman, the murderer may have even followed us home," Shar said, running to each of the windows and closing the shutters.

"We don't even know if the information in the letter was the reason Whalen was murdered. I say we sit on this until tomorrow," Laney said. "Don't tell a soul, okay?"

"Me? . . . tell a soul? The chances of me communicating with another disembodied spirit of a dead human being in my lifetime are zip. Woman, make a note of that."

Cilla fought the bedclothes. So much to think about—her promise to Toby to break up with Luke, to get a restraining order against him.

The full moon shot out from a cloud, its yellow light looming yellow through her open window. She shivered even though sweat soaked her nightshirt. She thought of Luke, of Laney.

She hadn't meant to eavesdrop. For the second time that day, she had heard words not meant for her when Laney had read the letter out loud. When Shar had said, "Paul Carson is Toby's father," Cilla had pressed her body against the wall in the center hall and listened to all of it. About the letter. About the stabbing in the park. About someone running away.

Through the window, clouds rippled across the moon like a choppy sea. She lifted her hands to the light and imagined blood on her fingers.

Only Toby knew about her Aunt Laney going to meet Whalen. Had Toby met Whalen in the park before Laney and Shar had gotten there?

Was Toby the person those kids saw running away? Did he . . . ? No, no. He couldn't have.

The blood on her hands waned and her fingers found her sore and swollen midriff. She clutched at the covers as fear consumed her. Fear of Luke, fear for Laney and Shar. Her eyes darted around the room picking objects out of the gloom. Her fears mounted and stirred the hairs on the back of her neck.

Toby's heart still pounded with the thought of it.

Laney and Shar crouching over the form. Laney removing something white from the man's pocket.

As the kids ran back to their car, Toby had slipped from his hiding spot behind the cabin and had run back up Opera Alley to his truck. Wildly, he had driven onto I-75 and was almost to Cincinnati before exiting at Florence and heading back. Nearing Hickory, he fumbled the dial on his radio. Unemotionally, an announcer was reporting the news as though just another murder—a mundane statistic. But to Toby, it meant that Whalen was dead and what he knew about Paul Carson was forever lost.

The crest on the hat in the trunk burned hot and deep in his brain.

Toby could hear Bucky's heavy breathing from his sleeping bag. How he envied his deep sleep. After tonight, he wondered if he'd ever close his own eyes again.

41

Even with the grim excitement of the night before, Laney had been up at dawn to print out her novel and compose the cover letter to send to Hammond Publishing. She boxed the manuscript and had it at the post office by ten o'clock. She planned to stop at Gray's to tell him about the publisher's letter, but first she had one more stop to make.

The rain had transformed the heat into a tropical oppressiveness. As Laney swung through the stone entranceway of Hickory Dock, Maddy was power washing the boat ramps. The two days of rain had raised the level of Stoney Creek about a foot and the quick recede had left a film of mud on the concrete. Laney's heart gave a lurch when she saw that her mother was not alone. Sheriff Powell stood at a safe distance to keep from getting splashed.

She parked next to the patrol car. Freddie sat in the front seat with his eyes closed listening to the dispatcher on the police radio. Gordon looked over as Laney exited the Whooptie and he approached her with a purposeful expression on his face.

"Hello, Gordon," Laney said uneasily.

"Laney," he said, tipping his cap. "I was just heading out your way."

That's what I was afraid of, Laney thought.

"Karen Thompson would like to meet with you this afternoon. Are you free . . . say about two at my office?"

"What's this about, Gordon?" Laney asked, her voice wavering. She cleared her throat.

"I think she should be the one to tell you. I assure you, it won't take long." Gordon forced a smile.

I might as well get this over with, she thought. "I'll be there," she said curtly and backed away.

Gordon tipped his cap again in parting, waved at Maddy and climbed into his vehicle.

Laney rushed to the hydrant and shut off the water. Maddy looked over at her when the nozzle lost its pressure, dropped the hose and moved toward her daughter, then stood tapping the toe of her soggy sneakers. Laney grabbed her arm and guided her to a group of white plastic tables and chairs on the picnic pavilion. Firmly forcing Maddy into a seat, she sat across the table from her. Maddy's freckles were olive against her overheated skin and her hair frizzled comically.

Laney lifted her own hair allowing her sweat to cool her neck

"Mother, what do you know about Ivy?" Laney asked.

"Ivy? Ivy Hart? Well, I don't really know her, honey."

"Tell me anything you do know." Laney dropped her hair and wiped sweat from her forehead.

"She housekeeps . . . nurses the elderly or sick. Isn't she takin care of Malcolm?"

"Not anymore. Has she always lived in Hickory?"

"Now that I couldn't tell you. I know she worked some for Sadie Davis after she broke her hip."

"How long ago was that?"

"A few years back. I remember Sadie tellin me what a great cook she was."

Laney smiled, remembering Ivy's Scottish cooking that Malcolm had loved so much. "Mother, how is Sadie getting along these days. Think I could pay a call?"

"She's gettin pretty frail. She must be about eighty-four or so. She has a small apartment in St. Clair Place but I'm afraid it won't be long before she's moved to the nursin wing. According to her son, Ray, she's on the waitin list. Honey, why all the questions?"

"Later," Laney said, hurrying to the hydrant and turning the water back on. She waved and loped to the Whooptie.

"Well, I never," she heard Maddy call as she ducked inside the car.

"Miss Sadie," Laney called through the door after knocking twice. The door creaked open a crack. Loud television sounds filtered out into the hall as Laney pushed it open. A slight smell of urine nudged her senses. Miss Sadie sat in a lift-chair in the halfway up position in front of the television set. Amazingly, with fingers swollen like tubers, she flipped channels with the TV remote like she was sending Morse code. She turned her head as Laney entered the room.

"Who are you?" she asked, looking over her spectacles as Laney moved closer. "Don't tell me. You're Maddy's daughter. Laney, isn't it? I remember now. I haven't seen you since you were a teen. You look just like her."

"So people say," Laney said, happy that Sadie's memory seemed to be intact.

"Grab a seat," Sadie said, pointing to a straight chair. "Can I get you something? . . . some tea? . . . coffee? It's a bit early for a stiff one."

Laney sat facing Sadie on the edge of the chair. She leaned to one side so that Sadie could still see the television. "I'm fine, thank you," she said.

But Sadie clicked off the remote and raised the lift-chair until she was standing. Instead of moving away from the chair, she stood leaning against the cushions as though she were the target for a knife thrower. Her intelligent hazel-colored eyes glistened behind onion skin lids. "Why you here?" Sadie asked.

Taken back by her bluntness, Laney stuttered, "I . . . I—"

"Speak . . . provided the conversation doesn't include bowel movements or who kicked the bucket last night." Her eyes crinkled merrily.

"Actually, I have some questions about a woman who cared for you after you broke your hip awhile back."

"Ivy Hart. Hell of a cook. Skin like a camellia. Temperament of a sniper. What else do you want to know?"

"Well . . . "

"What she do?"

"Nothing, really. I . . . er . . . do you know where she worked after she left your employ?"

"Several places. Just day work. No live-ins until that Scottish fellow hired her. You got something juicy on her?" Her eyes glittered with interest.

"Miss Sadie, I really don't have anything naughty to tell you about

Ivy Hart," Laney said, looking at her watch.

Sadie sighed. "I believe before my ticker gives out, I shall perish of boredom."

"I wish I had something to brighten your day. But I was hoping that you could enlighten *me* about the woman."

"Thinking of hiring her? I'm surprised she gave me as reference. We tangled on more than one occasion and she left in a cloud of dust and a hearty 'Hi-yo Silver.'" She slapped her leg.

Laney smiled. "Over her care?"

"Mostly over her boy, Toby. She didn't much like me getting too close to him."

"Why?"

"Couldn't tell you. She holds her cards close to her chest, that one."

"Toby's a nice young man. He's working on an archaeological dig out at Stoney Creek Farm this summer."

"He should feel right at home."

"Huh?"

"Paul and Alice Carson who used to own your farm were dear friends of mine."

"Really? But how—"

"While the Carsons were soaking up the sun every winter, Paul hired Ivy to check on the house regularly and get it ready for their return in April. But I imagine the boy wouldn't remember much about it. He could only have been about four years old the last winter she worked for Paul."

Laney gave a startled gasp and felt a rush of heat to her face.

"My goodness gracious! I did enlighten, didn't I?" Sadie said. "Want more?"

"Sure." Laney could barely contain her excitement.

"Ivy's family came from London, Kentucky but she moved to Hickory right out of high school. Don't know how she met the Carsons but they moved her south when they bought their condo. Ivy lived in it year round until Alice had a falling out with her and fired her. Later, Alice wrote me from Florida that she never wanted to see the woman again. When Ivy moved back to Hickory, I guess Paul felt sorry for her and allowed her to clean the house when Alice wasn't there."

"When was that?"

"About 1980. Toby was just an infant."

Shazam! Laney said to herself. The connection! Ivy had worked for Paul Carson in Florida, had his child, then moved to Hickory. She wondered whether the "falling out" was because Alice had discovered that Paul was the father of Ivy's baby.

"Do you know who Toby's father is?" Laney asked innocently, deciding not to reveal the contents of Whalen's letter that was tucked safely away in her purse.

"According to Alice, Ivy named some young man she had met down there, but evidently, she preferred to raise the child alone than pursue child support or force a marriage. You have to admire the woman for keeping the child and going it alone. I suppose it couldn't have been easy all those years."

Yeah, Laney thought, remembering the monthly interest Paul Carson had settled on the child. "Miss Sadie, are Alice and Paul Carson still living?" she asked, already knowing half the answer.

"Unfortunately, no. Alice died the year they sold the farm and Paul, the year after."

Laney was bursting inside with all this new information and couldn't wait to tell Shar. But first, she had to grab a bite of lunch and see Karen Thompson at the sheriff's office. Glancing at her watch again, she hurried her goodbye and thank you with a hug as Sadie slowly lowered herself into the depths of the lift-chair. As Laney quietly closed the door, Sadie's knobby forefinger was already telegraphing TV signals.

42

The trip to the salad bar was a waste of money. She couldn't eat because the thought of what might be facing her at the sheriff's office was gnawing inside. Wondering if something was wrong with her food, Jesse approached her several times but Laney assured her she just wasn't hungry. She finally left the Finish Line and walked to the courthouse, which was only a couple of blocks from the restaurant.

When Laney opened the door to the sheriff's office, Gordon, his hands behind his head and his legs crossed and propped on the desk, lurched forward. His shoes hit the floor with a bang, and Karen Thompson, sitting in a chair facing Gordon, looked over and smiled.

The forensic anthropologist was about forty years old with a trim figure and intelligent wide-set eyes the color of soft moss. This was only the second time Laney had ever seen her—the first encounter the day the infant had been discovered on her farm. Then, Laney had only seen her at a distance as the woman examined the tiny form in the excavation. With her sweetly expressive face and medium length honey colored hair pulled back and tied with a grosgrain ribbon, she certainly didn't appear to be someone who regularly autopsied maggoty corpses or boiled bones to discover forensic evidence.

Gordon stood to introduce them and only then did Laney see the fine careworn lines fanning from Karen's eyes that were the consequence of her job responsibilities and horrible things she had seen. Gordon waved for her to be seated next to Karen and when she settled into her chair, she noticed that the anthropologist held an Airborne Express mailer in her lap.

"Laney, Karen requested this meeting today, so I'm going to turn this discussion over to her. Karen?" Gordon smiled nervously.

"May I call you Laney?" Karen asked, turning sideways in her chair.

Laney nodded, her eyes riveted on the package in Karen's lap.

"I understand that Sheriff Powell has explained to you the findings of the Medical Examiner's Office. Our first responsibility in this case is to determine who the child's mother was. Your sister, Cara Collins, was the last female owner of the property where the child was found. She lived at the residence since the time that the burlap the child was buried in was produced."

"When was it made?" Laney demanded, determined to prove them wrong.

"Between 1960 and 1985," Gordon said.

"See! Cara moved there in eighty-nine," Laney cried triumphantly.

"We found some matching sacks still in the barn, Laney," Gordon said quietly.

"So you see it's only natural that we begin with your sister. Since she is deceased, I have decided to ask you to cooperate—"

"It can't be Cara's baby," Laney interrupted. "We would have known if she were pregnant. And she couldn't, wouldn't—" She burst into tears.

Karen reached for her hand but Laney yanked it away.

"I understand your anguish, Laney," Gordon interjected. "But I didn't think you would want your mother to be tested."

"No . . . no, you can't test my mother," she sobbed, her mind running in circles. Her recent knowledge about Ivy was burning to be told, but abruptly, she held out her arm. "Do it!" she shouted, knowing she had weeks before the results would be in.

"Laney, it's not a blood test any longer," Karen said, "and you can have your private doctor administer it, if you like."

"Yes," she said.

Karen slid her fingers under the Airborne Express seal and removed the transport kit.

"It's a simple procedure," she went on, explaining as she showed her the contents. "There are two forms you must fill out. The first is basically a Test Request Form marked with the case number. The second is a Chain of Custody Form for who is taking the sample to sign. If you go to a doctor's office to have it done, his name is put here, or if you go to a Patient Service Center, the technician's name."

"The test? What about the test?" Laney asked impatiently.

"There are illustrated directions and several sterile tip swabs," Karen said gently, slipping all back into the cardboard envelope. When you're finished, send it back to the lab, Federal Express."

Laney snatched the container from her hands and was out the door without even saying goodbye.

Gray could see Laney sitting inside the Whooptie in front of his clinic as he pulled along side her in his Jeep and opened the door. He gathered up Puccini and peeked through the Whooptie's passenger window. Even though he waved and made a funny face, Laney only turned her head slightly, expressionless.

"Damn it, now what?" he said under his breath. He let the tabby into the clinic and stood on the stoop waiting for Laney to alight from the Nissan. But she continued to sit behind the steering wheel staring listlessly through the windshield.

Gray jerked the car door open and before Laney could react, pulled her from the car. Accompanied by a stab of sciatic pain, he hauled her over his shoulder and with staggering, leg quivering strides, packed her into the clinic. With Laney's arms and legs flailing and her curse words blending with barks from the kennel cages, he stumbled up the steps. Several times, her elbow smacked him in the face.

"Let me down!" she yelled.

Careening against his apartment door, his shoulder slammed it open against the wall. Hurtling off-balance through the opening at full run, he plunged over the back of his sofa as Natine's hysterical laughter echoed up the stairwell.

As they sorted out their various limbs, Gray's nose began to bleed.

"Damn," he said, jumping from the sofa and pinching his nostrils together. He dashed down the hall to the bathroom. "Way to go, macho man," he said mopping his nose and mentally kicking himself for his he-man tactics. When he returned to the living room, pressing a huge wad of tissue to his nose, Laney was gone.

"Cute," said a voice edged with ice in the direction of the kitchen. Gray swung his eyes to the doorway where Laney glared with a keep-your-mouth-shut look. "What did you think you'd accomplish by that rakish display of domination? I was thinking through some really heavy stuff out there when your exaggerated sense of manliness ripped me out of the car and carried me up to your cave."

Gray opened his mouth to speak, then thought better of it. Instead, he stuffed a piece of the toilet paper into his nostril and assumed a manly stance. The end of the tissue trailed down to his waist.

"I am not going to laugh," Laney squeaked in ascending falsetto, her pupils dilating and a smile tugging her lips. She turned her head away. "Damn you, Gray Prescott," she sputtered and stalked into the kitchen.

Gray rushed back to the bathroom and cleaned up, hoping that Laney wouldn't completely recover her anger. When he walked into the kitchen, she was at the sink filling the teakettle with water. He hugged her from behind. She slipped under his arm and carried the kettle to the stove. He followed. She clicked on the burner and spun to face him. She had tears in her eyes.

Gray gave her distance. "I know I was a brutish son of a bitch, but I get so scared whenever I see that vague mood come over you," he said. "I guess I'm afraid you will disconnect from me like you did once before and up and leave." With his finger, Gray traced a tear down her face.

Laney took hold of his hand. "I know how I can run away from problems I don't want to deal with, but I'm going to stay with this one," she said and she related all that had been building up inside her—the mummified infant that she was determined to prove wasn't her sister's child and Luke's abuse of Cilla.

"Cilla! Good God! That son of a bitch! I'll fix his ass—" Gray slammed two mugs onto the table, then flung the tea bags at them.

"Gray, this is something that Cilla has to do herself. I believe she will finally decide to make the break. All we can really do is stand by her and keep the creep from harming her again."

"Where is she?"

"She spent the night at Malcolm's. Shar's keeping an eye on her."

"Does her mother know?"

"Not yet. Tina's out of town. I expect her to stop by this evening on her way home. That would be a good time for Cilla to tell her."

"This other . . . the baby remains." He saw her wince. "Where are you on this?"

"I just met with Karen Thompson. She already started DNA testing on the infant. She wants a sample from me."

"You?"

"Either I consent or she'll ask mother. I can't put her through that.

"When?"

"The kit's in the car." She began to cry again.

"Sweetheart, if it's not Cara's child, the DNA won't match."

"I can't wait six weeks to get the results. I'll go crazy." Tears streaked Laney's cheeks. "It's not hers," she whispered.

"What did you say?"

"Someone other than Cara is the mother."

"Laney—" Gray began.

"The burlap the child was buried in was produced between the years 1960 and 1985, and they found some matching sacks still in the barn."

"But only one other female lived in the house between 1960 and now. Alice Carson."

"Alice wanted children. She wouldn't have killed her child."

"Killed? What do you mean? The child was killed?" The breath caught in his throat.

"Oh, God, I wasn't supposed to tell you that. Karen Thompson thinks the child was murdered before being buried."

"Laney, my God . . . I can't believe. . . . No wonder you have been so interested in getting your sister cleared in the birth of the child." He gathered his thoughts before speaking. "But no one else but Alice and Cara lived in the house," he said, pouring water from the kettle with an unsteady hand. He looked up briefly.

Laney's expression was darkly exultant as she uttered the single name, "Ivy."

Gray reeled with astonishment and his hand pouring the tea water jerked. The steaming water soaked into Laney's place mat. "Did I hear you correctly? "Ivy Hart?" he choked.

Laney grabbed a sponge from the sink and mopped the spill. "Gray, she had access to the house and the farm for four years, from 1980 to 1984," she said, slipping into a chair. She squeezed lemon juice from a plastic lemon into her tea and stirred in a packet of sweetener.

Gray stood with the kettle in his hand, unable to move while Laney related what Sadie Davis had told her about Ivy working for Paul Carson.

"You can't believe every cock and bull story that a little old lady in a nursing home tells you. Especially that one. For God's sake, I recall that her family put Sadie there after she ate nothing but peanut butter sandwiches for a whole week because she didn't want to take the time to fix a proper meal . . . afraid she'd miss one of her TV shows."

"I found her very lucid."

Gray shrugged. "How the hell you got the notion that Ivy could have murdered her own child from information "dippy Davis" slipped you is beyond me." He sat at the table and stirred his tea, squeezing the bag against the side of the cup with his spoon.

Laney's face screwed into a frown as though she were debating whether or not to tell him something. She twisted an errant ringlet of red that had escaped her combs when they had toppled over the back of the sofa. Abruptly, she blurted, "Carson was Toby's father."

The absurd statement took a moment to register. "Yeah, and I'm Toby's little sister," Gray said snidely.

Her eyes downcast, Laney silently sipped her tea. When she finally looked at him, Gray could see disappointment. He saw it more often these days.

"Don't do this, Gray," she said.

"What?"

"Play devil's advocate."

"I'm not."

"You are."

And he knew she was right, the realization flaming his face. He thought back to a year ago. His caviling had almost resulted in her death. He wondered why he did it and why he hadn't seen it before it had begun to harm their relationship. "Aw Laney, I'm sorry. Let me hear all that you know."

She began and he was stricken by what she had endured in the park and amazed at all that she had learned from the letter she had obtained from the dead man. When she finished, he could imagine Whalen's body sliding to the ground, but could not cut through the thickness of the horror and panic she must have felt. But above all, he was surprised at the length she would go to try to prove that her sister was not the person who had borne, then murdered and buried that tiny form.

She went on. "I think Ivy and Paul had an affair while she was working for the Carsons in Florida and Ivy gave birth to Toby. Alice found out, fired her, and Ivy moved to Hickory about 1980 like Sadie said. Paul set up the trust for the child and unknown to Alice, allowed her to work in the house when they were in Florida those winters. On one of his trips to Hickory, Ivy must have conceived again. This time, I think she hid the pregnancy from him and when she gave birth, murdered the baby and buried it in the field, thinking no one would ever discover it.

Gray thought about what she said for a long time. The only sound in the kitchen was Puccini scooting his opened can of cat food across the floor with his lapping tongue.

"What does Whalen's murder have to do with this?"

"I'm not sure. Obviously, Whalen knew about Toby being Carson's son, hence the letter in his pocket. Maybe he knew something about the baby's murder, too, and Ivy found out that he was going to meet me. Gray, Whalen sounded terrified on the phone."

"Do you know what you're saying, Laney? Ivy a murderer . . . twice over," Gray said, fully aware of Laney's admonitory frown.

"I have to make a decision about the letter. The police should have it for evidence."

"My God, the letter! The police could arrest you for taking it . . . or worse! You and Shar were there in the park with Whalen!"

"My God, certainly they wouldn't believe . . ."

Secretly he wanted to upbraid her for deciding to meet Whalen in the park in the first place, but he stopped himself, knowing just how easily he could bring her down again. As he tried to assimilate all the information that Laney had told him, another thought, more terrifying to him rammed itself into his crowded mind. The person that the teens saw running away from the park may have seen Shar and Laney take the letter from the man's pocket. They could be in danger.

"Gray? You didn't answer."

"I just don't know, Laney. I just know you'd better turn the letter over to the authorities as soon as possible. If Ivy did murder Whalen and the infant, the police might be able to prevent her from killing again."

Laney breathed a question like a whisper.

"What?" he asked.

"Will you drive me to Mark Lyons's office so he can take the DNA sample?" She covered his hand with hers. He brought her cold fingers to his mouth and kissed her palm. He held her for a long time until her shoulders straightened as though bracing for what she had to do.

When they arrived at Dr. Lyons's clinic, the forms were filled out in short order and Mark read the directions. He removed one sterile swab and rubbed the tip firmly up and down on the inside of Laney's cheek. He then took another and did the same on the other side while Laney stared at a crack in the plaster wall. Mark took the swabs, put them into the kit, sealed it and gave it to Gray to mail.

43

The day spun like a dervish through her mind—Sadie, Gray, and the DNA test she had just taken. When she finally arrived home, she couldn't recall the actual drive and she wondered if she had driven safely. Malcolm's Olds was in the drive and Shar and Cilla, pumping together on the wicker swing, were close to setting a new world record for height. Kudzu clung wild-eyed to Shar's halter top, his sharp claws locked in the fuchsia colored fabric. After darting off the steps to greet her, Blackberry rolled onto her back to get a belly scratch but had to settle for a brief toe rub.

"I completely forgot to run by to get you after seeing Gray," Laney said to Cilla while unlocking the front door. "Shar, thanks for bringing her home."

Cilla forced the swing to a stop and snatched Kudzu from Shar. She flew by Laney at the door, quickly excused herself and ran up to her room. After brewing a pot of tea, Laney carried a tray into the library while beginning to relate to Shar all that she had learned since she had last seen her.

Shar was speechless. And when she finally spoke, her comment seemed extraordinary to Laney, considering how she felt about Ivy.

"So now that we know how Ivy Hart and Paul Carson met up with each other and that Carson was Toby's father, why would Ivy kill Whalen just to conceal Toby's paternity? It doesn't make any sense to me. Why all this secrecy about his father, anyway?"

"You're being very generous about a woman who almost stole your Scottish laddie away. But that's my point, Shar. There must have been another reason for such a violent act."

"Maybe Whalen read about the discovery of infant remains on your farm and when you called him looking for Carson, he thought there might be some connection with Ivy." Shar was thoughtful before adding, "Or knew there was."

Neither touched her tea.

"With Whalen dead, we may never know for sure. But how would Ivy learn that we were going to meet in the park last night?" Laney pondered.

"I've got it!" Shar said after several moments. "Ivy was here for dinner just after you found the trust department envelope in the attic with Whalen's name on it. Could she have seen it?"

"Shazam! It was on the kitchen desk. She went right by it, coming in and rushing out. If she saw it, she might have gotten in touch with Whalen herself."

"And scared the gizzards out of him . . . and threatened him to keep Carson's paternity a secret," Shar said.

"And killed Whalen when he told her he was going to let the cat out of the bag," Laney added.

Shar looked troubled. "But I still say why? And how did Ivy know Whalen was going to meet you at the park?"

"Maybe she followed him there," Laney said, then shook her head. "Guesstimate. We just need more to go on."

There was a knock on the library door.

"Come in," Laney called.

Toby stuck in his head. "Could I talk to you for a minute?" His thick brown hair, crying for a haircut, hung to his earlobes.

"Sure," Laney said.

"I'm out of here," Shar said, unfolding herself from the leather couch.

"It's okay," he said, striding into the room and looking around nervously. He wore his cutoff jeans with a gray T-shirt. Dark shadows beneath his eyes indicated a restless night.

"Sit down, Toby," Laney began. "Would you like—"

"Gotta get to the point before I lose my nerve," he said, sitting on the edge of the red plush chair. His eyes were strangely bright and glassy. "I was there last night . . . in the park," he blurted.

His words shot through Laney like a lightning bolt and Shar flinched, her jaw dropping.

Laney was the first to recover. She cleared her throat before speaking. "Park? Whatever do you mean, Toby?" she asked innocently, but worried that her breaking voice was giving her away. Shar collapsed back into the sofa.

Toby looked back and forth at them. "The murder. . . ."

Oh God, surely he wasn't the one seen running away, Laney thought.

"Wh . . . what were you doing there?" Shar asked.

He looked at Laney, his heavy lashes fluttering anxiously. "Cilla overheard your phone call from Whalen and she told me. I followed you there."

"What concern was it of yours?" Laney asked, rather put out at the kid's audaciousness, but relieved that if he followed her there like he said, he could not have murdered Whalen. He was already dead. Also, that Toby knew about the planned meeting could finally explain how Ivy also knew.

She was about to ask him if he had told his mother when tears suddenly streamed out of his eyes and his shoulders began to shake with sobs. He lowered his head in his hands.

Alarmed, Laney rushed to him, stooped and enfolded his broad shoulders in her arms. "Toby, what is it? You can tell us. Please let us help you." She looked over at Shar. Her friend's face was twisted with anguish for the boy.

His shoulders suddenly straightened and he struggled away from Laney and stood. "I'm sorry," he said, his eyes a startling blue against his red-rimmed lids. He took a quivering breath for control but the tears continued to race down his face.

"No need to be," Laney said, getting to her feet.

He turned his back to them as though it might help him get through it, if they couldn't see his pain. They waited.

"The crest in the attic," he whispered. "I know it somehow." His body began to heave again. "It's tearing me up." He spun to face them. "Sometimes the thought of it makes me feel good. Other times . . ." His eyes took on a haunted look. "When Cilla told me that Whalen wanted to meet you to tell you something about Paul Carson, I had to go . . . to find out something . . . anything about him." His eyes turned incurably sad, his voice a beseeching moan.

"Why do you think that is?" Laney asked, afraid to intimate what she knew that Toby should know, if indeed, he didn't already know.

"It's as though I knew him, somehow."

Ah, yes, she thought. Toby and the house. How well he seemed to know it. How he went directly to the library to use the computer. How he found Blackberry in the pantry to take her for walks and had no trouble finding the attic when the entrance was hidden from view. Add to that, the strange fondness he had expressed for the crest on the horse blanket and how his eyes riveted on the felt wide-brimmed hat when she had tried it on.

"Toby, you've lived in this house or have spent time here, haven't you?" Laney asked.

He blinked with surprise. "How could I . . . ?"

Her hand reached for her purse on the desk and slipped inside. She fingered the letter, then in a moment, pulled it out and handed the envelope to Toby. She heard Shar catch her breath but when their eyes locked, Shar nodded.

"What is this?" he said, just standing there. Then he removed the letter and read—his face slowly reflecting pain, illumination and finally, understanding. When he finished, the letter fell from his hands and his arms dropped. A smile as glorious as a sunrise spread across his features, his eyes radiating sunbeams. "My father," he whispered. Fresh tears poured down his cheeks.

Then abruptly, his face drew tight and his lips pursed with anger. "Mom knew Paul Carson was my father . . . and . . . and . . . she hid it from me," he stammered with rage. His eyes blazed murderously and every vein in his neck ridged.

Laney laid a restraining hand on his arm. "Toby . . . Toby, let's be fair. According to the letter, Paul Carson wanted it so. He was married and I guess he wanted to protect his wife, Alice." She told him how Paul had allowed Ivy to work at the house during the winter months when Alice was away, and that he probably remembered the house from the four years his mother was employed. "Maybe Paul visited here occasionally during the winter months to keep in touch with the business of the farm. Obviously, you remember him. And Toby, he must have cared for you. He provided for you very well. You've been receiving the money. . . ."

"Yeah, sure," he said coldly. "Mom gives me an allowance of a few bucks every week. I've worked somewhere after school and on weekends since I was twelve . . . and every summer." But his anger seemed to moderate.

"Toby, last week I saw you snatch an envelope away from your mother at Malcolm's," Shar said. "Was that some of the money?"

"My truck payment that I'd hidden at the apartment. Mom said she needed the money and wanted to borrow it," Toby said, his mouth curling in resentment. "Can you believe that, when she's been pocketing all that money—?"

"She seemed very upset about something when she came back into the house," Shar interrupted.

That's putting it mildly, Laney thought, recalling the unexpected glass of lemonade dumped on Kudzu.

"I had just told her about finding the baby remains out at the dig. It seemed to really shake her up."

Shazam, so that was it, Laney thought. She could just imagine how the remains' discovery could have unnerved Ivy, especially when she thought she had gotten away with destroying her child all those years ago.

"It hit everyone hard," Laney said, wondering how Toby would ever get through learning the truth about his mother.

His fingers combed back his hair. "Where did you get the letter?"

Shar flashed a look at Laney.

Toby's eyes followed. His face blanched. "Oh, no . . . that's what I saw you take from Whalen!"

He pushed back his hair again, revealing eyes marked with sorrow. "Jerome Whalen murdered," he said, his voice cracking.

"How did you know he'd been murdered?" Laney asked.

"The car radio on my way back to the farm." He paused, his mind far away. Then he murmured sadly, "He was always great to me."

"You knew him?" Laney tossed a look at Shar.

"Yeah, he and my mom used to go out . . . you know . . . date. But they had a big fight . . . so they split. I was real young."

Toby picked up the letter and scanned it again. "I knew he worked at Georgetown Bank but had no idea he was a vice president." He folded the letter and placed it back into the envelope. "I guess this is what he was going to tell you in the park. But why did someone kill him before . . . ?" An unreadable expression crossed his face.

"Toby, what has your mother told you about your father all these years?" Laney asked.

He shook his head to bring himself back to the conversation. "She didn't . . . I mean, anytime I asked, she would only tell me he was dead and she wouldn't say anymore than that."

"Well, you must have a few good memories of Paul Carson and according to the letter, he certainly thought enough of you to leave you a lot of money when you turn eighteen," Shar said.

Good God, Laney thought. If his mother is implicated in the murder of Whalen or the infant, Toby might lose his mother too. Her heart ached, wanting to make everything all right for him. "Toby, if you would like to keep the items in the attic box, you may," she said.

With her offer, his face lit up for the second time. "Gee . . . thanks." Then the cloud descended once more. He stared at the letter in his hand. "I have to show this to my mom. I want her to know I finally know."

"Would you like me to go with you?" Laney asked.

He started for the door and hesitated. Then like some lumbering football receiver retrieving a fumble, he bungled Laney's body with a graceless hug. "Thanks," he choked, his eyes spurting again as he ran out of the room.

Shar closed the door behind him and faced Laney. "Poison just dropped a couple more notches on my list for mother of the year," she said.

Laney nodded. "She gives the boy little more than zip, then tries to get his meager savings . . . all while she's getting $30,000 support money. I just bet she was concealing more than just the name of Toby's father."

"And I bet it has to do with money," Shar said, adding, "It always does."

44

Laney slid into the only parking spot left on Main between Fourth and Fifth Streets.

"She's home," Toby said the same time that Laney recognized Ivy's car—two spaces further up the street.

Without waiting for Laney, Toby jumped out of the Whooptie and rushed to the doorway next to Second Hand Rose's shop. Laney locked the car and raced to catch up with him. Anger propelled him up the steep narrow steps to the second floor apartment over Frank's Drug Store. He unlocked and shouldered the door open in one forceful thrust.

Laney, just reaching the landing, heard Ivy say, "Toby . . . I thought it might be you. You've never once walked up those stairs." Through the open door, Laney could see her walking down a long dark hallway toward them. When she moved beneath the cheap, light fixture in the foyer, Laney saw that she wore her same navy uniform trimmed in lace and the white cap controlling her hair. She must have a new position, Laney thought.

One thing was different. Beneath Ivy's eyes, blue-gray crescents filtered through her china doll skin. Was it the lighting, she wondered. Ivy's body stiffened when she saw Laney behind Toby and sucked in a loud breath. "What are you doing here?" Ivy said, her eyes narrowing.

Laney opened her mouth to reply but Toby answered, "She offered to come with me!" he said, his fist clutching the letter. Afraid to say more, he thrust out the letter.

Ivy's eyes shot to it, then up to his face, but she made no effort to take it. "What, Toby?" Her eyes reflected a curious mixture of naivete and wariness.

"Take it!" Toby demanded, forcing it into her hand.

"I don't like your attitude," she said, trying to gain control while briefly scanning the envelope. The tiniest spasm flashed in her cheek.

"Read it, damn you!" he said.

The letter rustled as she slid it from the envelope, unfolded and held it up to the light. As she read, a tiny tremor shuddered through her body "Toby, I can explain—" she attempted to say when she had finished.

"There is nothing . . . *nothing* in the whole damn world you can say."

"Toby, if I had told you his name, I would have jeopardized your trust fund."

"What could they have done if you had told me? Take back money that I never even got?" His anger threatened to explode. "What *did* you do with the money all these years?" he said savagely.

"Toby, that's not a lot of money. It takes money to live. Food. Clothes," Ivy said.

"Mom, have you looked around lately?" His arm swept a nasty flourish at the dirty walls, the broken linoleum on the floors, the tiny living room with its cracked, vinyl covered sofa and shabby chairs.

Laney, amazed by his cold, fierce attack, shrank into the shadows. A lot of support I am, she thought, wanting to crawl away under the door like the cockroach she had just spotted darting under a baseboard.

"You always worked. Still, there was never anything extra. Where did it go?" Toby continued.

Ivy didn't answer as she continued to focus on the letter, her heavy dark lashes almost touching her cheeks. Abruptly, they fluttered and she glared wide-eyed at Toby. "Where did you get this? This is not the original. I always burned any proof."

Toby swallowed loudly and shifted his feet uncomfortably.

"Jerome Whalen," Laney said, expecting a reaction, but she couldn't read the emotion that passed briefly over Ivy's face.

"Jerome is dead," Ivy said.

How did she know, Laney wondered. The radio? TV? Or was she there as Laney suspected? She decided to throw caution to the wind, fully aware that she was again breaking a confidence. "Murdered, Ivy, just like the infant that was buried in the field."

Toby gave a startled gasp, but Laney's eyes riveted on Ivy.

Ivy's eyes flickered—a barely faltering waver followed by a glazed pause before resuming their steady, cold stare. Her mouth trembled but she said nothing as she turned and unsteadily began to walk down the hall.

"Ivy, I'll have to take this letter to the police," Laney called to her.

"Do what you have to do and I will do what I have to do," she said emotionlessly as she disappeared into the darkness.

45

After the rains, the temperature had risen steadily until the air, saturated with extra humidity, made Laney feel as though she were inhaling great gulps of moisture with every breath.

By the time Laney and Toby left the apartment in Hickory, it was seven o'clock, too late, Laney reasoned, to deliver the letter to the police department. Anyway, she was rung out by the confrontation with Ivy and just didn't want to deal with what she was certain would be an unpleasant meeting with Gordon.

Even at the late hour, heat-generated mirages appeared ahead on the blacktop as they drove Hickory Pike. To her surprise, when they arrived at the house, Shar and Cilla were preparing a bountiful spaghetti dinner for them by means of Paul Newman's Sockarooni Sauce, Cilla's garlic bread and Shar's only specialty. Laney invited Toby to join them and called Gray. Gray declined because of an unexpected Health Department Board meeting that had been called to discuss the low drinking water situation in Hickory. The recent rain hadn't alleviated the water situation much and Gray said restrictions might have to be put on lawn watering and the washing of vehicles.

Shar jumped into the Oldsmobile to pick up Malcolm. As Toby and Cilla set the table in the dining room, Laney deliberated whether or not to invite Bucky for dinner. It was his last night in Kentucky, she rationalized, and darted out the screen door into the dusk.

As she approached the carriage house, she thought she heard voices. She couldn't see past the house to see whose car was parked in the drive. She opened the door and took a few steps into the carriage house. A woman, her back to the door, turned her head with the sound. It was a moment before Laney got the complete picture. The woman was Ivy. And the gun in her hand was pointed at Bucky.

"I told him," Cilla said, as she placed a silver fork to the left of Laney's dinner plate.

"Told him? Who?" Toby asked, his mind elsewhere, back in the apartment when he had told his mother he finally knew who his father was. Her excuse for keeping it from him wasn't good enough. He thought of the time lost that he could have been with him. The hell with losing the trust. Some things are worth more than money.

Cilla's fingers trembled as she placed the knife and spoon on the right of the dinner plate. "Luke," she said.

Instantly, Toby was back. "You told him? When did you see him? He's not allowed—"

"I didn't. I called him."

Relieved and happy that Cilla hadn't given up her resolve, he hugged her with his free arm. "Bet he was pissed," he said, placing a napkin at each place setting.

Blackberry, her nose pressed to one of the floor length windows, growled.

"He didn't say much at first. Just listened when I told him it was over . . . that I wasn't ever going to let him hurt me again."

"Cool." Then remembering Luke's history, he asked, "Did he threaten you?"

"Not at first . . . I mean . . . he tried to tell me he was sorry . . . that he wouldn't ever again."

"You better believe he won't."

"He won't accept this. It didn't end nice, Toby."

"What else did he say," he asked gently, while wanting to kick the guy's teeth in.

"He said he would kill himself. That he couldn't live without me. Then in the next breath, said he'd kill me . . . my mother . . . Aggie."

"Jeez, Cilla. Did you tell him you were getting a restraining order?"

"He said it wouldn't matter . . . that we belong together, forever."

Blackberry barked and her fur bristled.

"Man, Cilla, I don't think you should wait. Get a restraining order now."

"My mom will be here later tonight to get me. She's going to have a cow, but I'll tell her everything. We'll go tomorrow morning."

She looked so pretty. That pale hair like spun gold pulled up behind her tiny ears.

Cilla had dimmed the overhead chandelier before lighting the candles—those in the hurricane globes on the mahogany table and the double candelabra on the sideboard. Their pendants flashed rainbows and made the crimson walls flicker flames.

Toby grasped her arm gently and pulled her to him. "Cilla," he said into her hair, "I'm afraid. Let's talk to Laney. Bet she'll agree you should do it now." Cilla reached up with her thin, soft arms and clutched his neck tightly. He moved his lips against hers. "Jeez, Cilla," he whispered when their lips finally separated. He cleared his throat and pried her arms from his neck.

"I want to share something with you," he said. "My father, I finally know who he is, I mean, was. He was Paul Carson."

"You just found out?" she asked.

What a strange thing to say, he thought. The way she said it, it was as though she already knew. "Yes, today," he said.

Cilla looked relieved. "How do you know for sure?"

"Laney showed me a letter from someone who really knew."

"Oh," she said. She studied his face acutely, as though she expected him to say more. And he did have more to tell her, but not now. He didn't want to reveal anything about the trust just yet.

"What's taking Laney?" he said instead. "Cilla, check the sauce. I'll get her."

Laney backed toward the door, one hand palm outward, the other searching for the doorknob behind her while a cruel video tape of a past terror in this very place raced through her mind.

"Stay and listen," Ivy invited Laney—those cold eyes never leaving Bucky's face. "Bucky's about to unburden himself."

"I don't think—" Laney said, her sweaty hand on the knob. How did Ivy know Bucky? The gun. Where did she get it? Somewhere in

Laney's brain, Gray's words were in playback: "You'd better turn the
letter over to the authorities as soon as possible. If Ivy did murder
Whalen and the infant, the police might be able to prevent her from
killing again."

She had to get help, fast. She didn't doubt for one minute that if Ivy
had some score to settle with Bucky Gage, she was going to settle it.

"Don't you want to hear why Bucky killed Jerome?" Ivy said, her
voice suddenly breaking.

What in the hell was Ivy talking about, Laney wondered? Wasn't Ivy
the one? And the loving way she said Whalen's name. . . .

"Ivy, let's talk privately," Bucky said, taking a tentative step toward
her.

Ivy, a sob catching in her throat, raised the gun with both hands
until the barrel pointed at Bucky's head. "Don't move or I won't wait
until after you tell all of it. Let's begin with last night, Bucky."

Bucky shrugged his shoulders while tossing her a questioning look.

Ivy answered by cocking the gun, the click clean and neat.

The smug look rushed from Bucky's face. "I . . . I did you a favor,
Ivy. Whalen was about to spill the beans. . . ."

Oh my God, Laney thought. Bucky? Not Ivy?" Her head spun with
confusion. "Wait," she said. "How did you even know Whalen was at
the park?"

"Cilla overheard your phone conversation with Whalen and con-
fided in Toby," Bucky said. "Toby just happened to mention it to me
so I was waiting at the park when Whalen arrived about ten-thirty."

God almighty, she thought. Just a half an hour before I arrived.
"But kill him? . . . what possible reason . . . ?" Laney said. She felt nau-
seous as she recollected Whalen sliding to the ground, his eyes staring
lifelessly.

"Shall I, or do you want to do the honors, Ivy?" Bucky sneered as
Ivy lowered the gun a few inches.

Ivy took a step toward him. "We'll hear it from *you*, you bastard."

Bucky stepped back, staring at the five and a half-inch barrel. "Toby
told me Cilla thought Whalen sounded frightened on the phone and
that he was going to divulge something about Paul Carson to Laney."
His face glistened with sweat. "I knew immediately what that was.
Only three people knew—Ivy, Whalen and me. Even Paul Carson
died without knowing the truth—that he wasn't Toby's father."

"What?" Laney gasped.

With the admission, Ivy sighed as though a great weight was lifted and she dropped her hands lower. The gun wavered. "The two of us met while I was living in Louisiana working for Paul and Alice Carson and Bucky was working on his masters at Tulane," she began to explain, her eyes never leaving Bucky's face. "We dated for quite a while, didn't we, Bucky? Until that night when I discovered why he would never take me out in public. I saw him with another woman— his wife, I later found out." Her mouth curled. "I was devastated. I was pregnant with Bucky's child."

Ivy swallowed hard and continued, "I'm not proud of this, but in desperation, I slept with Paul one night while Alice was away and later told Carson that the baby was his. For some reason, he never questioned the paternity. I think he just wanted to believe he was a father. Paul really loved Toby. He saw him every chance he could, gave me money to support him. When Alice fired me after Toby was born, I believe it was because of all the attention Paul was giving the baby. It's possible that Alice even believed that the child was Paul's."

Laney couldn't believe what she was hearing. Her mind raced recklessly. Bucky, Toby's father, a murderer.

She collected her thoughts enough to ask, "I thought the Carson's winter home was in Florida." She remembered that Sadie had said Alice had written her from there.

Ivy smiled as she explained. "After Paul moved Toby and me to Hickory, they sold their house in New Orleans and bought a condo in Florida. Paul continued to allow me to work here at the house when Alice was down south. He set up the trust for Toby. That's how I met Jerome Whalen. He was Toby's trust officer."

"Let's not forget he also knocked you up," Bucky added.

Laney gave a startled gasp and felt the blood rush through her veins.

As though he hadn't commented, Ivy continued, her voice soft, caressing. "Jerome and I were planning to get married before the baby came. Toby and I had been staying here at the house, getting it ready for the Carson's return in April. No one knew about the pregnancy. I barely showed."

Ivy briefly massaged her forehead with the fingers of one hand and said, "About the same time, while Bucky was visiting friends in Lexington, he called me and I told him I was getting married and about the trust Carson had set up for Toby. I thought he would be happy for Toby. Big mistake. He threatened to tell Paul that he wasn't

Toby's father if I didn't give him monthly cash payments to keep his mouth shut. That's where all the money went—into Bucky's pocket."

"Ivy, you were the one who lied to Carson and told him he was Toby's father. Don't put that one on me," Bucky said.

"This nasty tale isn't finished, Bucky. Tell the rest of it," Ivy said, motioning impatiently with the gun.

Cilla checked the spaghetti sauce and then wandered out onto the front porch. Strange, she thought when she recognized Ivy's car behind Toby's truck. Ivy must have caught up with Toby as he left the house to look for Laney, she thought. They're probably in the carriage house. She thought she might join them there but remembered the verbal explosion coming from the kitchen the night of the dinner and Ivy's fast exit. She decided to wait on the porch for everyone.

She swung a while on the porch swing and watched the night approaching. She recalled what Toby had said about discovering who his father was. What a load off her mind. He couldn't have killed Whalen, after all. He had learned about his father from the letter that Laney and Shar had taken from his body.

Blackberry, inside the screen door, began to bark. A faint smell of skunk drifted from the direction of the creek so she decided to leave the dog inside. "Blackberry, hush," she said.

Finally, she stretched and stepped off the porch into the night. Above her, the stars punctuated the night like luminous ellipses. Still feeling Toby's kiss, she raised a forefinger to her lips. All at once it occurred to her that who ever did kill Whalen was still out there somewhere, maybe even lurking, waiting for Aunt Laney and Shar. Cilla's breath quickened, her heart fluttering in her chest.

"I saw ya, this time," a voice behind her said, but before she could cry out, one of Luke's hands smothered her mouth while the other brutally twisted her left arm behind her back. She felt the cold hard outline of his knife tucked into his belt against her back. "If ya make a sound, you and your family are history," he rasped into her ear.

Under his hand, she nodded and he released her mouth. He dragged her toward the trees beside the house and then shoved her along the narrow path worn by Blackberry's daily jaunt to the creek.

Weak with terror and a knifelike pain tearing through her shoulder, she stumbled ahead of him.

Down through the trees he propelled her. When she heard the ripple of water slapping against the floating boat dock, he released her arm and jerked her around. His body was an inky form in the darkness and his rage spluttered from his mouth like a growl.

"His slimy paws were all over ya," he snarled.

"Luke, I told you over the phone that I can't see you anymore," Cilla said in a terrified whisper.

He shoved her and she fell. She shrank into the weeds, praying he wouldn't hit her.

He didn't. His foot slammed into her thigh and she thought she would die with the pain. "Luke . . . no . . . please," she pleaded, curling into a tiny ball, her arms hugging her knees. Afraid to scream, she moaned and cried.

Luke, a black shadow, stood over her. "Give it up, Cil. Ya ain't ever leavin me. Ever."

Luke's words sliced into what little confidence and hope that she had felt just a few short hours ago when she had mustered the courage to tell him over the phone that it was over between them. With tears coursing down her cheeks, she wondered whatever she had seen in Luke.

With her heart wrung with fear and hopelessness, her mind flashed back to when she had first moved to Washington and her first day in the new school after Christmas break—a bleak and hollow holiday just weeks after her father's suicide. Climbing onto the bus, she hadn't known a soul. In her geometry class, Luke had winked at her and later sat next to her at lunch. After school, as she lined up behind the others to board the bus, he had pulled her out of line and offered to drive her home. He had been so good to her then, calling her everyday, helping her deal with the anguish of losing her father. They became inseparable. When they made love for the first time, he'd been considerate and the passion she had felt was real, exciting. She couldn't get enough of him. She hadn't needed anyone else in her life.

When had he begun to change? The checking up on her. His rage when she didn't do what he wanted. His heavy drinking. The violent sex after he had hit her the first time just because she had tutored one of the class jocks one day after school. Why had Luke become this monster who made her fear for her life and her family?

Suddenly, she knew. Luke hadn't changed at all. She had been so depressed and desperate for some ray of comfort, she hadn't taken the time to know him, hadn't seen his early signs of abuse—snide remarks about her family, discouraging her from making new friends and slowly drawing her away from the old. He disapproved of all her outside activities until just the mention of going anywhere without him would set him off. When she was offered the summer field school, he poohpoohed it, remarking that it would be like children playing in a sandbox in the hot sun and that it would take away from their time together. She told her mother that she had changed her mind about working at the dig, but Tina had already signed all the permission papers and insisted that Cilla fulfill her obligation.

Luke yanked her to her feet and shoved her across the dock and into a small johnboat tied to a cleat. He patted his knife, daring her to make a sound. God, where was he taking her?

He released the towrope and as they moved upstream through the dark water, Cilla's heart thrashed against her ribs, masking the hum of the trolling motor. She heaved a groan of despair and pain while the house lights high on the bank faded along with all her hope.

The door knocked against Laney's back as Toby burst into the carriage house. "Oh, sorry," he said, then froze when he saw his mother with a gun pointed at Dr. Gage. His gun. The Ruger single six revolver looked huge in his mother's hand.

His throat closed spastically and his pulse roared out of control. Dizzy and sick with fear, he choked, "Mom!"

"Son . . . we were just getting ready for chapter two," Bucky said.

When his mother saw Toby, her eyes glazed over with horror then seemed to beg silence from the professor as she shook her head no. Her finger quivered on the trigger. In a breaking voice, she said, "Toby, I . . . I don't want you to hear this."

Bucky realized he had the advantage even though Ivy held the gun. He smiled. "Toby, you were too little to know this, but your mother called me in the middle of the night to help deliver her little bastard." His voice dripped with spite.

"What in the hell . . . ," Toby muttered.

"Please Toby . . . it was so long ago . . . you couldn't remember," Ivy stammered. "Go back to the house."

"Stay put," Bucky said. "You should know about your mother."

"Don't do this, Bucky," Ivy warned.

"After she told me about the trust money, I came to the house to collect my first payment," Bucky said.

Payment? What is he talking about, Toby wondered. Why would she give him money? Blackmail? Maybe he knew Carson was my dad and he threatened to ruin the trust by revealing it. But the other . . . Mom having a kid?

"She met me at the door and said she was in labor. I could see she was frightened . . . all alone in this big house with you, Toby. She didn't want you to see."

All at once, Toby's recurring nightmare flashed in his mind. Forgotten words and scenes began to swirl, then drift through his consciousness.

"Hide and seek time, Toby. Bet I can't find you," Toby remembered his mother saying one night, long ago.

"You sorry human being," Ivy said to Bucky.

"What are you bitching about. I helped you when the child's own father wouldn't come," Bucky bellowed.

"I went into early labor. Jerome would have come, but he was in the hospital with pneumonia."

"The—point—is," Bucky said sardonically, precisely. "I was the one who helped you." A curiously elusive emotion flickered across Bucky's face.

"You killed her," Ivy choked. "Laney told me." Tears that Toby had never once seen on his mother's face poured from those suddenly tragic blue eyes.

"The child was stillborn," Toby heard Bucky say through the buzzing in his ears.

"She wasn't!" Laney yelled. "Karen Thompson determined the cause of death a fracture of the skull . . . occurring before or at death."

"The baby never took its first breath!" Bucky shouted at Laney. "Ivy, you remember. She never cried."

"You took her away so fast. I never saw her," Ivy said.

"She was dead, I tell you," Bucky said, his eyes widening innocently, his mouth forming a nervous, insipid grin.

Toby peeked out from the closet beneath the stairs. The man, his back to him, was shoving a doll into a sack in the front hall. As the man turned, Toby shrank behind some coats. He heard the man rummaging inside the closet and a hanger fell at his feet. Above his head, the man grabbed at something from the shelf. The sack in the man's other hand was inches away from Toby. The doll mewed like one of the new kittens in Mr. Carson's barn. The man stomped away from the closet and when Toby peeked again, he was jamming the felt hat with the pretty colors and two big letters down over his yellow hair. The man opened the front door and the cold rain blew in. When the door slammed shut behind the man, Toby climbed over the boots and shoes to look through the sidelights of the oak door. As the man stepped off the porch, he savagely swung the sack at the porch post and Toby heard the doll break.

Toby lunged at Bucky at the same moment that Bucky moved at Ivy. Laney screamed as the gun cracked.

The window to Laney's right shattered as the bullet ran wild. Bucky, with Toby's arms in a tackle hold around his waist, crashed into Ivy. With the impact, the gun flew from Ivy's hand, skidded across the floor and slammed against the carriage house doors. It clattered and spun to a stop. Laney dived for the gun as Bucky suddenly squirmed and wrestled his upper body free from Toby and scrambled for it. Writhing on the floor, the two of them battled for possession.

Familiar voices exploded behind Laney as the door to the kitchen garden struck the wall and two figures rushed in.

"Get the son of a bitch," came from Shar.

"Take that," Malcolm said, his crutch cracking down on Bucky's forearm, just barely missing Laney's fingers. Bucky screamed and rolled to his side clutching his arm while Laney grabbed the gun.

Sitting astride Bucky's back, Shar's fingers yanked at his golden locks then shoved his face hard onto the brick floor.

When Gordon and Freddie stormed the garage a moment later, they found Ivy stunned and sprawled unladylike on the floor with taffeta billowing about her spread-eagle legs. Bucky, effectively hobbled by Toby's sinewy arms, was howling expletives while Shar, like a child riding horsy, continued to straddle Bucky's upper back. His arms were pinned to his sides by her knees and whenever he raised his head, Shar would brutally thrust it down again.

If Laney hadn't been so terrified, she might have found the scene amusing. Instead, as she held the gun on Bucky with shaking hands, her teeth rattled in her mouth like mechanical toy dentures. Just as she thought her quaking knees would buckle, Sheriff Powell gently pried her fingers from the gun.

Malcolm used the jagged end of his broken crutch to struggle to his one good leg. The Scotsman smiled big at the officers. "Bloody glad to see you."

"I leave for a lousy hour and all hell lets loose," Shar said as the last police car rolled down the driveway. "How did Ivy get in here without you knowing, anyway? The car wasn't in the drive when I left to pick up Mal."

"We were busy in the back of the house fixing dinner," Laney said. "I guess Ivy was so eager to get at Bucky, she went straight to his tent and when he wasn't in there, cut across to the carriage house." She struggled to control the quavering in her voice

"I can't believe all of this," Laney said, collapsing on a front porch step. "My legs feel like macaroni that's been cooked too long."

"I can't believe that no one got seriously hurt with Ivy waving that revolver around," Shar said. "And speaking of pasta, our dinner with Paul Newman must be a lost cause."

"I have to thank you and Malcolm," Laney said.

"When I saw Ivy's car in the drive when we got back, we knew only something earth-shaking could have gotten her back to this farm. Then, when we didn't find you in the house, we came looking for you."

"Looking in the window of the carriage house, saved the day 'Mighty Mouse,' " Laney said. "I'm only glad that you had the foresight to call the police before barreling in. Still, it was hairy for a few seconds—Bucky knocking the gun from Ivy's hand as Toby knocked Bucky to the floor. You sure moved fast—but then, you're built for speed."

"The only injury was to Bucky's arm when Mal swung that crutch after Toby got him down," Shar said, with a half-hearted laugh.

"And to my crutch," Malcolm smiled.

"Shar, did you and Malcolm hear much of the conversation while you listened at the window?" Laney asked.

"Evidently, as much as Toby did—enough to know that Bucky was the bad guy even though Ivy was holding the gun."

Laney was pensive. "I'm afraid you only heard half of it," she said. "Bucky murdered Whalen."

"Huh?" Shar said.

"Bucky is Toby's father."

"Woman, you're full of it."

"Will you just shut up a minute so I can get on with this?"

Shar opened her mouth, then closed it.

"For now, just take my word on this. Bucky was blackmailing Ivy for the money she was getting from Carson. Only three people knew about Toby's true paternity—Ivy, of course, Bucky, and Whalen. She must have told Whalen some time when she was planning to marry him. And when Bucky found out Whalen was going to meet me in the park, he presumed Whalen was going to tell me about Toby being his son."

"End of his money, right?" Shar said.

"Right."

"So Bucky knocked off Whalen."

"Right." But Laney remembered the wounded look Bucky had given Ivy when he reminded her that he had been the one who had helped her. Could Bucky have been jealous of Jerome Whalen? Could that have been the real motive behind Whalen's death? In some morbid way, it made more sense than Bucky killing Whalen because his money might be cut off. After all, Toby would soon be eighteen and Bucky's extortion money would cease. Could jealousy have also been the motive behind the death of Whalen's infant?

"Did Toby hear the part about Bucky being his father?" Shar asked.

"No. But I bet Bucky will spread the word when he gets charged with two murders."

"It will be the end of Toby's trust money when it gets out," Shar said.

"Probably so. Think how devastated he'll be to find out Paul Carson wasn't his father after all."

"Poor Toby ends up the victim in all this," Malcolm said finally. "He not only loses the money, his mother will be charged with concealing the death of an infant, and his biological father will be charged with both the murder of Toby's half sister and Jerome Whalen."

"My God, Mal, you make it all sound like a soap opera," Shar said.

"I read somewhere that concealing the birth of a child is only a misdemeanor," Laney said. "Ivy may get off with just a short sentence or no time at all."

"You know, ever since Toby remembered how Bucky killed the infant, I feel more empathetic toward Ivy . . . and I believe Toby does too. I'm pleased he went to the police station with her," Malcolm said.

"Toby's statement to the police about what he remembers in the past just may help his mother," Shar said.

"And clinch Bucky's fate," Laney added. Suddenly, she felt tears pool in her eyes. "Shar, the infant wasn't Cara's child." Her tears spilled over and ran down her cheeks. "Even though I said it couldn't be her baby, I have to admit I feel relief now that I know for sure." She hiccuped a sob.

"I believe what we need is a toddy," Malcolm said, working a single crutch as he led the way into the house. Laney struggled to her feet, grasping the post that Toby had identified to the police as the one that Bucky struck with the sack. Her hand involuntarily recoiled.

Before Laney could close the door, she saw a car pull into the drive. "Tina," she sighed." With all the turmoil, she had completely forgotten about Tina and Eugene stopping by to pick up Cilla after their trip.

"Shar, would you run upstairs and tell Cilla her mother and Eugene are here?"

Shar packed Kudzu and covered the flight in giant strides.

While Shar was gone, Laney introduced Eugene and Tina to Malcolm. She decided to keep the night's excitement under wraps. There would be enough of it if Cilla decided to use this opportunity to tell Tina about Luke's abuse.

Malcolm offered them a drink, but they declined. He had just handed Laney her Bloody, when Shar came galloping down the stairs and rushed into the parlor. She peered at Laney wild-eyed and motioned with her head to meet her privately in the back of the house.

"Excuse me," Laney said, smiling her way out of the room in the direction that Shar had gone.

When Laney turned into the hall, Shar—Kudzu under one arm—dragged her into the pantry and closed the door behind her. Blackberry looked up from her dog dish.

In a voice high and hysterical, Shar said, "Cilla's gone!"

46

"**I** won't forgive you for not telling me sooner, Laney," Tina cried with a voice shrill with horror when Laney told her that her daughter was missing and that it was possible that she had sneaked away to be with the boy who had been abusing her for months. Tina collapsed on the sofa, her face ashen with shock. Limping to the credenza, Malcolm poured a double shot of Scotch for her which she downed too quickly. Coughing and choking, tears ran down Tina's face.

Laney called Gray and Shar phoned Toby and was surprised when Ivy answered. Laney surmised that someone had posted bail or that she had been released on her own recognizance. Toby got on the line and promised to be there in a few minutes. Tina called her mother in Washington and explained the situation, asking that she not tell Aggie that her sister was missing.

By the time everyone had assembled, it was after eleven and no one had seen Cilla for three hours.

After Tina and Eugene made a list of Cilla's friends, they went into the library to call them. It was clear by the short list of names, that Cilla had dropped many of the friends she had had in Hickory when she moved to Washington, and the few she had made at Mason County High School had slowly stopped calling her because she was so preoccupied with Luke.

"Back off," Toby suddenly said. "You're assuming Cilla ran off with that cockroach on her own accord."

"What are you saying?" Gray asked.

"Cilla told me that she told Luke earlier today she was breaking up with him," Toby said. "I think she meant it."

"Well, amen!" Shar said.

"But the scum threatened her and her family. She was scared to death."

The ensuing silence loomed over the group until the clock in the hall chimed on the half hour.

"When Mal and I got here, I assumed she was up in her room," Shar said.

"Th . . . there's no way Toby's truck could have gotten by Aaron," Laney stammered desperately.

A child-like whimper came from Tina standing in the doorway. All eyes shot to her. She swallowed dryly. "Call the police," she said. Tina had the final word.

It was after midnight when Gordon and Freddie arrived at the farm for the second time. Gordon listened patiently as Laney told him how Luke had been abusing Cilla but he didn't seem convinced that she had been abducted. Still, he sent Freddie out to check around the house when Toby told him Blackberry had been barking at something while he and Cilla had been in the dining room. Could Luke have been out there, Toby wondered nervously.

While waiting for Freddie, Gordon asked Tina if any of the calls to Tina's friends had produced any information about places that the kids haunted when they were together. Tina reported that only one girl had even seen Cilla that summer and that encounter was at church. Tina turned to Eugene who stayed with her girls a lot on the weekends when Tina was at antique shows.

Eugene Finley, a handsome man with graying brown hair had been holding tight to Tina's hand ever since Gordon had arrived. "I try to keep a good eye on the kids when they're in my care," he said. "Most weekends when Cilla's home, I keep them busy . . . taking them to the movies, picnics or swimming. A few times, I've let Cilla go to the mall in Lexington with Luke on a Sunday. Personally, I don't care for the kid. He's calling Cilla constantly. He won't let her breathe."

Freddie burst into the parlor. "Sheriff," he said, while chewing vigorously on his chewing gum, "some bushes in the back of the house have been trampled. Not badly, mind you, more like someone might have stepped on a branch or two trying to get close to the dining room window. I followed a path down to the creek and found this lying near the floating dock." He held out a blue hair barrette.

Tina looked at it, her eyes frightened. "I don't recognize it. But then, Cilla had so many of them."

"The boards on the dock were damp like someone had maybe tied up a boat recently—maybe got splashed when the barrels rocked," Freddie continued.

"Let me see that," Toby said, reaching for the barrette. One glance was all it took. "It's Cilla's," he said. "She had two of them in her hair this evening." He recalled seeing the blue plastic bows as he buried his face in her hair in the dining room. To Toby, this cinched it. Luke Tucker had found a way onto the farm and now he had Cilla.

Gordon had come to the same conclusion and initiated action immediately. He contacted the state police and the Mason County Sheriff's Department to be on the lookout for a gray Ford pickup with Mason County plates. While he waited for the tag number, Tina began to tremble. Eugene grabbed her around the waist to steady her.

When Gordon wrote down the plate numbers, he hung up and turned to Tina. "There's still the possibility that Cilla spoke to Luke by phone and they arranged a rendezvous," he said, trying to soften the possibility of an abduction. But he followed his remark with a question directed at Laney, "What was Cilla wearing when she was last seen?"

Toby was the one who answered. "She had on denim cutoffs, a pink short sleeve T-shirt and blue sneakers with yellow laces in them."

"Do you have a recent picture of her?" Gordon asked Tina gently.

A moan escaped her lips but she reached for her purse and slipped Cilla's junior class picture from her billfold.

Seeing Tina's distress, Gordon advised her to go to Washington in the event her daughter attempted to call home. As she and Eugene left, Tina's stricken face seemed to have aged in a single hour. As though made of fragile cut glass, her pain-etched features seemed close to shattering and her tragic eyes drilled blame into Laney's. She only nodded a brief goodbye.

Gordon ordered everyone remaining to stay put until Cilla was found, his eyes centering on Toby as he spoke. With one last cautionary look at the teen, Gordon nodded to Freddie and they left.

Filled with guilt over Tina, Laney retreated to the kitchen where she fed the scorched tomato sauce to the garbage disposal. She removed Shar's salad, chilling in the refrigerator, and placed it on the kitchen table along with a package of bologna, a loaf of wheat bread, mayonnaise, dill pickles, and a bowl of eight hard-boiled eggs for anyone who might want it. She wasn't hungry herself, nor did anyone else seem to be. She tossed packages of paper plates and plastic forks next to the salad and sat down.

"Toby, you're a teenager. Where would you go?" Gray asked.

"How would I know where the monster would take her?" Toby answered, then quietly added, "But probably somewhere remote."

"When I was a teen, my boyfriend and I once broke into his uncle's cabin at Seven Springs near Pittsburgh with a bunch of other kids and spent the night. We ate some of the guy's canned goods and roasted marshmallows in the fireplace. We left before dawn because we were so scared of getting caught," Shar said. "I don't think his uncle ever found out."

"There's lots of places out there like that. Secluded. Isolated. Oh God, we've got to find her," Laney cried in frustration.

"Laney, this is something for the police," Gray said. "They have an APB out. They'll find her."

Shar cleared the table and put the food away.

"I think we'd better go, dear," Malcolm said. Shar helped him to his feet and acted as his second crutch as they went to his car.

"Call me, if you hear anything, Laney," Shar said, after settling Malcolm into the passenger seat.

"Please, me too," Toby said, struggling for control. He walked slowly toward the tent that he would no longer share with Professor Bucky Gage.

"Laney, try to get some sleep," Gray said.

"God, I can't," she said, rolling away from him and turning on the bedside lamp. The misty blue shade cast shadows on the walls.

She relived the whole evening's events with Gray. He held her spoon-style, his arms tensing when she came to the part where Toby had struggled with Bucky and the gun had discharged. But for the first time, he listened without criticism and she appreciated his new efforts. And that he had insisted on staying with her meant the world to her. She didn't want to be alone tonight.

"Where could she be?" she said again out loud.

"I think Toby hit it right," he said. "He's taken her someplace where they can be alone. If Cilla told Luke earlier that it was over, I bet he either doesn't believe her . . . or that if he can just get her away from her support system—you and Toby—he can brainwash her again."

"In a way, I hope he can."

"What?"

"At least I hope she'll play it smart. Maybe if she can pretend she's the same old submissive Cilla, she can stay safe until she's found."

'Don't count on it' would normally have been Gray's response and to be honest, she was telling herself the same thing.

She turned out the light and snuggled back into Gray's arms. She eventually fell into a restless sleep, and in a dream she was back in the kitchen garden marching with Cilla, Toby, Aggie, and Bucky to the beat of the Dixieland number—a light-hearted time before she knew that Luke abused Cilla and that Bucky was a baby killer.

47

The boat trip ended at Jeff Irwin's place, two farms upstream from Stoney Creek. They passed the sign on a post near the tiny dock with a message that read: *Night fishermen: Please deposit $4 in lock box.* The Irwin house high on the bank was dark as Luke dragged Cilla to his truck in the small gravel parking lot, leaving his father's johnboat hidden behind some weeds.

Luke drove fast but didn't exceed the speed limit in case the radar guys were out. When they reached the Mason County line, Cilla knew their destination—the farm where Luke had taken her the first time they had made love—love, now what a distortion, she thought as he pulled into the lane. He drove past the greenhouse, around and into the partially burned feed barn. He parked and after closing the barn doors, forced her into the darkness. His flashlight led the way around the barn and across a small barnyard to the foot of the towering grain bin. His beam caught the metal ladder and followed it upwards.

Luke jabbed her with the flashlight and she knew what she had to do. Higher and higher she climbed until she felt the rim of the grain bin where the roof began. She was grateful that it was nighttime so she couldn't see the ground far below.

Luke reached around her and opened the manhole cover situated on the edge of the roof to the left of the ladder. The cover clanged open. "Get in," he ordered.

"How?" she asked, hanging onto the ladder desperately.

"There's another ladder like this one on the other side."

She obeyed and backed through the oval opening. Her trembling legs felt for the rungs below.

"Hurry up," Luke said, following close behind. She had only lowered herself a few rungs when her feet crunched ankle deep into the dry corn. As soon as Luke dropped beside her he dug into the corn to the left of the ladder, exposing a stash of beer. She suppressed a cry, knowing that his drinking usually resulted in either battering or sex. Luke tucked the flashlight under his arm and snapped a tab.

"Want some, Cil?" he asked and flipped her a can. It landed at her feet and sunk into the corn.

"I don't like—"

"Drink it," he ordered, so she retrieved it.

He played the light across the sea of gold and up the metal cylindrical walls. Musty gray clumps of corn clung here and there. "Spiders," he said, the beam catching their webs trembling with corn dust.

She stepped away from the sides. "Luke, this is crazy. Please . . . let's go home," she said, her words hollow as they reverberated off the bin.

His hand snapped out like a whip and the flashlight caught her cheekbone. She cried out, crumpling to her hands and knees, the hard kernels covering her wrists, the pain in her thigh resurfacing. The beer can buried deep and she left it there.

"Cil . . . ya ain't never going back there. I'll kill ya first."

The sun still hadn't made it over the trees when Laney wakened. Gray lay on his side facing her, his arm flung over her body. His hair was mussed and even in sleep, frown lines creased his brow. Gently, she lifted his arm and moved away from him. She slipped into her robe and left the room, closing the door softly behind her.

Padding into the kitchen, she searched her address book until she found the number of Tina's mother. She dialed.

"Lucille, this is Laney McVey," she said when a woman answered.

"Have you found Cilla?" Tina's mother sounded fully awake as though she had been up for hours or perhaps hadn't been to bed at all.

"Not yet. At least I haven't heard anything. Could I speak to Aggie?"

"Well, she's still in bed . . . and Tina asked that I not tell her—"

"Lucille, she might be able to help. I won't tell her, I promise.

Please."

"I'll get her."

"Hi, Aunt Laney," a sleepy sounding Aggie said a few minutes later.

"Aggie, honey. I need some information about a mystery I might write. I thought maybe you could help."

"Sure . . . if I can . . . but I don't see how."

"If you were a teenager and wanted to be alone with your boyfriend, where would you go?"

"Gee, Aunt Laney," she giggled. "I don't have any boyfriend except dumb Denny in my class who always teases me."

"Then pretend you're Cilla. Where would she go with Luke if they didn't want anyone to know?"

"Is this book like Goosebumps? I've read ten of them."

"Well, kind of." Think, Aggie, think, damn it, Laney thought impatiently.

"I know they go to a mall in Lexington. But that isn't alone. One Sunday we went to the movies there. Cilla didn't want me to go but Eugene made her take me."

God, this isn't going to work, Laney told herself.

"Oh, I know!" Aggie said.

Laney held her breath.

"On the way home after the movie, Luke took us out to some farm he works on. It was really spooky. It had one of those glass houses on it—you know—a greenhouse. Most all the windows were broken and it didn't have any plants in it. Only little pieces of glass all over. And there was a barn that burned in a fire."

Laney couldn't believe what she was hearing. "Aggie, do you think you could find the farm if someone drove you?"

"Gee, I don't think so, Aunt Laney. I was only there once and we didn't stay long. But Luke could show you. He knows the place real good."

I bet he does, Laney thought. The son of a bitch. "I may ask him, Aggie. Thanks a lot. You've been a real help. I'll give you an acknowledgment when I write that book."

She hung up the phone. It's a long shot, but what the hell, she thought. I've got to do something. This waiting is driving me mad. She next phoned Shar and told her to meet her in Hickory at Gray's clinic parking lot.

She dressed in jeans and a white T-shirt. She didn't even try to work her hair. Gray slept on.

She scribbled a short note to him, leaving it on the desk in the kitchen. She grabbed her address book and ran out on the front porch while Blackberry dashed for her favorite squirrel. Toby, sitting desolately in the porch swing, looked at her with expectant eyes and she shook her head no.

But when she started up the Whooptie, he leaped in beside her.

48

Laney held off telling Toby what Aggie had disclosed until she picked up Shar at the clinic.

"Way to go," Toby said, when Laney told them about their conversation. "But if you don't ask Luke, how do you expect to find out where this farm is?"

"That's where you come in," Laney said, handing her cell phone to Toby. "When we get near Washington, you're going to call the Visitors' Center and tell them you just got hired on at some farm and you don't know how to get there."

"Get out of here," Shar said from the back seat.

"Tell them all you know about the place is that it has a broken down greenhouse on it and a burned out barn. Believe me, they'll know the place," Laney said.

"Never in a million years," Shar said.

"Steak dinner at the Finish Line?" Laney asked Shar.

"You're on."

Laney looked at the dash clock. Nine a.m. She wondered what kind of night Cilla had experienced. Was she frightened? Was she cooperating with Luke? Had he hurt her again?

Toby must have been thinking such things as well and he said, "I wonder if the police questioned Luke's father."

"I'm sure they did or plan to today. I sure as hell won't tip them off by calling him to ask where Luke works. But in any event, I bet the police are watching the house in case Luke shows up," Laney said.

When they crossed the Mason County line, Laney handed over her address book and pointed to a number. "Do your thing, Toby. A free meal rides on it," she said while thinking the bet might help break Toby's distress.

He dialed and said his lines. A tight smile tugged the corners of his lips. He turned off the cell phone and gave Laney a thumbs up.

Turning to Shar, Laney said, "Medium rare."

Luke drank most of the night, tossing empty cans behind them. Cilla stopped counting at six. As she watched him down one beer after another, she wondered if anyone had found the barrette that she'd dropped near the dock. Unless they did, no one would ever think that Luke had found a way onto her Aunt Laney's farm. But maybe Toby would figure it out.

As she feared, after Luke had all the beer he wanted, he shoved her back against the corn, his fingers pinching and prodding until her breasts were sore. He tore off her shorts and over and over he rubbed his sweaty body against hers until he fell into the corn, frustrated and unsatisfied. "You bitch," he said.

When she thought he was asleep, with minimum movement, she put on her panties, shorts and T-shirt and inched her way towards the ladder until Luke's cold voice shattered the quiet.

"Don't think I don't know whatcha doin, Cil. Ya goin to make me hit ya again?"

"Luke," she said, beginning to cry. "What are we going to do? We can't stay here forever."

"I ain't decided yet. Shut up."

At some time, she must have slept because surprisingly, a gray dawn poured through the open manhole and pinpricks of daylight spotted the walls where bolts were missing in the metal skin. Cilla fingered the painful swelling under her eye and was grateful that only one eye was swollen shut. Across from her, Luke's scrawny, naked body lay fish-belly white against the corn, his hands folded behind his head, his wet, matted underarms dirty yellow like his hair that had escaped its rubber band. The beak of his baseball cap lay buried in the corn. Shiny thin slots for eyes stared at her. At that moment, Cilla wished he would die.

"This is it," Shar cried out and Laney screeched to a stop. She backed up a few feet, pulled onto the gravel and stopped. The mailbox had been whacked and straightened numerous times, but G. Mullins was still legible.

"I think it's time we call the police. What if Luke is here? What in the hell would we do? Ask him nicely to hand Cilla over?" Shar said.

"If the scum's here, I'll take care of him," Toby growled under his breath.

"Toby, we all want a juicy share of Luke, but you're right, Shar," Laney said. "This is something for the police. But I suggest we at least try to find his truck first. I sure don't want to send the police on a wild goose chase. Agree?"

"Woman, I remember another time, another place," Shar remarked sarcastically.

"I have my cell phone this time," Laney said, starting down the lane.

"Greenhouse straight ahead," Toby announced, "and the burned out barn in front of the grain bin. Aggie wasn't kidding . . . the place is out of a Stephen King novel."

"Let's hope not," Shar said uneasily while Laney swung a right, passed the greenhouse and stopped beside what was left of the feed barn.

"Do you see what I see?" Toby remarked. "Rows and rows of shrubs and bushes. Laney—taxus! Cilla told me that Luke's dad owns a garden center near Washington. This must be where he grows the stock," Toby said.

"I just bet Luke was the one who poisoned Malcolm's bull and planted the notebook Bucky gave you," Laney said. "He must hate you with a passion, Toby."

Toby was silent, a vein in his neck pulsing, his expression fierce.

"Damn, I don't see the truck anywhere," Laney said.

"Pull around to the far end of the barn," Toby said. "He could have parked inside the part still standing."

Laney turned the Whooptie left and stopped in front of the double doors. She jumped out of the car and ran up to the doors and peeked inside. She motioned to the others and Shar and Luke scrambled all over each other to get out.

"It's awfully dark, but there's some kind of vehicle in there," Laney whispered.

Toby shoved on one of the doors until it moved enough to allow them to skinny through.

Dust motes hung in the rectangular beam that struck the rear of Luke's gray Ford truck.

"Call the police," Laney breathed, but Shar was already at the Whooptie, punching in the digits.

49

"Let's get this show on the road," Garvin Mullins said to his son as he took a last sip of his coffee and placed the mug in the sink. "Weather report says we'll be getting some rain before evening so I want to get this corn loaded and to town."

"Good thing we set up yesterday," Steve said. He grabbed a third powdered donut from the box on the table and scraped back his chair. "What will you do when I'm away at college this fall?" He held the screen door for his dad and let it slam behind them.

They walked together up the gravel drive, the man's hand resting on his son's shoulder.

"I made it okay when you were little and couldn't help, no reason why I can't do it again," Garvin said, reaching the crest of the slope then continuing down toward the bin.

"But mom was here to help."

For a moment, a flash of sadness clouded Garvin's eyes as he remembered her long painful illness. "I may have to hire someone on once in a while. Juan Gonzales offered to help when he could. And Tucker leasing those acres helps some."

They reached the heavy grain truck parked in front of the bin. Garvin checked out his equipment—the unloading auger jutting from the side of the bin that would carry the corn from a center well under the perforated floor through the bin wall to the outside. There, the corn would drop into a large triangular hopper. Garvin's eyes traveled up the twenty-four foot long portable transfer auger that would lift the corn upwards and drop it into the bed of the truck.

"Ready?" Steve asked at the switch box.

"Yep," Garvin said.

Steve shoved in the breaker handle. The motor of the portable transfer auger cut on, rattling a rhythmic tune. He flipped the switch that started the unloading auger underneath the bin floor. Initially, there was a loud clanking noise as the metal auger, without any corn to cushion it, banged against the housing.

Garvin pulled at an L-shaped pipe in the side of the bin and heard the center well trap door open with a clunk. Instantly, the sound of the auger softened to a drone as the corn began to move through.

The two of them watched as the corn poured into the hopper and on up the transfer auger. Above, the kernels of corn flowed into the truck like nuggets from some magical gold mine.

Cilla heard something. Voices? She looked at Luke. Unaware, he lay back in the corn and pulled on his jeans—lifting his hips as he zipped. Maybe she had imagined it. No one would ever find them here.

Luke sat up and stuffed the knife lying on his tank top into his waistband. He pulled the shirt over his head. He slapped his baseball cap on his head and reached for a cowboy boot half buried in the corn. He lazily poured the kernels out.

Suddenly a rattling sound somewhere outside the bin startled them and Luke put a finger up to his lips. "Shit," he said. "Someone's here. Must be Garvin on his tractor. I dare you to open your trap," he spat, a hand touching the handle of the knife.

Cilla heard a clattering followed by a clank, then a rhythmic low drone. She glanced at Luke, rushing to pull his boots on.

Suddenly, a small dimple appeared in the center of the corn immediately in front of Luke. What is that, Cilla thought and scooted away from it. Luke, preoccupied with his boots, didn't seem to notice.

The depression sharply funneled and grew by the second. "Luke," she shouted, digging wildly with her heels. In front of her, the corn rushed toward the enlarging cone like pebbly quicksand. Flipping to her hands and knees, she clawed desperately as the surface fast became a sliding slope. Faster and faster she dug, feeling the slipping corn beneath her, seeing the ladder just feet in front of her. The vortex inhaled and sucked behind her, the kernels clattering a death rattle as they filled the beast.

Luke screamed.

The three of them climbed back into the Whooptie to wait.

"Laney, maybe we need to search. Luke can't get the truck out as long as the car blocks the entrance to the barn, and the cops will be here in a few minutes anyway," Toby said, dying to get his hands on Luke.

"Please, let's wai—" Shar started to say.

"What's that noise?" Laney said.

Another clanking noise started up followed by a rumbling.

"Sounds like an auger," Toby said, jumping out of the Whooptie. Laney and Shar followed Toby as he quickly made his way around the side of the barn toward the sound. They stopped at the corner of the barn and three heads peeked around toward the bin.

"Someone's unloading corn," Toby said, and they approached the two men.

The older man spotted them and walked over." He smiled broadly at the threesome. "Can I help you?" he shouted over the din.

As Shar began to explain the situation and to ask him if he had seen the two teens, Laney spied something blue lying in the grass near the bin's ladder.

Another blue barrette!

Grasping it, she ran over to Toby and Shar, pointing to where she had found it. All eyes shot up the ladder. The manhole cover was open!

Like a soulless wail from the grave, a hollow scream echoed through the walls of the bin. Garvin's face turned white. As he raced toward the switch box, Toby with Laney right behind, began to ascend the ladder as though propelled by rockets. Shar stood frozen in horror, one hand shaking on a ladder rung.

"Cilla!" Toby screamed, his feet stumbling on the rungs, his powerful arms not pulling his body upward fast enough. As his hands grabbed the top rung, he heard the thud of the center well trapdoor and the abrupt silence as, below, the augers ceased their rumbling.

He reached the manhole and peered inside. "N-O-O-O!" he screamed and felt Laney's hand fiercely grasp his ankle.

"God no, Toby!" Laney cried.

Tears sprung from Toby's eyes and for a moment he couldn't see. Suddenly, a whimper drew his gaze downward and he stretched his neck to see. He saw blue sneakers with yellow laces. And flattened against the inside ladder, Cilla clung as though part of it.

"Cilla," he choked, then yelled, "Laney! . . . thank God . . . she's okay!"

Toby dropped into the corn and helped Laney down. Together they pried Cilla's white fingers from the rung and held her close. Toby heard the sound of sirens in the distance and outside, Garvin and his son frantically climbing the ladder with their clanking shovels.

But inside the bin, the rushing funnel of gold was still. And beyond the wide, deep depression in the corn and scattered near the walls of the bin, lay crumpled beer cans—Luke's futile legacy of his miserable life.

Not twenty men with shovels nor the hot brilliant flames of four acetylene torches cutting through the grain bin's corrugated skin could save Luke. The smothering funnel had carried his body within a few feet of the center well trap door and when the torches had done their job and the corn had burst from the opening, Luke's blackened body was finally freed from its cylindrical metal tomb.

Laney had phoned Tina immediately in the event that word of the accident might have reached her before she had heard that Cilla was all right. Tina claimed her daughter on the spot and whisked her away before Luke's body was ever found. When Luke's father moved toward his truck to follow the ambulance to Maysville, and one by one, the volunteers and emergency vehicles pulled away, only then did Toby, Shar, and Laney climb into the Whooptie. They drove silently back to Hickory—the horror of the day too dreadful to speak about.

Shar left Hickory two days later. She phoned Laney two days after that to announce that she had given John Bernard her resignation notice. Two weeks to the day, she packed up her belongings, Kudzu, and her West Highland terrier, Nessie, climbed into a U-Haul and descended on Hickory, Kentucky. Malcolm was delighted.

50

Three Weeks Later

"What time is the reburial ceremony?" Gray asked as soon as Laney opened the front door.

"In a half hour." Laney stepped out onto the front porch and together they watched as yet another car pulled into the grass and parked in the pasture next to the field of stones.

"Who's that?" Gray asked, his arm creeping around her waist and pulling her close.

"The blue and white mini-bus? NAAD. Remember the group from North Carolina that protested the dig? See, there's Orenda Griffin and her husband," Laney said, nodding her head in the direction of the makeshift parking lot and the people spilling out of the bus. "This time, I invited them."

"I've thought a lot about that," Gray said. "Can you imagine how Ivy must have panicked when she heard about the dig and discovered that her own son had been chosen for the junior field crew? No wonder she called NAAD. She hoped they'd stop the dig before the child was found."

"Bucky took a great risk in planning the dig in the first place. I guess he thought his site measurements were precise and the infant would lie outside the perimeter," Laney said.

"He made a second blunder—he didn't reckon on some red-head-ed innkeeper nosing around and uncovering it." Gray buried his face in her hair and she felt his warm breath through its bulk. "M-m-m," he soughed in her ear and she shivered. "I guess they're happy that the dig is over and that no Indian remains will be unearthed." He raised his head as another car drove in. "But who are all the other people?"

"The two couples at the fence are my guests this weekend. They just arrived from Missouri this afternoon and will stay until Monday. The other cars—I have no idea. But after the article in the _Hickory Times_, I suspect curiosity seekers want to see the covering up of the dig and witness the reburial of Bones. I really don't mind."

"I don't see Cilla and Toby."

"They're in the carriage house getting Bones ready."

"What's happened with the kids' theory that Bones is really James Harrod?"

"Cam approached a couple historians about it. They said the skeleton is the right height and age and the two healed broken thigh bones make it an interesting supposition. But no proof. Like Bucky, Cam thinks the remains are of a Caucasian male who was buried in a shallow grave with his brass compass in the late eighteenth century. Whoever buried him maybe wanted people to believe he was part of this Late Woodland stone grave. Perhaps that someone was an early historic Native American who held the guy in high enough regard that he buried him in a site that might be protected because it was an Indian burial ground."

"That theory could apply to Harrod," Gray said. "Remember the arrowhead that was found near his bones? If Harrod just died in an accident, Indians might have buried it with him because of the times he befriended them."

"Toby said it may have been his cause of death but most people believe one of Harrod's companions did him in on that final hunting trip," Laney said. "I like to think not. Enough violence and death."

"Couldn't they do DNA testing to identify him as Harrod?"

"That would be up to Harrod's descendants. I believe a relative was told about the discovery but no request has been made."

"So, they are just going to put him back into the earth?" Gray said.

"I think it's the best solution. I'm having a headstone made and I'll build a fence around the whole graveyard to protect the site."

It seemed forever before either of them spoke again. Then it was Gray, directing the conversation to her writing. "This time next year, you'll be a published author. Knew it would happen for you."

"I still can't believe it but I'll have a lot of rewriting to do."

"Got a second book in you?"

"I've already begun."

They watched as Cam Dalton retrieved a large box from his van parked in front of the carriage house doors and disappeared inside again.

"When did Professor Dalton get here?" Gray asked.

"Yesterday," she answered. "Parker Webb University sent him up to make sure that the Late Woodland stone grave isn't disturbed when Bones is reburied."

"How's Cilla?" he asked.

"Getting stronger every day. Tina has her in grief counseling."

"To get over Luke?" Gray frowned.

"Actually, more to get over the death of her father. She never really dealt with his suicide—part of the reason she turned to Luke in the first place. She has a lot of unresolved issues to sort out."

"What about you? You okay?" His arm tightened around her waist.

"I just want all of this to be over." She thought about the funeral at St. Clair Cemetery just two days before when Ivy's tiny daughter was finally put to rest. She had attended the private service with Ivy, Toby, and Gray in a steady rain. Jerome Whalen, the child's father, had been buried two weeks before in Georgetown. Laney had not attended that funeral, but Toby and his mother had gone.

"Why do you think Ivy and Jerome Whalen never married? I know she loved him once," Laney asked.

Gray thought a minute before answering. "Whalen was in the hospital when she delivered the child that she thought was stillborn—and Bucky was there, not him. Could it be that all the pain of losing their child just pulled them apart? It happens, sometimes."

"Hmm. Look. There's Gordon and mother. He sure gave me hell over that letter I took from Whalen. He was going to charge me with tampering with evidence." Laney waved.

"Why didn't he?"

"I think because Bucky made a quick confession to Whalen's murder when he found out about the letter. It was as though Bucky wanted to protect Ivy from being charged with Whalen's death. Don't you think that's strange?"

"What I think is odd is that, so far, Bucky hasn't revealed that he is Toby's biological father. My God, Toby provided the main evidence against him with his latent recollection of Bucky's murder of his half-sister."

"I wonder if the man actually might have feelings for his son after all and want to preserve Toby's trust," Laney said, chewing on the side of her cheek.

"You have time to do a lot of thinking when you're sitting in a jail cell. I believe he's trying to protect Toby from the fact that his real father is a murderer."

Laney hadn't thought of that possibility. But Toby had another problem to deal with. Ivy had been indicted for concealing the birth of a child, only a gross misdemeanor which, in the state of Kentucky, is punishable with up to a year in jail. Her trial would begin after her DNA was compared with the child's. Karen Thompson had also obtained DNA samples from Jerome Whalen's body to try to establish paternity of the infant.

Laney was pensive, then decided to go for it. "Getting back to James Harrod. Cilla told me another theory about Harrod's disappearance—that he might have just up and left his wife because he was jealous of the attention she gave other men. Jealousy—the green-eyed monster. Funny how different people cope with it." She glanced up at Gray. No reaction from him.

She continued. "Luke turned violent when Cilla paid the slightest attention to another guy." She sneaked another look at him to see if he was paying attention. He gave no indication he was even listening.

"Shar fought back like a tiger when Ivy threatened her relationship with Malcolm." Still there was no response from Gray.

"And I'm convinced that Bucky's prime motive for murdering his baby and Whalen was his jealousy of the man." She paused, taking a breath. "You—"

Gray's fingers tensed against her waist. "Tell me, Laney." His tone was laced with sarcasm.

She plunged. "When you thought I was attracted to Bucky, you withdrew," she admonished cautiously, looking up at him.

Gray's eyes flickered and turned dark. "I had no cause?"

"I suppose I did flirt a bit with him," she said, recalling the midnight swim. "And rattled on about him endlessly . . . and told him about my manuscript being considered for publishing even before I told you . . . and—" Possibly she *had* gone too far. He'd never distrusted her before.

Gray let her wallow.

All at once she recalled Bucky's kiss on the porch and her face flamed. No sense telling him about *that,* she decided on the spot.

So, he pouts instead of fights, she thought. Maybe it's part of his charm.

"You either want me or not, Laney."

She took his comment as a question and answered by wrapping as much of her body as she could around him. In her arms, he felt warm, comfortable.

"You betcha," Laney said.

Blackberry nosed her from behind. "You know, we get no privacy around here."

"If you marry me, we could take a honeymoon," Gray said, then fell sharply silent as though he had surprised himself with the words.

"What did I hear you say?"

"You heard me," he said, recovering and looking rather pleased with himself, now that he had said it.

"Is this a proposal?" she asked him.

"Guess you could call it that."

"You guess?"

"No . . . I mean . . . I love you and I want to marry you. No guessing about it," he stammered. "It's the God's truth, Laney." In an awkward motion, he held her at arm's length and she saw in his turquoise eyes that he expected her answer to be yes.

"Malcolm just pulled up," Gray said, rather hoarsely after an intimate kiss.

Though she wanted to prolong the heat of their embrace, she tore herself from his arms.

"Shar—" Laney said, her mouth exploding her joy at seeing her friend after almost three weeks. Shar and Malcolm planned to be married before Christmas.

Shar worked her way out of Malcolm's Olds and disregarding the curved brick walk, scorched a new path to the porch. She and Laney hugged as though they hadn't seen each other for a year. Malcolm hobbled his way toward the porch, his cast ragged and dirty with autographs and Shar's lipstick kisses.

Laney heard the bulldozer start up in the pasture adjacent to the site. Roger Masterson of Grover Construction eased the machine toward the largest pile of back dirt at the side of the excavation and stopped. Cam, Toby and Cilla were walking across the yard, Cam carrying the large rectangular box that Laney had seen him remove from his van. It was just large enough to hold the skull and individual bones of an adult skeleton. She knew Bones lay inside.

Shar and Malcolm made their way slowly toward the dig site. Gray and Laney followed.

Cam laid the box next to the dirt base on which Bones had been discovered and then the three of them walked to where the grass began at the edge of the excavation. Suddenly, Toby broke away and, grabbing Cilla's hand, returned to the box. He whispered something to her and Cilla smiled and nodded. Stooping next to the raised pedestal, the two of them whisked away stray leaves and discarded a pebble or two with their bare hands as the dozer dropped scoop after scoop of dirt over the blue-gray stones while inching closer and closer. Toby yanked at the lid of the box and tossed it aside. Reverently, Cilla and Toby removed bone after bone and positioned them on the raised area. The skull was last, placed where it was originally unearthed and where they felt was the only fitting resting place for Bones. As the dozer approached with another load of soil, Toby and Cilla stepped aside. As the earth fell and covered the remains, a cheer rose from the crowd but a sigh like a lament escaped from Laney's lips. The sound was a long, deep breath of weariness and relief—that from this moment on, the field of stones would only be a memory.

Afterword

Toby lifted what he and Cilla had at first thought was a flat black pebble from the fifty-fifty solution of ammonia and water and dropped it into the ten percent solution of formic acid and water. The caustic liquid let off an irritating odor as Cilla's little souvenir she had picked up from the dirt pedestal fumed in the porcelain dish. Exactly two minutes later, as per Bucky's field notebook instructions, Cilla lifted what looked like a silver button from the acid with the tweezers and dropped it into the soft felt. With her eyes shining at Toby in expectation, she rubbed and rubbed it in the cloth, then opened the cloth to the light. The wire shank was missing from the button but when she turned it over, it gleamed like a new dime. The hand-stamped initial was unmistakable—the letter H.